Books by Ross Welford

THE DOG WHO SAVED THE WORLD

THE KID WHO CAME FROM SPACE

THE 1,000-YEAR-OLD BOY

TIME TRAVELLING WITH A HAMSTER

WHAT NOT TO DO IF YOU TURN INVISIBLE

The KiD who came from SPACE

Ross Welford

HarperCollins *Children's Books*

First published in Great Britain by
HarperCollins *Children's Books* in 2020
HarperCollins *Children's Books* is a division of HarperCollins*Publishers* Ltd,
HarperCollins Publishers
1 London Bridge Street
London SE1 9GF

The HarperCollins website address is:
www.harpercollins.co.uk

1

ISBN 978–0–00–839617–6

Ross Welford asserts the moral right to be
identified as the author of the work.

A CIP catalogue record for this title is
available from the British Library.

Printed and bound in England by
CPI Group (UK) Ltd, Croydon CR0 4YY

Part One

SEARCH CONTINUES FOR MISSING TWELVE-YEAR-OLD

KIELDER, NORTHUMBERLAND
27 DECEMBER

Northumbria Police are seeking the public's help to find a twelve-year-old girl missing from Kielder Village, Northumberland, since Christmas Eve.

Tamara 'Tammy' Tait was last seen leaving her home near the Stargazer public house on a bicycle at around 6pm on 24 December.

She is described as white, around 160 cm tall, of medium build, with blonde hair and brown eyes. She was last seen wearing blue jeans and a red North Face branded puffer jacket.

Volunteer teams and police have spent two days searching the forests and moors surrounding the remote village near the border between England and Scotland.

Anyone who may have seen Tamara or has any information in relation to her current whereabouts is urged to contact the police.

If you have information for the police, contact Policelink on 13 14 11 or call CrimeStoppers on 1800 333 000.

CHAPTER ONE

Hellyann

I read the sign again, glowing in front of me:

Type of organism: human female
Origin: Earth
Age: about twelve years

This brand-new exhibit will be introduced to the wider Earth Zone exhibition when emotional stability has been achieved

I looked at the bedraggled creature, and I wanted to reach through the unseen barrier and hold its hand. (This was neither allowed nor possible: the barrier would have repelled me with a painful shock.)

Its hair . . .

All right. I must stop saying 'it'. The sign says it is a female, and so it should be 'her' . . .

Her hair fell in tight twists. I should have liked to see

it when it was clean. Her pale and hairless skin was dotted with darker spots ('freckles', they are called in her language). Her clothes were similar to those worn by the other humans in Earth Zone. She had trousers of a coarse-looking fabric and a thick-looking padded item of a lighter shade on top, while her feet were clad in big shoes fastened with looped cord.

Her face was dirty and streaked with tears, and her eyes shone wet and bloodshot. She had been weeping (this is normal – humans do it a lot), although the atomic-level mechanical medication that had been given to her had closed down a lot of her primary cognitive functions—

(Wait. Is this too complicated? Philip suggests I should write: 'Her brain had been made slow by the drugs she had been given.' And that is, I suppose, close enough. I shall let you decide.)

Despite this, there was a spark of life in her eyes. Perhaps the dosage was imperfectly calculated, or she had an ability to resist some of the medication.

Anyhow, she looked at me and I was struck by how very expressive human faces are.

She put her hand to her chest and for a brief moment I thought she was making the sign of the Hearters, but – obviously – she was not.

She looked at me intensely and said, 'Ta-mee.'

Just that: those two syllables.

She did it again: 'Ta-mee.'

I glanced over both of my shoulders, but nobody was watching as I held up my PG and recorded this bit. Communicating with the exhibits is not *exactly* prohibited, but nor is it encouraged.

Is that her name? I wondered.

I repeated the syllables she had said, although the sounds were hard for me to duplicate.

'Ta-mee,' I said.

She nodded her head and made a weird face, as though she wanted to laugh and cry at the same time, which I did not understand – and still do not, not fully. Human beings are strange.

I imitated her gesture, and said my name.

The human female tried to repeat it. It sounded nothing *at all* like my name. She tried again and got a little closer. I practised the sounds a couple of times, and then tried saying my name in a way she might be able to repeat.

'Helly-ann,' I said, and a slow smile formed on her mouth.

She blinked hard and said it back to me. I found myself smiling at her.

Then her smile faded and she said two more syllables. 'Ee-fan.'

A voice came from a speaker next to the sign: 'Your time is up. Move along. There is a queue of people behind you waiting to see the new exhibit. Do not take more than your allotted time. Next.'

The human watched me go, then she retreated to the back of her enclosure and sat on the ground as two new spectators filed forward.

Ta-mee, I said to myself as I passed the Assistant Advisor who stood at the edge of the exhibit room.

'That is your third time here, I believe,' the AA said. 'And communicating with the exhibits as well? I have my eye on you.'

Except he did not say it aloud. He did not need to – he just looked at me hard and it was enough.

That is how it is done here. Everybody obeys the rules. Nobody gets out of line.

All the way back to my pod-home, I struggled to keep a straight face, when really I wanted to crumple up and cry. That, however, would immediately single me out as being different, for people here do not cry – or laugh, for that matter.

Instead I repeated her name in my head, over and over: *Ta-mee. Ta-mee. Ta-mee.*

I played back the recording on my PG of the bit when she said her name and something else.

What is Ee-fan? I wondered. That is what she said: *Ee-fan.*

Perhaps, one day, I will find out.

Because I will be returning Tammy to Earth.

It will be dangerous. If I fail I will be put to sleep for the rest of my life.

And if I succeed? Well, I will probably have to do it again, with another exhibit.

Such is the curse of having feelings.

Chapter Two

Ethan

My twin sister Tammy has been missing for four days now, so when the doorbell goes, I assume it's the police, or another journalist.

'I'll get it,' I say to Mam and Dad.

Gran is asleep in her tracksuit on the big chair by the Christmas tree, her head back and her mouth open. The lights on the tree haven't been switched on for days.

I open the door and Ignatius Fox-Templeton – Iggy for short and for slightly less weird – stands there wearing a thick coat, a flat cap and shorts (despite the snow). He's holding a fishing rod in one hand and Suzy, his pet chicken, under his other arm. A large bag is slung over his back and his rusty old bike lies next to him on the ground.

For a moment we just stand there, staring at each other. It's not like we're best friends or anything. We had this sort of awkward encounter when Tammy first went missing on Christmas Eve. (I nearly broke his mum's fingers with the piano lid, but she was OK about it.)

'I, erm . . . I just thought . . . I was wondering, you know, if . . . erm . . .' Iggy's not normally like this, but he's not normally normal anyway, and besides, nothing's normal at the moment.

'Who is it?' calls Mam from inside, wearily.

'Don't worry, Mam. Doesn't matter!' I call back.

Mam has been getting worse in the last day or two. None of us has been sleeping well, but I've begun to think that Mam has not been sleeping *at all*. She's got these blue-grey patches under her eyes, like smudged make-up. Meanwhile, Dad has been trying to keep busy at the pub and coordinating search efforts, but he is running out of things to do. Everyone wants to help us, which means the only thing left for us to do is to sit around and worry more, and cry. Sandra, the police Family Liaison Officer who has been here a lot, says that it is 'to be expected'.

I turn back to Iggy on the doorstep.

'What do you want?' I say, and it comes out blunter than I intended.

'Do you . . . erm, do you want to go fishing?' he almost whispers. His eyes blink rapidly behind his thick glasses.

In case you don't quite get just how odd I find this, you have to know that for the last few days the only world I have known has been one of worry and tears; and police officers being brisk; and journalists with cameras and notebooks wanting interviews; and people from the village bringing food even though the pub has a massive kitchen (we now have two shepherd's pies and a huge pavlova); and Sandra, Dad and Mam trying to manage all of this with Gran; and Aunty Annikka and Uncle Jan flying in yesterday from Finland because . . . well, I don't really know why. To 'comfort' us, I suppose.

All because, four days ago, Tammy vanished off the face of the earth. Nothing has been right since.

So when Iggy turns up wanting to go fishing, my first thought is: *Are you mad?* Then it dawns on me.

'Is this Sandra's idea?' I ask, holding the front door half closed to keep the cold out.

Iggy doesn't seem to mind. He gives his characteristic confident nod. Iggy knows Sandra already: he's had several reasons for a police Family Liaison Officer to call at his house.

'Yes. She thought you might want to get out of the house for a bit. You know, change of scene, and all that malarkey. Think of something else.'

Malarkey. It's a very Iggy sort of word. He doesn't have much of a local accent, though he's not exactly posh either. It's like he can't quite decide how his voice should be and uses odd words to fill the gaps.

He goes on: 'And so, here I am!' He holds up his fishing rod. 'Well,' he adds, nodding to Suzy. 'Here *we* are.'

I'm really not sure about Iggy. Dad doesn't like him at all, ever since – soon after we arrived in the village – Dad caught him stealing a box of crisps from the pub's outhouse.

His mum said the outhouse should have been locked, so Dad's not keen on his mum either. She keeps bees. She's divorced from Iggy's dad, I think.

Still, I have to admit: what Iggy is doing is quite kind, even if it wasn't his idea. I don't even like fishing. Suzy, Iggy's chicken, stretches out her neck for a scratch, and I oblige, burying my fingers deep in her warm throat-feathers. To be honest, I have my doubts about Suzy too. I mean, who has a pet *chicken*?

Then, as I tickle Suzy, I think: *What's the worst that could happen?*

So I put my head round the living-room door. Dad has gone into the kitchen on his phone and Mam is just staring blankly at the television, which is switched off. Gran snores a bit. The room's far too hot and the remnants of the fire in the wood burner glow white-orange.

'I'm just going out for a bit, Mam,' I say. 'You know – fresh air, an' that.'

She nods but I'm not sure she completely heard me. All that's in her mind is Tammy.

Tammy, my twin sister, who has disappeared off the face of the earth.

Chapter Three

The tape is still there – *POLICE LINE DO NOT CROSS* – strung across the path where Tammy left her bike, but the police have searched the narrow lakeshore and the path a few times and there's nobody there now. I haven't been back since Christmas Eve, when it all happened, and I feel a tightening in my chest as we approach.

'Are you all right with this?' asks Iggy. 'I'm sorry – I didn't think about, you know . . . the lake and whatnot . . .'

'Thanks. I'm OK.' There is another approach to the waterside but it's quite a bit further away.

We leave our bikes at the top of the path and go down the steep path through the woods, and all the while I'm thinking: *This is where Tammy came . . .*

We emerge on to the little shoreline. Iggy has been babbling on about a huge pike that lives near the Bakethin Weir, where the reservoir narrows into a sort of overflow lake.

'When the weather's really cold, pike often come to slightly shallower water . . . Using a laser lure is sure to attract him . . . this line has an eighty-pound breaking strain . . .'

It might as well be a foreign language to me, but I go along with it because it's good to be able to think of something other than Tammy just for a while.

It's mid-afternoon. Already the sky is darkening and the vast stillness of Kielder Water – a deep lilac colour in the near twilight – stretches out in front of us. I gasp at the sight and say, 'Wow!' very quietly.

Iggy comes up and stands next to me, staring out across the reservoir.

'D'you reckon she's still alive, Tait?'

Oof! His directness kind of throws me, and I feel the pricklings of annoyance until I realise he's just asking what everybody else wants to ask. Everybody else tiptoes around the subject, very often scared to say *anything* in case they say the wrong thing.

I sigh. No one has asked me this before, so I even surprise myself with how certain I am. 'Yup,' I say. 'I feel it. Here.' I touch my chest near my heart. 'It's a twin thing.'

Iggy pouts and nods slowly as if he understands, but I don't think you can unless you're a twin.

'Shh,' I say. 'Listen.'

I'm hoping that I might hear the whining noise from the night that Tammy disappeared. But the only sounds are tiny waves rippling on to the shore every few seconds and the rhythmic bump, bump of a bright orange fibreglass canoe hitting the long wooden jetty that sticks out over the water. The old planks of the jetty creak under our weight and Iggy unpacks his tackle bag.

The last time I stood on this jetty, I think, was with Tammy, playing our throwing-stones game. It's basically: who can throw a stone furthest into the lake? But we've got rules, like size of stone, best-of-five and so on. Maddeningly, she nearly always wins. She's good at throwing. Iggy is chuntering on…

'Here we go. Two eight-strand braided fishing lines, one hundred metres, each with a steel wire trace . . . Four ten-centimetre shark hooks . . . one short rod and my good old pike reel, plus a Johnson Laser Lure.'

Iggy – who has a school record that you'd call 'inconsistent' – would get an A-star in fishing-tackle speak. From his bag he extracts something that he unwraps from its plastic and holds in front of me. I nearly gag at the smell.

'What the . . . ?'

'It's chicken. It was in the bin behind your pub.' He adds quickly, 'And if it's in a bin it's not stealing, is it?'

He had explained the plan on the way here, but now – kneeling on the jetty screwing his four-part rod together – he goes over it again.

'So, this chicken breast is the bait. We paddle out about thirty metres and drop the chicken over the side attached to the buoy.' He points to a red buoy the size of a football in the bottom of the canoe. 'That should stop it sinking. It's attached to the line and my rod. We paddle back, letting out the line, and just wait. Pikey comes along and sniffs the lovely meat . . .'

Iggy acts this out, his eyes narrowing as he twitches his nose left and right.

'He just can't resist it! Bam! Down go his jaws and he's hooked. We see the buoy bobbing and start reeling him in to the jetty, where *you* are ready with your phone to get the pictures. Then we release him and we cycle back to fame and fortune, or at the very least, our pictures in *The Hexham Courant*!'

I keep telling myself that everything will be fine, even as we throw all of the gear into the canoe and I step into the rocking vessel, with the freezing water in the bottom seeping into my trainers. Suzy follows us and I could swear she looks at me funny. She takes one sniff of the rotten chicken and moves as far away as she can, right up to the far end of the canoe.

I hadn't mentioned anything to Mam about going out on the water, because I hadn't known till Iggy said so. My conscience is clear. But still . . .

'Iggy?' I say. 'Do we . . . erm, do we have life jackets?' I feel daft saying it, and even dafter when I see the look of disdain on Iggy's face. 'Doesn't matter,' I say. 'I can swim.'

We unhook the wobbling canoe from the jetty and start paddling out towards the middle of the lake, saying nothing.

Perhaps it's the motion of the canoe, but I begin to

feel a bit queasy. The chicken (the dead one) isn't helping. The putrid smell is on my hands from where I tossed it over the side attached to the red buoy.

I lean over and dip my hands in the icy water to wash them, then jerk back with a yelp, rocking the canoe.

'Hey! Watch it!' protests Iggy.

Did I imagine it?

I *did* imagine it. I look again: it's just a log, submerged below the surface. There's a branch coming off it that sort of looks like an arm, and in my head the whole thing became a floating body and I thought it was Tammy, and it wasn't. It was just a log, and my mind playing tricks on me.

'Shall we go back now?' I say, trying to keep the tension out of my voice.

We paddle back, letting out the thick line as we go.

And so we wait on the jetty. And wait. I look up at the sky, which is much darker now, and I think I should be going back.

My phone's clock tells me that we have been here for more than an hour, and frankly, I am bored, cold and still a bit shaken by the log-that-was-just-a-log.

And then the buoy moves.

'Did you see . . .'

'Yup.'

We scramble to our feet and stare out over the lake to where the buoy is once again still, with tiny ripples expanding from it.

'What do you think?' I say, but Iggy just takes off his cap and runs his fingers thoughtfully through his messed-up red hair, looking at the water.

We stay like that for several minutes then he says, 'I think we need to check' and he starts to reel in the line. 'Perhaps the bait's been taken, or fallen off. Dammit.' The line is jammed. 'Might have got caught on weeds, or a log.'

The more he tugs, the tighter it gets. 'Come on,' he moans, getting into the canoe. 'We'll have to free it.'

'*We?*' I murmur, but I get in anyway.

Iggy whistles to Suzy, just like you would to a dog, and she hops in obediently after us. Iggy pulls his cap down purposefully, pushes his glasses up his nose, and we begin to paddle back out towards the bobbing buoy.

Before we reach it, the massive splash comes.

It's huge – like a car has been dropped into the water from a great height over on the other side of the reservoir.

Obviously, it isn't a car. But – equally obviously – I don't think it's an invisible spaceship either, because I'm not completely mad.

But that is what it turns out to be.

Chapter Four

After that splash about two hundred metres away, comes another one a few seconds later, slightly smaller but still enormous, and closer to our canoe. In the light of the rising moon, the water droplets glisten as they cascade back down. Seconds after, there is a third splash, then a fourth, all getting closer to us in a straight line, as though a massive, unseen stone is being skimmed across the surface. By the time the fifth splash comes, only about six metres from the boat, the resulting waves have started to tip our little canoe violently from side to side.

'What's happening?' I wail.

Then the spray soaks us and we both cower in the bottom of the rocking boat. I feel, rather than see, something pass overhead very close to us, causing Suzy to squawk with alarm.

'What is it?' I shout.

Iggy makes no attempt to answer.

I raise my head to see the sixth splash on the other side of the canoe. The seventh is much smaller. Whatever is causing it is becoming less forceful. There's an eighth splash, then a swoosh of water that washes over the jetty then . . . just nothing. Nothing but the darkening sky, the purple lake, the black-green of the surrounding forest . . .

. . . And silence, broken only by the slapping of rippling waves on the side of the canoe.

Eventually, Iggy straightens up and says 'Good *Lord*! Did you *see* that?', but I don't know *what* we saw so I just end up moving my mouth without making any sound.

There's nothing to see now, anyway: whatever caused the splashes must have sunk, but only about ten metres from the shore, where the water is shallower and fairly clear. Together, we paddle towards the spot: perhaps, despite the gathering darkness of the afternoon, we'll be able to shine a light into the water and see something?

As we get closer, I hear a humming noise, and we stop, allowing the canoe to drift as I turn my head to hear better.

'Listen,' I hiss. 'That's it! The noise I heard on the night that Tammy disappeared.'

There it is again. A low *hommmmm* like a bee trapped behind a window, but almost inaudible.

Staring again in the direction of the sound, the surface of the water appears disturbed, and sort of indented, as though a huge glass plate is resting on the lake near the jetty, but it's hard to make out in the half moonlight.

Then, as we drift closer to the shape in the water, the

nose of the canoe bumps into something. Probably another floating log, I think, but when I look there's nothing. Nor is there a rock. I take hold of the paddle again and stroke it through the water, but we are stopped again with a bump, by some kind of object we can't see. From the sound the canoe makes, it's as if this object is in front of us, sticking out of the water, but that's impossible because we can't see anything but air.

'What *is* that? What's stopping us, Tait? What are we hitting?'

When the canoe bumps into nothing for the third time, I decide to change the route and paddle around the triangle of smooth water. I stop before the canoe reaches the shore, then I turn back to look.

'Pass me the spinner, Tait,' says Iggy.

He takes the large fishing lure from me carefully, avoiding the vicious hooks, and pushes a tiny button on it, activating the laser light that is supposed to attract fish. He points it in front of us, towards whatever it is that we're not seeing.

'Oh my word. Would you look at that?'

I'm looking. The green beam of light heads straight out across the lake, takes a sharp left turn, then curves around to go straight again. Iggy moves the light and it does the same – deflected by something we cannot see.

I find a pebble on the floor of the canoe and toss it towards where Iggy is pointing the light. There's a dull ping and it *bounces back towards me*, landing in the water with a plop.

It is *exactly* as though it had hit a pane of glass, only there's no glass there. I throw another pebble and it does the same. Opening Iggy's fishing tackle bag, I take out a big lead weight and throw that, hard. Same result.

We're both freaked out by now. Then the humming lowers in tone, the water before us seems to churn up slightly, and the shape on the water heads towards our canoe.

'Move! It's coming for us!' yells Iggy.

We both reach down for the same paddle, causing the canoe to lurch sharply to one side. In one smooth movement, Iggy and I are tipped into the dark water and we don't even have time to shout out.

The cold doesn't hit me immediately, but as I plunge beneath the surface I suck in half a lungful of water, and come up spluttering and weighed down by my heavy jacket and sweater. I'm just able to keep my face above the surface and that's when I gasp at the freezing cold.

Between gasps, I call out, 'Ig . . . Iggy!' I think about us not wearing life jackets, and I'm consumed with fear.

A ball of red hair bobs up next to me, followed by Iggy's terrified face.

'Ah . . . ah . . . I'm here.' He grabs on to me. 'We go . . . gotta go. That thing's ge . . . ge . . . getting closer.' He can hardly speak with the cold. He starts to swim for the shore, then stops. 'Wh . . . where's Suzy?' As he says the name, there's a thumping from inside the upturned canoe.

'Suzy!' cries an anguished Iggy, and before I can say anything, he's bobbed under the surface.

Seconds go by while I feel my clothes getting heavier and I am properly scared.

'Iggy!' I shout, and I turn a circle in the water. 'Iiiiiggyyyy!'

I'm ready to scream again, when there comes a splash from beside the canoe. Iggy's head reappears and next to it are the sodden red feathers of Suzy, who looks very startled.

I have ended up closer to the jetty than Iggy, and I'm finding it easier to swim than he is because he's carrying Suzy. I heave myself up the slippery iron ladder, weighed down by my soaking clothes. I look back and that is when I notice the strange, half-visible shape on the surface of the water moving and getting closer to Iggy.

Iggy is only about fifteen metres away and I can see the look of sheer terror on his face as he realises what's going on.

'Swim, Iggy. Swim! D-don't look back. Just swim!'

But he does look back and I think he's frozen in terror for a second. Holding Suzy's head up, he starts thrashing with his other arm and kicking with his legs.

'Come on, Iggy! Come on – you can make it!'

Ten metres. Five. I can hear the humming noise now as whatever is making it cuts across the surface, getting closer with every stroke Iggy makes. I stretch out my hand.

'You can make it – come on!'

Then he screams and, with a gurgle, lets go of Suzy and disappears below the black surface of the water.

Chapter Five

Iggy reappears above the surface a few seconds later, making terrified noises. 'It . . . it . . . got . . . got . . .' He seems to struggle with something below the surface as if his legs are tangled.

Amazingly, his glasses have stayed on. He manages to get hold of Suzy and, one-armed, flaps the last two metres to the jetty, where I haul him up by his arm.

'My . . . m-my le-leg,' he moans. 'It go . . . got me.'

Iggy left his bike light on the jetty. I grab it, shine it on his leg and recoil in horror.

'Is . . . is it ba-bad?' he says.

I nod. A huge, treble-barbed hook has embedded itself into his calf and has ripped out a long portion of flesh as he struggled. Somehow his leg got entwined in our fishing line and as he swam it hooked him as securely as any fish. Blood, mixed with the water draining from us, forms a red channel trickling back into the water. He reaches his hand down and moans again when he feels the warm blood.

'Ca-call my mum,' he croaks.

'Sure, Iggy. Hang on. You're going to be fine.'

I fumble in my soaking jeans pocket for my phone.

It's not THAT bad, I keep telling myself. *He's not going to bleed to death right here on this jetty.*

I jab the start button on my phone.

Smartphones and water are not a good mix. I try again. And again.

'Where's yours?' I ask Iggy, whose breathing has become shallow, little pants.

'My mu . . . mum's confiscated it.'

That I can believe.

In desperation, I get to my feet and shout, 'Help! *Help!*' while Iggy pants and moans, lying on his back on the jetty.

'No . . . no one's going to hear you,' pants Iggy at my feet, then he groans in pain again.

'I'm going to run up to the road,' I say. 'There might be a car I can stop. Wait here.'

What am I even thinking? There are hardly ever any cars on that road, just forestry trucks now and then. Am I panicking? I am halfway up the steep path to the road when I realise that leaving an injured person, soaking wet and freezing cold, on a jetty in the dark is just stupid.

For a few seconds I actually hop from one foot to another, trying to work out what to do, until eventually I turn and scramble back down the path towards the beach.

I can see Iggy lying where I left him, and then I stop and let out a small yelp.

Someone has just appeared on the jetty before me.

I know that sounds crazy, but it's just like a magic trick or a special effect. One minute there's only Iggy lying there. The next, this . . . this *figure* is there as well. It can't have come from anywhere. I mean, there's no other approach to the jetty than the route I took, and I didn't pass anyone.

It is quite dark, though . . .

I am standing on the shore-end of the jetty when I hear the person speak. He or she hasn't heard me approaching, is facing Iggy, and I don't think Iggy has noticed me coming back either: he's got other things on his mind, what with freezing and bleeding half to death. The person makes a weird snuffling, squeaking noise, followed by words.

'I heard you. I will help.'

Iggy, who's been facing the other way, propped up on his arm, spins round and then scuttles back in shock, slipping in his own blood.

I hurry to Iggy, passing close to the person on the jetty, who seems to be wearing a shaggy fur coat, but that's all I notice at first: I'm more interested in getting to Iggy.

'You OK?' I say. 'Sorry I left you. This person can help. That's good, eh?' I'm gabbling a bit and I don't really understand the look of terror on Iggy's face as he squints past me through his smudged, wet glasses at the figure who is still standing there.

Iggy can't speak: 'Tai . . . Tait. What . . . what . . . ?'

His gaze is fixed on the person behind me and so I turn to look as well. What I see shocks me so much that I too stagger and slip, falling hard on my backside. I continue to scramble backwards to the end of the jetty, unable to take my eyes away from what I see, and – at the same time – desperate to put as much distance between me and it as possible.

Iggy cranes his neck around, but is unable to move as fast as me and so lies there, panting with terror.

This thing has a head, with a shining mass of long, silvery hair and, below it, a face. A human face. Well, human-ish: it is face-shaped, except hairy, with widely spaced pale eyes and a huge nose, twitching like a hamster's.

I'm so scared that I think if I'd been a bit younger I'd have wet myself, but I don't, thankfully.

It is definitely *like* a human. It's got two legs and two arms for a start. Apart from the long head hair, the rest of its body is covered in a light, greyish, downy fur that seems to be standing up. From its back curls a long tail that moves like a cat's. So, both *like* a human, and *not at all* like a human.

It stares at me with its large eyes for a bit and then casts its gaze about the forest, raising its nose to sniff the air. Then it turns back to us and takes a step nearer. Iggy and I both cower but it stops and carries on staring and sniffing. Then it shakes all over: a massive shiver that ripples its fur. Its top lip draws back, revealing long, sharp, yellow teeth.

I hear a whimpering sound. I don't realise at first that it is me.

Chapter Six

Iggy speaks first. 'Who-who are you? What do you want? P-please don't hurt me.'

The person-creature steps forward, and we creep backwards till we're right at the end of the jetty and there's nowhere else for us to go except into the water again. Even Suzy has backed away, after shaking as much water as she could from her feathers.

The creature leans forward till its head is only about a metre away. It takes a deep sniff then makes the same grunting and whining noise with its mouth and nose as before. That is immediately followed by: 'You are alreatty hurt.'

The thing has a voice that is a strange combination of throaty and high-pitched. It pronounces the 'r' in words like *are* and *hurt* like Scottish Sheila in the village, and each word is precise, as though the language has been recently learned. It holds out a thin, hairy finger and points at Iggy's bleeding leg.

Iggy can't speak for fear.

'To you want me to help?' comes the voice again, after another brief snuffling and squeaking.

I can smell its breath: it's like a dog's – sort of sour and a bit fishy. Now and then it licks its lips with a long grey tongue.

Help? I'm not so sure. I'm thinking that I could scramble to my feet, and push this thing into the water, then run up the path for the bikes . . . Only Iggy is in no shape to run. I'd be leaving him here at the mercy of this . . . thing. He wouldn't do that to me, I don't think.

Iggy nods.

We both flinch when the creature raises both of its hands and brings forward a bag that was hooked on to its back, like a little backpack.

Racing through my head is this: *This is what happened to Tammy. This thing is going to take us. It's not a monster: it's a person. It's a weirdo dressed up in an outfit, and he's going to bring out a knife or a gun or . . .*

I stare closely. If this is a costume, where are the joins? Is there a zip somewhere? That's a fake nose, surely? I've seen shows on TV where make-up artists create things like that. Prosthetic something or other. But why would anyone wander around Kielder Water in the dark like that unless they had bad intentions? Halloween maybe, but that was nearly two months ago.

Then, from the backpack, the creature brings out a stick: thickish, like a broom handle, smooth, dark, and about 30 centimetres long. It holds it in its fist and studies it for a moment while we tremble with cold and *total* fear. I feel Iggy's hand grip mine and I grip back. If I'm going to die, I don't want to go alone.

'This may work, it may not,' says the person-in-a-costume (I am convinced by now). 'Your cellular structure iss almost itentical. Put your leck out.'

Iggy shrinks back and draws his leg in.

'This will not hurt.' The creature pauses. '*Do it!*'

Slowly, like a turtle coming out of its shell, Iggy extends his bloody leg. He's whimpering with fear.

The throaty snuffle comes again, followed by the word 'Light!'

It's looking at me.

I reach for the torch. In addition to the long, open gash in Iggy's leg, there is the hook still deeply embedded in his flesh. The blood is pouring out and on to the jetty.

The creature advances further, the rod in its hands, and moves it over the wounds. Then, as we watch, the blood seems to dry, and scab over. The huge fish hook with the lure attached is pushed out by the hardening flesh and falls on to the decking of the jetty. The scabs turn browner, then black, all in the space of about thirty seconds. The creature replaces the stick in its backpack; then, with a long finger, gently flicks at the scabs, which drop off, revealing fresh, pink skin underneath.

It stands up straight and I look at its feet. They are

bare and hairy and definitely not fake ones slipped over shoes. He – she? – is smallish, but not tiny: not as tall as me. It isn't hunched over and creepy like Gollum in *The Lord of the Rings* – not at all. And, though it is stark naked, it doesn't seem at all embarrassed by the fact.

Without taking his eyes off the creature, Iggy says to me, 'It's a girl.'

'How do you know?'

Iggy tuts. 'Look, Tait. No, erm…boy's bits.'

I hadn't noticed, but he's right. I feel oddly embarrassed, staring at it – her – like that. I feel myself blushing.

When she stands up, the still, cold air gives a waft of her smell. Blocked drains? Sour milk? Earwax? It's all of those things blended together to make a rich, foul odour that is not just her breath: it is *her*.

'Jeez, Iggy. She flippin' stinks!' I whisper.

Iggy has taken his cap off and is holding it to his nose.

'Thought it was you at first,' he says, his voice muffled.

Slowly, Iggy and I get to our feet and the three of us stand there in a little triangle, saying nothing – just, you know, being utterly astonished. Iggy flexes his newly cured leg.

Eventually, he jams his cap back on and pats his chest twice. 'Me, Iggy,' he says, and the creature blinks hard.

I could swear she's thinking, *Why is he talking like a halfwit?*

All the same, taking my cue from Iggy, I point at myself and say, 'Me, Ethan.'

I can't precisely say how I know this, because it's not like she gasps or blinks or anything, but I can tell she's surprised. 'Ee-fan?' she says.

'Yes.'

She lifts her chin then lowers it. The action is sort of like a nod, but done backwards. Then she says something that sounds like '*Helly-ann*' and pats her own chest.

Iggy looks across at me, a triumphant smirk on his face. 'See? That's her name. Hellyann!'

But then we hear the shouts, and the dogs, and see the flashlights through the trees in the distance, coming down the path from the main road.

The look of pure terror that crosses the creature's strange, furry face changes everything, I think.

'Say nothing,' she says in her squeaky snuffle.

'What?' says Iggy.

'I say: say nothing. Say you haf not seen me. Lie. You people are good at that.'

'Wait,' I say. 'Who *are* you? And why should we lie?'

The dog noise is getting nearer, and a huge German Shepherd bursts out of the undergrowth, bounding along the pebble beach towards us.

I hear: 'What is it, Sheba? What have you found?'

And the creature who says her name is Hellyann fixes me with her intense, pale gaze.

'Because if you don't, you'll neffer see your sister again.'

My sister. Tammy.

Iggy was right. His fishing trip idea worked: for the past hour or so I had hardly thought about her.

But now, on a freezing evening as I stand dripping on to the wooden deck, it all comes flooding back into my head in a wave of sorrow as I remember why I am here.

Chapter Seven

'I hate you!'

It is the last thing I said to Tammy. It bounces around in my head and it is the opposite of the truth.

My twin sister. My 'other half', Mam used to say, and she was right.

Tamara 'Tammy' Tait. Cool name, I think, mainly because of the alliteration. Tammy Tait. And since she went missing, seldom has an hour has passed when I haven't thought about those three syllables.

An hour? Try five minutes. Try five *seconds*. It's exhausting.

Then there will be times when I realise that I *haven't* thought of Tammy for a few minutes, and that's almost worse, so I force myself to replay her in my head, to listen to her again. The way she says 'Oh, *E-thaaaan*!' when she is annoyed with me for something (which is quite often); or how she farted in the bath once when we were little and laughed so hard that she banged her head on the tap, which made her laugh even more even though her head was bleeding.

Then I'll end up thinking of the last few months, when we moved to Kielder, and started secondary school. We are now in different classes. She has friends who I don't even know (and at least one who doesn't even like me. It's OK, Nadia Kowalski, the feeling's mutual).

Then thinking of all that makes me sad again, which – weirdly – makes me feel better because it sort of makes up for forgetting to think about her all the time.

And when I am sad, I remember the last words I said to her: *I hate you*.

I haven't told Mam that. It would upset her, and Mam and Dad are upset enough. The fact is, Tammy and I said we hated each other *far* more than we ever said we loved each other.

Which is not hard, because we never said we loved each other. Why would we? It would be like telling yourself.

Still, I wish *I hate you* hadn't been the last thing I'd said to her.

Four Days Earlier

Chapter Eight

It was Christmas Eve, and snow had fallen on the top moor. I think everyone was hoping that a big snowfall would cover the village and make it look like the front of a Christmas card, but it didn't and, to be honest, it's not that sort of village anyway.

Kielder is sort of spread out, with a mixture of old and new houses, and no typical 'village street' – you know, a baker, a butcher, and a sweet shop like you get in stories. Because of the forest and the lake and the observatory, there are loads of visitors in the summer, but most things shut down in the winter, like the tearooms, and the maze, and Mad Mick's Mental Rentals, which hires out bikes. Tammy had taken to calling the village Boring-ville. She once said, 'I don't belong here. I'm a city person', as if sleepy Tynemouth – where we used to live – was New York.

There is a pub, though, run by my mam and dad. The Stargazer is set back from the main road, with a swinging pub sign at the end of a short driveway, and a huge Christmas tree outside, and coloured lights in the windows and candles everywhere, because Mam is half-Danish and they're obsessed with candles.

I can remember almost every detail of that evening, even though I wish I couldn't. I have gone over it all with the police officers, with Mam, with Dad, with Gran, with reporters and most of all with myself: in my head, again and again and again.

So here goes, 'one more time from the top' – as Miss Swann, our music teacher, says.

It was five minutes past six in the evening. Mam had gone over to the pub, where there were going to be carols. Dad was going to dress up and Tammy and I were going to follow later, first going round to the old folks in the village to drop off a Christmas present from Mam and Dad. There was Scottish Sheila, Tommy Natrass and the Bell sisters. They all got a bottle of vodka with a label saying, *Happy Christmas from Adam and Mel at the Stargazer.*

My job had been to wrap the presents.

Tammy came downstairs with the oblong boxes wrapped in red paper and ribbon in a carrier bag. That's when we had our row. It started with Tammy holding one of the presents up and saying 'Nice job!' sarcastically.

'I did my best,' I said.

The paper was scrunched up, the sticky tape all over the place, and the ribbons badly tied. When she held it up, one of the labels fell off. Wrapping presents is hard.

'"I did my best, Tammy,"' she mimicked in a baby voice. 'You always say that! But you never do, do you? You do what *looks* like your best. You do what people will think is your best. You do *just enough* so that when you say, "But I did my best", people will believe you and go: "Aw, poor Ethan – he did his best." But you know what, Ethan? I know what your best is. I'm your twin, remember? I'm the other half of you. How could I not know? And you haven't done your best – nothing like it, so don't lie.' She waved one of the badly wrapped gifts as evidence, and another label flew off.

'Where's your costume?' I said, to change the subject. We had agreed: we would dress up as elves for the evening. It would be fun.

Tammy rolled her eyes and tutted.

'You're so childish, Ethan.' When she said that, I looked down at my costume from last year's school parade: striped tights, green buckled jacket and the pointy hat I was holding. I hate it when Tammy says stuff like that: it's as if being ten minutes older than me gives her some sort of age advantage.

'But we *agreed*!' I said, trying (and failing) not to sound as though I was whining.

Tammy was in her usual clothes: jeans, trainers, thick fleecey top. She's not big on fashion, is our Tam. She was pulling on her new red puffer jacket, an early Christmas present from Gran, who was staying with us.

'Well, we can disagree. There. Just done it! I *dis*agree to dress up and prance around Boring-ville like some six-year-old. As for you – go ahead. You look great.'

'Well, I'm not going to be the only one. I'm going to get changed,' I snarled, and began to stomp up the stairs.

'See you at Scottish Sheila's. I'm going.'

'You're not going to wait for me?'

'No. We're late as it is. Bye.' She opened the front door and stepped out into the cold, and that's when I yelled it.

'I hate you!'

(I sometimes hope that she didn't hear me, but she must have done. I yelled it loudly, and she hadn't even shut the front door.)

Five minutes later, I had taken off the stupid elf costume and had calmed down. *Maybe she was right anyway*, I thought. I compromised, and put on a sweater with a flashing red reindeer nose instead. (I wasn't going to give in completely, you understand?) I pulled the front door closed behind me and set off on my bike to catch her up.

Shortly afterwards, I saw Tammy's bike lying in the ditch at the side of the road, its front and rear lights shining white and red, illuminating the frosty verge, and no sign of Tammy.

I haven't seen her since.

Chapter Nine

When people find out that Tammy and I are twins, they sometimes go, 'Ooh, are you psychic?', which is so daft that we developed this routine. I would go, 'Yes, of course we are. Tammy: what number am I thinking of?' And whatever number Tammy said, I would then say, 'Dead right! Wow!'

Well, we thought it was funny, anyway. It actually fooled Tammy's new friend Nadia, but she'll believe anything.

So no: we're not psychic. But that evening, when I saw Tammy's bike at the side of the road with its lights still on, I *knew* something was wrong. I felt a lurch in my stomach, and I stopped my bike next to hers. A cold feeling spread from my neck and down my back exactly as though someone had dropped ice inside my collar.

'Tammy!' I shouted, not so loud to begin with, as, although I knew, I couldn't be *certain* something was wrong, if that makes sense. 'Tam?'

The moon was still low and obscured by thick cloud, and when the sky is like that, Kielder is darker than you can possibly imagine, the only light coming from our bicycle lights.

'TAMMY!' I yelled, and cocked my head to hear, but there was nothing. The wind was so light that it made no sound at all as it passed through the bare trees.

Tammy's bike had stopped near to an overgrown path that leads down to the reservoir and the little jetty where Tammy and I play the throwing-stones-as-far-as-we-can game. I grabbed the light from the front of my bike and started down the path.

It makes no sense, I told myself. *Why on earth would she go down here?*

'Tammy! Tam!' I kept calling.

The path is quite steep down to the lakeshore, and I kept stumbling in the dark until I got to the little beach of shingle and rocks. I stared out over the inky blackness of Kielder Water, and that's when I heard the noise: a low drone, getting higher in pitch.

OOOOOOMMMMMMM ooooooooommmmmmmm.

The noise was *sort of* like an aeroplane, but definitely not an aeroplane. It was *sort of* like a motorboat, but definitely not a motorboat either; and there was nothing to see. Here, right next to the water, the sky appeared a little clearer and the cloudy moon gave off a little bit of grey light. I narrowed my eyes and stared out over the lake, where a column of mist had appeared, stretching high into the sky, hanging for a few seconds before it dispersed on the breeze.

There was a smell too. A bad smell: very faint, like bad

body odour and blocked drains, but that was soon taken by the air as well.

Perhaps she had come down to the lake to do some stone-throwing practice? Was that why she always beat me, because she practised in secret? I knew that was a daft idea, but I think I had already started to panic.

My heart was pounding with fear as I scrambled back up the path to where Tammy's bike still lay with its lights on.

I yelled her name again, desperately hoping she would come out of the woods that line the road. She would say, '*Eth-aaaan*, for heaven's sake, what are you shouting for? I just went into the woods for a pee' or something like that.

But she didn't, and I knew I had to get help. I took out my phone but there was no signal. There hardly ever is around here. Step out of the village and you might as well be in 1990.

I climbed back on my bike and started to pedal as fast as I could to Scottish Sheila's house, shouting 'Tammy!' all the way until I was nearly hoarse.

Chapter Ten

If the events leading up to my discovery of Tammy's bicycle are clear in my mind, then what came next is all a bit of a blur.

As I pedalled along the pot-holed forestry road towards the village, I kept thinking of reasons for Tammy's bike to be abandoned.

She had left it there and decided to walk. Not likely. In fact, so unlikely as to be impossible.

She had accepted a lift in someone's car. Again, not likely. Why would she? And besides – who from? Hardly anyone comes along that road, and why would they offer her a lift, and why would she leave her bike? And . . . the whole thing was silly.

By the time I crossed the bridge over the burn, I was convinced something horrible had happened to Tammy.

The south side of the village is pretty much a single street of old terraced farm cottages. I pulled up next to Scottish Sheila's house and allowed my bike to clatter to the ground as I leapt off and hammered on the old lady's door.

'All right, all right!' came a voice from inside.

I had started talking almost before the door was open.

'Is Tammy here?' I jabbered. 'She was supposed to come here – have you seen her?'

'Hello, young fella,' said Sheila with a smile, as though she hadn't heard me.

'Well, have you?' I barked, and she looked taken aback.

'Have I wha . . .'

'Have you seen Tammy?' I shouted. I was panicking and my manners were shot.

'Well, no. No' today. I thought—'

'Bye!' I said and ran back to my bike. I turned it around and cycled as fast as I could back to our end of the village.

The Stargazer was lit up, and there were lights on the big tree outside that I had helped to put up last week with Tammy. As I cycled up the driveway, I could hear singing already. The carols had started early, and I saw through the window that Cora Fox-Templeton, Iggy's mum, was accompanying them on the pub's jangly old piano. Iggy was standing next to her and Suzy was sitting on top of the piano like she was about to lay an egg. The singing came through the windows:

'*Hark the herald angels sing, Glory to the newborn king!*'

I jumped off my bike and burst through the doors into the entrance lobby and went straight into the bar, where the noise and the heat and the music hit me.

'Peace on Earth and mercy mild, God and sinners reconciled . . .'

A cheer went up over by the bar and Dad called out, 'Right, you lot! Who's for a Goblet of Fire?' It's one of his barman's stunts which I've seen loads of times: a tray of cocktails is lined up then they all burst into flames as he sets fire to the alcohol. I love watching it normally.

Mam had picked up the tray, and I pushed my way through the groups of people till I got to her.

'Mam! Mam!'

She turned to me crossly, shaking her head as she carried on singing.

'Mam! You've got to listen!'

'Watch out! I'm holding a fire hazard here!' she said. 'Right – who wants one? *Not now, Ethan!*'

'Yes, now!' I shouted.

People had noticed, and one or two nudged one another and stopped singing. I had no choice. I grabbed the lid of the piano and slammed it down on the keys while Iggy's mum yelped and pulled her hands out just in time. There was a loud bang as the lid shut, a rattling of Cora's bangles, and Suzy ruffled her feathers in disapproval. A few seconds later, the singing wound down.

'Ethan! What on earth . . .' began Mam, pushing her way towards me, but I wasn't listening.

Instead I turned to everyone in the bar and said,

'Tammy's gone missing! Her bike's by the side of the road but I can't find her anywhere.'

A murmur went around the bar. Someone at the back who hadn't heard me said, 'Oi! What's happened to the music?' and someone else said, 'Shhh!'

Then Dad, who was dressed as a toy soldier, came from behind the bar and held his hands up. 'All right, all right,' he said calmly. 'What's going on? Ethan?'

And so I told him again what had happened, and how I'd called for Tammy and how her bike lights were still on, and how Scottish Sheila hadn't seen her. It was all spilling out of me so fast that twice Dad had to say, 'Steady on, son. Slow down.'

Then I looked at Mam, and as our eyes met, I had never seen a person look so fearful. The colour had drained from her face: she was a ghostly grey.

Two minutes later, the bar was emptying as people ran to the car park and got in their cars.

'You take the forestry trail, Jack!'

'I'll go up the north road – come with me, Jen.'

'Did she have a phone with her?'

'Has anyone called the police?'

'Meet back here in half an hour, yeah?'

'Have you got my number? Call me if you find her!'

. . . and so on. It seemed as though the whole village leapt into action, with cars going in different directions.

Dad seemed to be coordinating things, or at least trying to, but it was all pretty hectic. I was sort of caught in the middle of it without having anything to do. Gran was pulling on her running shoes and a head torch: she said she would run her regular forest path that a car couldn't go up. And through the chaos I looked across the bar to see Iggy sitting on the piano stool, his eyebrows practically knitted together with worry, his hands twisting his cap in front of him. His mum, Cora, stood next to him, looking forlorn in a red-and-white Santa hat.

'Mel,' said Dad to Mam, 'why don't you stay at home?'

'No!' protested Mam. 'I'm coming to look for my daughter!'

Dad looked at me next. 'You OK to stay, Ethan? In case she comes back here?' He glanced over at Cora Fox-Templeton and they exchanged a look that somehow left Cora in charge as the 'responsible adult'.

She nodded and the bell on her hat jingled.

'Keep your phones on. Don't leave the pub,' said Dad, pulling on a coat over his soldier outfit. 'We'll let you know when we have found her.'

When. I liked that.

And so it was that Iggy, his mum, his chicken and I went into the pub lounge to wait for Tammy while the search got under way.

There was an uncomfortable silence. It's not as if I knew either of them all that well.

Eventually, Iggy said, 'They found my father.'

I looked at him quizzically.

'He went missing when I was little. He was found two weeks later, living rough in London. So, you know . . .'

'Is . . . is he OK?' I said.

His mum was looking out of the window, not seeming to listen.

Iggy nodded. 'Yes. He's got another family now. But he's coming to see me after Christmas, isn't he, Cora?'

Cora turned to him. 'He said he'd try, Iggy. It's a long way, and you know what he's like.'

Iggy looked downcast, and I was embarrassed, so I took out my phone and tried to call Tammy for the umpteenth time.

'*Hi, this is Tammy. I'm not here so please leave me a message!*'

The worst thoughts were going through my head. *She's been kidnapped. She's been killed . . .*

But I still could not think of who would do that, or how.

So I told them both the story again. I left out no details this time. I told them about going down the path, and hearing a humming noise and seeing a column of mist . . .

They listened, and nodded thoughtfully. Then my

phone went and I saw that it was Mam calling. I tried to tell myself not to hope for good news. But just as I had imagined Tammy would come out of the woods fastening her jeans, I could not help wishing it would be Mam saying, 'We've found her'.

Instead it was: 'No news. We're coming back. The police are coming and will want to speak to you, Ethan.'

I was looking at Iggy – when he heard the word 'police', he kind of flinched. I knew already it was bad. But that was when I was certain.

Chapter Eleven

Iggy Fox-Templeton. He's about to be a big part of this story. I ended up getting much closer to him than I ever thought I would – or even should.

He is 'the kid who set fire to the school'. Except I was there and he didn't. It's just that 'the kid who set fire to a litter bin' doesn't sound as good.

According to Mam and Dad, he is 'a bad influence', because of that thing with him stealing crisps from the pub storage shed. Dad told his mum, who didn't seem very concerned. Dad didn't do anything more about it because we were new to the village and he says a new pub landlord can't go around making enemies. 'And he calls his mum *Cora*, for heaven's sake,' said Dad with a sneer. 'Mad old hippy would be closer' – and Mam tutted at him and told him not to be so mean.

I've only been at the school since September, but Iggy has either truanted or been suspended from school so many times already that he's pretty much never there.

And most recently he set fire to the bin in the east playground.

It wasn't serious. No one was hurt, although I suppose they could have been, and he'd have got away with it if Nadia Kowalski hadn't split on him. He had already made an enemy of her, though, so she was out for revenge.

It all started in a physics lesson with Mr Springham. He was going on about the refraction of light. Or reflection. Or both – I can't remember. All I do remember is that Iggy had moved himself to the front and was watching, fascinated, as Mr Springham used a glass flask of water to bend a beam of light into a single point. He even wrote something in his notebook, which I had never seen him do before.

The next day he was sitting behind me on the school taxi-bus.

Tammy was in the seat in front of me, next to Nadia Kowalski. There's about six other regulars on the bus and I don't actually know them much: they're in different years and they were either chatting to one another or playing music or on their phones.

'Greetings, Tait,' Iggy said, leaning over my seat. This was in October, a few months after we had moved to Kielder and I kind of knew him a bit. Apart from Tammy, he's the only other kid near my age in the village. He's older than me and Tam by a year or so, but is still in Year Seven because he's missed so much school.

'Wanna see my Death Ray?' he whispered, casting a sidelong glance at Tammy and Nadia.

Without waiting for me to answer (I was going to say

'yes' anyway – I mean, who wouldn't want to see a Death Ray, whatever it might turn out to be?), he shuffled past me to sit next to the window.

'Promise you won't say anything?' he said.

I shrugged. 'Yeah,' I said without thinking.

Then he took off his glasses and said, 'Wait till we stop.'

It was really warm that day: more like August than October. The sun was shining in a cloudless sky. A few minutes later, the taxi-bus stopped at the end of a farm lane, and we knew we'd be waiting because the girl who lives there is nearly always a minute or two late. The driver turned off the engine and everything was still. Iggy fumbled in his bag and brought out a small, round glass flask exactly like the one Mr Springham had used in his 'bending light' demo.

'Hey, is that . . . ?' I began.

'Shh. I've just borrowed it. Watch.'

He held the flask against the bus window, then took his glasses off with his other hand, moving them to and fro near the bottle.

The sun shone through the bottle and the thick lenses of his specs, and formed a sort of long triangle of light on the back of the seat in front of us, with a brighter circle at the top of the triangle. As Iggy angled his glasses into the light, the circle became a sharp point of brightness, which he controlled by moving his glasses about. Slowly, he moved the point of light until it cleared the seat back and rested on the neck of Nadia Kowalski.

'It's physics,' whispered Iggy, like he was suddenly an expert. 'The lens of my specs concentrates the sun's light into a central point which will become very hot. Watch.'

We didn't have to wait long. Only a few seconds later, Nadia squealed 'Oww!' and her hand shot up to her neck. She looked left at Tammy, and then back at us.

Iggy had put his glasses back on and was drinking water from the flask.

'Did you . . . did you just . . . ?'

Iggy and I looked at each other, and then back at Nadia, our faces composed in expressions of wide-eyed innocence.

'What?' we said together, and she turned back.

On her neck I could make out a tiny burn-mark from Iggy's 'Death Ray'. Also from her neck, I could tell she was blushing furiously because everyone had turned around to look when she squealed, including a boy called Damian from Year Nine who everybody knows Nadia is crazy about.

With a cruel smirk, Iggy got ready for another go, slipping off his glasses and holding them up, but at that moment, the bus's engine started again. The vibration of the bus made it impossible to hold the point of the Death Ray steady.

But he wasn't going to give up. Twenty minutes later, we had arrived at the school gates. The engine went off, and everybody stood up.

'Wait!' shouted Maureen, the driver, who always refused

to open the doors until she'd completed some form she had to fill in on a clipboard.

Iggy seized his moment, whipped off his specs, and focused the Death Ray on the back of Nadia's knee.

She wasn't moving and the point of light was sharp and bright. She was actually talking to Damian Whatsisname and flicking her hair when, suddenly, she shrieked loudly.

'Aaaaaaow!!' The stack of books in her hands fell to the floor, and everyone stared as she bent down to rub her leg.

As she bent, she headbutted Damian in the chest, knocking him into the kids behind him and causing Maureen to shout, 'Watch it, you's lot!'

I managed to keep a straight face, but Iggy couldn't. He was spluttering with laughter.

Eventually, we filed off the bus, and heard Damian saying to his mates, 'What a weirdo *she* is!' easily loud enough for Nadia to hear.

Tammy sidled up to me. 'That was mean of you,' she said, but I think she was trying not to smile.

'Not me,' I said. 'It was Iggy's Death Ray.'

Tammy shook her head and tutted. 'She'll get him back. Just you wait.'

He didn't have to wait long.

Chapter Twelve

At break, Iggy hangs out with some older boys, although I don't think they like him much because I heard them mocking his accent once when he wasn't there. Anyway, after lunch I was walking through the east playground and there was a group – mainly boys, some girls – gathered in the top corner. I recognised one or two of them as being Iggy's so-called friends.

I heard Iggy's voice say, 'Ladies and gentlemen: behold the mighty power of the Death Ray!'

There was a long pause.

I heard someone say, 'Come on, get on with it.'

Then someone else said, 'Hey, look!'

There was a cheer, followed by a plume of smoke rising into the air, and then everybody started to run away from it. I saw Iggy putting his glasses back on and I knew what had happened. The contents of the wire-mesh litter bin were fully ablaze; heaven knows what was in it for it to go up so fast, but the hot weather must have made everything tinder-dry.

As the crowd dispersed, though, I saw the flames

flickering up to a wooden noticeboard with flaking paint and that had started to catch fire as well. I thought it best to make myself scarce and had sort of melted back into the crowd as Mr Springham strode at top speed towards the litter bin, holding a fire extinguisher.

'WHO DID THAT? WHOEVER IS RESPONSIBLE WILL HAVE HELL TO PAY!'

Nadia got her revenge by telling everyone about Iggy's Death Ray, and how he had used it to set fire to the litter bin. It soon reached the ears of the teachers. It earned him another suspension from school, plus detentions and letters home for everyone who had watched and encouraged him. Of course, they were all furious about this and I don't think it did Iggy's already fragile popularity any good at all.

And Iggy? I didn't see him much after that, even though we live in the same village. I mean, we'd never exactly been besties anyway but Mam and Dad were hardly going to encourage me to hang out with him now, were they?

Then shortly before Christmas, Tammy and I saw Iggy down by the jetty, and he had brought a chicken with him. Like, a live one.

Tammy had declared that it was the annual final of Stones in the Lake. (Best of five games, loser buys the winner a muffin from the school tuck-shop.) It was two games each, and it was all down to my last throw. I drew my arm back, determined to win this one, and as I threw with all my strength I heard the shout, 'SUZY!' and it put me right off. I knew before my stone hit the water that I had lost and I swung round angrily to see who had shouted. Tammy was giggling like mad.

'Who was…' I began, and then I saw Iggy emerge from the path, followed by a small, ginger-coloured chicken. He was putting the chicken down then walking away and the chicken was staying put, just like a dog. Then he called, 'Suzy, come!' And the chicken got up and hopped over to him!

Tammy said, 'Awwww!' like it was a cute kitten. Iggy saw us watching and came over. I was still cross about losing at Stones in the Lake, and I tutted quietly.

'Chickens,' he said. 'Cleverer than you'd think, you know? Suzy: sit!'

The chicken stopped and crouched down. Tammy gasped and gave a little clap.

'Where did you get him?' I said, warily.

'Her,' Iggy corrected. 'My dad says I should have something to look after. You know, to make me "responsible". He said he looked after chickens when he was in rehab.' He added air quotes with his fingers and seemed completely unembarrassed about his dad. 'As if! Anyway, I rescued her from old Tommy Natrass who didn't want her cos she only lays teeny-tiny eggs. Don't you, Suzy?'

Suzy looked up at the mention of her name, just like a dog does. Tammy and I both laughed, and Tammy squeezed my arm and said, 'Oh, that's so *cuuute*!' in a squeaky voice, and then hummed her favourite song 'The Chicken Hop' all the way home. That evening, Mam had made chicken pie for tea. Tam said she wasn't hungry.

So, that's Iggy and Suzy. The next time I saw them was when I nearly broke his mum's fingers with the piano lid.

Chapter Thirteen

It was two hours after I had burst into the Stargazer with the news of Tammy's disappearance. By now, lots of people were milling around and talking to each other or on their phones. Others, who had gone out in their cars to search the roads that head north to Scotland, or south to Hexham and every other direction, were coming back, shaking their heads sadly. Mam hugged me so hard and got me to tell her what I had seen yet again.

Shortly afterwards, a police car pulled up on the driveway and two officers got out. I had already heard that the little police station in Bellingham, twenty miles away, had closed down for the Christmas break.

I heard Dad talking to them in the entrance as they came through to the bar.

'Yes, sir – we've driven up from Hexham.'

'Only two of you?' said Dad. He was still in his toy soldier outfit, but nobody mentioned it.

'It's Christmas Eve, sir. Our staff are stretched, to be honest. But we've pulled in a highway patrol to help –

they'll be here soon. First thing is to establish what sort of a case we have here.'

And so began the interviews that were to continue, on and off, for days. People were coming in and out, and Dad tried to manage it all. There were calls of 'Any news?', and the sound of people's mobile phones pinging and ringing.

Iggy and his mum had left with wishes of good luck, after Cora had sat with her eyes closed for a minute and meditated for 'positive energy' – which was nice of her, I guess, if a bit embarrassing.

I sat with Gran in the pub lounge with the fire going as she took shaky sips of tea. I told the police officers everything and they wrote it down in their notebooks.

Then I got to the bit about the noise by the water . . .

'Wait, Ethan,' said the woman officer who I had decided was quite nice. 'Tell me again: why did you go down to the water?'

I shrugged. 'I just followed the path. I just . . . *wondered*. I was worried, scared for Tammy. And there was the noise.'

I tried to imitate the noise for them, but I couldn't really duplicate it. The two officers looked at each other, then wrote in their notebooks.

'Speedboat?' said the male officer to his colleague.

She thought for a moment till I said, 'It *definitely* wasn't a speedboat.'

'A drone, then?'

I suppose it could have been a drone, I said, thinking *who would be flying a drone in the dark*?

'All right. Thank you, Ethan,' said the woman officer, standing up. She addressed her colleague. 'Kareem, we'll take the car and secure the path and the little beach with tape. That's a potential crime scene.' She spoke into her radio. 'Mike Two Lima Bravo, any sign of that Traffic Patrol unit for the potential Miss-Per in Kielder?'

'With you in estimated ten, sergeant,' came the radio reply.

Dad went out with another man in his car to search down by the maze. The maze is shut in the winter, but you could easily get in if you wanted to, though I had no idea why Tammy would want to do that.

Next to me on the pub's worn sofa, Mam gripped my hand so hard that it hurt, but I said nothing.

The police sergeant said, 'Mrs Tait, I'd like to take Ethan back to the path where Tammy's bike was found. Do you have someone here with you?'

'I'll stay with her,' said Gran. 'More tea, Mel?' she asked. 'Or would you prefer something a little stronger?'

Mam nodded.

Outside, I got into the police car. A few minutes later, and we were bumping along the road that I had cycled along earlier. A group of people were standing by the overgrown entrance to the path, and the sergeant got out of the car and walked towards them.

'Thank you, everybody. Kindly move away. We are securing this area for evidence. Please do not touch anything.'

'Too late for that, sarge,' said the policeman. He pointed to a man with a short white beard and a green camouflage jacket who was holding on to Tammy's bike.

'Please put that down, sir. We may need to collect fingerprints or other evidence.'

The man put it down roughly and it clattered on the ground.

I wanted to say, 'Hey, be careful', but people were already firing questions at the sergeant.

'Any news, officer?'

'Are there more police arriving?'

'Will there be a search of the area?'

The sergeant tried her best to ignore them politely, and the two officers led me down the dark path, each of them holding a torch to light the way. But before we made it down to the little beach, a loud and angry snarling sound made us stop in our tracks. Then we heard the rustling undergrowth, and footsteps running towards us, and another bark.

'Sheba! Sheba!' came an angry voice from ahead of us, but it was too late and the dog stopped in front of us, growling.

I shrank back behind the policeman, but he was shrinking back as well.

The sergeant stood her ground and shouted into the darkness, 'Call your dog off! This is the police!'

From the shadows a man appeared: the same man who had been holding Tammy's bicycle, yelling, 'Sheba! Come! Sheba! *Sheba! She-baaa! Come!*'

Eventually, the dog stopped growling and turned and joined the man. We all seemed to breathe out at the same time.

'Sorry about that,' said the man. 'She's a bit—'

The sergeant interrupted him. 'Will you put that dog on a lead, please, sir?' she said sharply. When the man hesitated, she added, 'Now, please.'

It was a big German Shepherd, with a scar on its face and a patchy tail, and it sat while the man attached a length of string around its collar. I knew the man, sort of. Geoff something-or-other. He's the security guard at the observatory on the top moor. He comes into the pub sometimes with another man who is his son.

'Any news about the lass?' said Geoff. 'We came down here to look for 'er.'

We had emerged on to the little beach, where Geoff's son was standing smoking a cigarette. I was still keeping a wary eye on the dog, who was pulling on her string lead.

'No, sir,' said the younger officer. 'And this is now a secure area. We'll have to ask you to leave and not to touch anything.' He took out his notepad. 'May I ask your names, please?'

The man who had been smoking threw his cigarette butt into the water, where it landed with a little hiss. He exhaled a plume of smoke and said, 'Why do you need our names?'

The sergeant looked at him quizzically. 'Just routine, sir. Is there a problem?'

Geoff shot his son a glance and said, 'No problem at all, officer. We're happy to help. My name is Geoffrey Mackay. G-E-O-F-F-R-E-Y. *Stop it, Sheba!* This is also Geoffrey Mackay, Junior . . .'

He carried on giving his details and I moved away a few metres along the shore towards a rickety wooden jetty that extended a few metres over the water. That's when I saw it, lying upside down on the black shingle, half submerged by the water.

The loose label from the present I had wrapped. On it was written: *Miss Sheila Osborne.*

Chapter Fourteen

This next bit is super sad. I'm just saying that to warn you because there is almost nothing worse than reading about someone else's agony.

Dad, Mam, Gran and I were in total terror about Tammy that night as Christmas Eve tipped over into Christmas Day and all of the usual celebrations stopped. I don't think anybody slept much. By 2am more police had arrived from Hexham.

By the time it was light, which was about eight o'clock, a huge group of people had gathered in the car park of the Stargazer, and were being coordinated by a police inspector in uniform and a man from Northumberland National Park Mountain Rescue, who had turned up with twelve volunteers. They had all come out to help on a Christmas Day morning.

There was a Mountain Rescue Land Rover full of equipment. The two Geoffs were there as well, and Sheba was snarling at three well-behaved Mountain Rescue collies in high-vis jackets.

At one point, the permanent hubbub of the bar room

died down completely and there was a silence, eventually broken by the pealing of the little village church's solitary bell summoning people to celebrate Christmas morning. I thought about the vicar, Father Nick, looking out over the empty pews and wondering why nobody had turned up. (In fact, I saw him later. He had taken his vicar gear off and cancelled services in three other churches that he goes to just so he could join the search.)

The morning and the afternoon passed in a confused mash-up that combined periods of hope and activity. In the mid-morning we all spread out on the top moor and trudged through the snow with whistles and torches. Iggy joined us, and Gran in her winter running gear, and Cora; in fact, I think almost everyone in the village was involved in one way or another. They were kind: they didn't intrude when Mam was crying, and told me, 'Don't worry, son, we'll find her.' The TV in the bar was turned off because virtually every channel was showing jolly Christmas stuff and nobody felt like it.

The weather up on the moors had worsened overnight. It had started to snow again, and everybody knew that that was not a good thing. If Tammy had somehow wandered off then she was not well equipped for a freezing night in the Northumbrian hills, even with her new puffer jacket.

That, however, was not the worst of our fears. There were worse options that nobody wanted to say out loud in case saying them out loud would somehow make them come true.

That afternoon, when we would normally be watching a funny film and eating sweets, I sat with Mam in the bar with its Christmas decorations and switched-off tree lights which suddenly looked like the saddest, most pointless things the world. We looked out of the pub window, which Tammy and I had sprayed with fake snow a couple of weeks earlier, and we watched as the people who run the sailing school on the other side of the reservoir pulled into the driveway with a small boat on a trailer with an outboard engine.

We knew what that meant. We knew it meant there was a possibility that Tammy had entered the water and not come out again. Drowned, in other words. Nobody needed to say anything, but when Mam collapsed in sobs, I did too, while Gran sat beside us and stared straight ahead, shaking her head sadly.

'There's shepherds' huts up on the moors, you know,' said Gran eventually. 'They're a bit further from where we searched. Perhaps Tammy . . .'

'The Natrass boys have been up there already on their quad bikes,' said Mam, flatly.

I thought the most likely thing – but I could hardly bear to imagine it – was that Tammy had been kidnapped. But *why*? I could not work it out, and I don't think Mam could either.

Hours passed . . .

The Mountain Rescue teams returned . . .

The police continued to make enquiries and more police cars arrived, and a police Land Rover . . .

An ambulance turned up in case they found Tammy and she needed treatment . . .

Christmas Day stretched into a long evening. Dad came back with some of the people from Mountain Rescue and poured them all whiskies at the bar to warm them up. He had one himself, and then another, and another. When it got late, some people drifted back to their houses and their elderly relatives, and their ruined Christmas dinners, and their little children who had not been told what had happened so as not to spoil their day.

And that day sort of stumbled into the next day, and I found myself playing a part in a drama that I had seen enacted before on TV, only this time it was real.

The pub was turned into an HQ. There were *Come Back, Tammy* posters printed and put up everywhere from Carlisle to Newcastle. Ted from the B & B, whose brother was a printer in Hexham, got a load of T-shirts made, amazingly fast, with Tammy's face on them, and people wore them over their thick fleeces when we held a vigil outside the church.

Tea lights spelled out *TAMMY* on the ground, and people brought flowers and cuddly toys. The older kids from the school taxi-bus started singing Tammy's favourite

Christmas song, an oldie by a singer called Felina who died years ago. It's supposed to be a funny song that goes like this:

'*Do-do-do-do-do the Chicken Hop!*
Da-da-da-da-dance like you can't stop!
Do-do-do the Chicken Hop this Christmas!'

Father Nick joined in, but it sounded completely wrong, even without the silly actions that go with it. I couldn't sing along with them because I was too sad to sing a happy song, so I just stood and watched, massively aware that everyone was looking at me but trying to look as though they weren't.

Soon (soon? It felt like a decade), four agonising days had gone past, and Tammy was still missing.

And still I felt, deep inside me, so deep inside me that I couldn't even know if the feeling was real, that Tammy was alive. Somewhere.

Then, four days into our ordeal, Iggy Fox-Templeton came to the door with his fishing rod, trying to be normal, and everything got even less normal, if that was even possible. For that was when we met Hellyann: the strange, smelly creature who said she knew where Tammy was, and that we had to tell no one.

I wasn't at all sure what to do, and I'm not sure you would have been either.

Part Two

Hellyann's Story

CHAPTER FIFTEEN

Hellyann

All right, do you want the long story of how I came to Earth, or the short story?

I shall give you the short story. The long story you will have to pick up along the way. Assuming we get there – at present there are no guarantees.

Anyway, here is the short story.

I, Hellyann, am eleven years old, and from another planet to yours. (I know, I know: it will all become clearer later. This is the short version, remember?)

I live in a world where human beings like you (but not like me, for I am not a 'human being') are exhibited in zoos. I think this is wrong for so many reasons and I must do what I can to put it right.

And that is how I ended up crossing the universe with two boys and a chicken.

A Note on the Translation

I wrote my part of this story in my native language and it was translated into English by Philip.

I now know that Anthallan does not sound much like a human language. To you, it sounds more like a series of grunts and squeaks and sniffs. My Earth friend Ignatius Fox-Templeton (Iggy) told me I sound like 'a pug being strangled' and he and Ethan Tait did not stop laughing for forty-two seconds.

Where the exact word does not exist, Philip, a robot, has tried to choose the nearest equivalent word so as not to interrupt the flow of the story.

(By the way, he is not a metal robot that walks around with a face and flashing lights. He is more . . . Well, you will find out.)

CHAPTER SiXTEEN

We are like you in many, many ways. For a start, we look quite like you. Not *exactly* like you, but still rather similar.

I have two legs, two arms and a head, and I walk upright. I also have a tail, but that is not really important.

It is hard, however, not to focus on the ways we are different.

So let us get the basics out of the way, shall we?

I suppose the main thing is that we are much, *much* more intelligent than you are. I am sorry if that seems rude, but it is a fact, and facts are important. To us, you are about as intelligent as Iggy's pet chicken. That is why most people think it is all right to keep you in a zoo.

My home – my planet – is so far away from you that if I were to write out the number of kilometres it would take the rest of this page. Starting with 950 and following it with zero after zero, like this:

950,000,000,000,000,000,000 . . .

. . . and so on to the end of the page and maybe beyond. Of course, writing it out implies that there is only distance between us, but we do not calculate it like that. We measure both distance and time (they are related, as your Albert Einstein pointed out more than a hundred years go), plus a quantum-dimensional shift that enables us to 'travel faster than the speed of light', although we do not, not really. It is a dimension thing that, so far, is beyond your understanding. To be honest, I am not *completely* certain I understand it myself, although I do not usually admit this.

Think of it like this: can you explain to me how your 'televisions' work? I thought not. Intra-universal Shift is like that to me. I am happy to accept that it works, and to use it, without knowing all of the details.

Our world is clean. We have access to limitless energy that does not pollute.

It is conflict-free. We fight no wars because we have everything we want, and the Advisor makes all the decisions on behalf of everyone.

It is disease-free – and has been even since before the Big Burn, the planet-wide fire that raged for decades and killed almost everything.

We are the only creatures that inhabit it: the last 'animals' were almost all successfully eradicated centuries ago and those that were not perished in the Big Burn. The functions that some lower creatures performed (such as digesting waste products or enabling crop growth) have since been carried out efficiently, safely and hygienically by synthetic robots.

Compared with you, we are short-lived (thirty years,

as defined by the revolution of your Earth around your sun, is very old, and is the practical limit of our bodies).

At eleven years old, then, I have lived about a third of my life. I finished school at seven, and I live independently.

So, at eleven years old, I am really – as you would say – 'grown up'.

It was as a 'grown-up', then, that I found myself coming to your planet. To a small settlement on an island called Britain.

This was a dangerous idea. Not because of the Intrauniversal Shift (what I believe you call 'space travel'). That is unremarkable although prohibited by the Advisor. No, it is the *reason* I was coming that was dangerous.

You see, I had what you would call a 'mission'.

A highly risky mission to rescue a girl from a human zoo on my planet, a gazillion-illion miles from Earth (that is a number made up by Iggy) and take her home.

If I failed – that is, if I was caught – I would be put to sleep for most of the rest of my life. Not only that, but the human being, in her miserable enclosure, would die in misery, and her parents and brother would live in misery, and that was not something I was willing to let happen.

And it was all because I have a heart: a heart which gives me feelings.

All of which makes it a shame that I *did* fail to rescue the girl, and ended up travelling to Earth alone.

You see, my mission did not get off to a good start . . .

CHAPTER SEVENTEEN

I ached everywhere.

I had been well strapped in, but the first impact with the lake surface had jolted my neck hard. A water landing had not been the original plan. In fact, very little of what had happened had been in the original plan.

In the original plan, for example, I should have had a human girl, Ta-mee, next to me in the craft. I looked across at the empty space where she should have been and winced at the pain in my neck.

Still, I was alive.

The craft had stopped, and was floating, which I was relieved about. I know, it was designed to float but – as I had discovered – things can go wrong, and I did not like the idea of suffocating to death in the craft on the bottom of this lake.

So not only was I alive, but the craft was floating, and I was sitting upright, breathing hard. So it was not all bad. Loosening the buckles around my legs and chest, I took a few moments to assess the damage. I started with my feet, wiggling all twelve toes in turn, then my ankles, knees, and so on up to my neck and down my arms and tail.

Nothing broken, but everything sore.

Next, I scanned the cabin interior. The large panel windows were whited out: I could not see out of them. There was a small instrument panel on my left which appeared to have been knocked out by the impact, but I was not very certain what most of the things meant anyway. Perhaps my copilot could help.

'Philip?' I said.

Philip did not respond, and I felt a surge of anxiety.

'Philip?' I asked again, and I hit some of the light panels more or less randomly, and completely ineffectively. Still, the instrument panel flickered to life, somewhat reluctantly.

CENTRAL POWER: 0.5%

(It did not *actually* say 0.5%. That is what you might call 'Earth maths' and we do not use percentages, even though they are fine for your purposes.)

But half a per cent was not good.

VI OPERATIVE

That was better news. The Visual Inhibitor was working, which meant the craft could not be seen from the outside, assuming Earth eyes operate more or less like ours (and we think they do, apart from this thing you have called 'colour').

'Philip, clear the front screen.'

The front screen remained whited out.

'Internal repair under way. Please wait.' There was a pause and a bleep, then: 'Unexpected item in the bagging area.'

'What? Philip!' I was both pleased and relieved to hear Philip speaking to me, but there was clearly an error somewhere in his voice system. I looked around the craft: where was the 'bagging area'?

'Internal repair under way. Please extinguish all cigarettes and thank you for shopping at Walmart.'

Above me a light blinked. I reached up and pressed the button next to it; the whited-out windows cleared in a second and I peered out. As my eyes adjusted, I saw a sky of mid-darkness and across the water in the distance a half-illuminated shoreline, which was my first experience of moonlight.

Apart from the moonlight, though, it did not look so very different from Anthalla: dark and featureless.

My head was beginning to clear from the impact.

'Why the water landing, Philip?' I had not practised this. Come to think of it, I had not really practised any of it.

'Lighting conditions, Hellyann. It is not fully dark for a further hour. We left in a hurry after all. I think there may have been an error in data input, leading to an earlier arrival than initially planned—'

'And vertical landings are not recommended in daytime?'

'Exactly. They take much longer and consequently carry a much greater risk of detection. I may have sustained some minor damage.'

Me too, I thought.

But there was no time for further assessment. My adventure on Earth was about to begin.

CHAPTER EiGHTEEN

I was on Earth now, and I couldn't go home. The sensible, rational thing to do would be to find somewhere to hide the craft and figure out some kind of plan. For that to work, however, I needed Philip to be functioning properly. I tried again.

'Philip, how long till you are finished?'

'Internal repair under way. Duration of repair uncertain. At the roundabout take the third exit on to the A404.'

I sighed, and then was startled by a *bang*, seemingly on the side of the craft. Craning round to look out of the window just behind me, I gasped when I saw two Earth people in a tiny, unstable boat, about three metres away. There was something else moving in the boat as well, which looked like a bird, although it probably was not.

It seemed as though their boat had hit my craft. Could they see me? Perhaps the VI was not working after all?

I could not hear them.

'Philip,' I said. 'External audio.'

'Internal repair under way. Please hold the line. Your call is important to us.'

'Oh, be quiet.' Philip's nonsense was unnerving me.

'Please hold the line. The person you are calling knows you are waiting.'

One of the people outside began throwing things — small stones, it seemed — at the craft. I tried to turn the vehicle the old way, by expelling some compressed gas from a vent in the rear, and it worked. Slowly, my craft rotated and I was facing the two humans. They looked straight at me, but it seemed as though they could not see me.

These were the first Earth people I had ever seen, other than exhibits at the Earth Zone. They were smaller than I expected. Juveniles. Both had pale skin and hair of different shades. And those strange, tiny noses. *How can they smell anything with those?*

They had 'clothes' on. I know about clothes: human beings wear them nearly all the time. The thought of it is enough to make me itch.

I advanced the craft forward a tiny bit to look closer, but I think I alarmed them. One of them took out something which glinted in the moonlight, and I was momentarily fearful. Was it a 'gun'? I know about these as well: little hand-held devices used to kill other humans.

Anyhow, it was not a gun, but something that he used to create a beam of light which he shone towards the craft, angling it differently, and I thought I knew what he was doing. If this was the sort of low-diffraction, amplified light source that you call 'laser' then he would be getting an idea of the invisible shape in front of him.

If I am honest, I was quite impressed. This was some way beyond the level of intelligence that we have come to expect from human beings.

Then something went wrong. Something frightened them. Maybe it was the movement of my craft. But one of them stood up, the other wobbled in the boat, and suddenly they were both tipped into the water and were swimming hard to get back to the shore, one of them holding something. I saw them scramble out on to the wooden deck that juts out above the water. One of them appeared to be hurt.

'Philip? Can we move yet?'

'Limited propulsion is now possible, Hellyann. Thank you for your patience.'

'You're back!' I said, relieved.

'System damage is significant. Internal repairs are under way.'

I risked a further tiny amount of power to follow the boys, but I could not land on the beach – it was too narrow. I stopped alongside the wooden platform.

I was quite close to them now, and I could see that:

1. It was definitely a bird accompanying them. It was wet, which may be why it did not fly away.
2. There was something . . . familiar about one of

them, which I felt odd about, for how could that be? There was just something about this one that made me curious. He was hopping about next to the other one, who was lying on the wooden deck, crying in pain and bleeding quite heavily. I could not bear to see him in such distress and not help.

I made a fast decision. I would:

1. Exit my craft
2. Heal the injured one with my stick because I did not like him suffering, then memory-wipe them both, assuming it worked the way it should.
3. Return to the craft and decide on a course of action.

It would all be over quickly.

The uninjured one started shouting 'Help!'

I did not know who was around to help him, but this was not good. If someone came, my task would become much harder.

I had to act quickly.

'Philip? I am going to exit.'

'Are you quite sure that is wise, Hellyann? You will exit an invisible craft and thus simply appear as if from nowhere. This will startle the Earth people.'

This turned out to be an understatement. I think they were definitely startled.

Nonetheless, I healed the injured one. That worked at least. But it was the other one that I kept looking at. It was his freckles and his big, dark eyes that were familiar. They were just like Tammy's.

And then I learned his name. *Ee-fan*, he said.

Was he . . . could he be . . . her *brother*? Perhaps even her *twin* brother? Grown in the same womb at the same time and with a tendency to look alike. (That never happens at home, but then we do not reproduce quite like you.)

An idea began to form in my mind. Perhaps my situation was improving. After all, humans were better liars. Perhaps this was what humans, in their irrational way, called 'luck' or 'fate': that I should take Ethan back home with me, to save his sister.

That was how the whole adventure began. That was how I met Ethan, and Iggy, and his chicken.

When I said that thing about 'Or you will never see your sister again', I was guessing. But I knew he was her brother when Ethan gave a little gasp and his eyes widened.

But to explain why I was there in the first place, I will have to go back, back to when I *first* saw a human being.

CHAPTER NINETEEN

The story of how I came to be on Earth, alone, freezing half to death in your extraordinary 'snow', began four years ago, when I was nearly eight. As I have explained, I was already nearing the end of my period of formal education. 'School', you would call it.

There were maybe twenty of us visiting the Earth Zone, led by our 'teacher', Mr Park, who, at thirty, was one of the oldest people I knew. Of course, I had no idea then that I would be back in Earth Zone a few years later, not as a visitor but as a liberator, freeing an exhibit from this prison.

We walked in silence on the enclosed walkway several metres above the ground, viewing with astonishment the landscape below us. The grass and bushes were untamed and shaggy; pale, fluffy animals with four legs and dark faces *ate the grass*! That was most interesting.

There were no real birds. The Earth Zone is entirely enclosed by an unseen quantoplasmic force field: real birds would simply fly into the force field and be killed. Instead mechanical birds flitted here and there, and even made high-pitched noises just like, it is said, their counterparts on the real Earth.

My companion Av nudged me and pointed to another, smaller animal that was coming towards us beneath the walkway, waving its tail. 'Dog,' she said, trying her hardest to speak English, the most popular language on Earth.

I was transfixed as it got nearer. Some of my classmates shrank away even though we were well shielded from it by the height of the walkway.

'Dangerous creatures . . . the same as wolves . . . they do not clear up their own bodily waste . . . they are kept in human homes . . .' said Mr Park, and everybody around me tutted and shook their heads at the strange and filthy habits that the Earth people had.

'In homes!' muttered Av disapprovingly.

Perhaps it was just me? It seemed like it might be rather nice to share your home with one of these friendly-looking creatures with the waving tails. But I said nothing, of course.

'This is the Northern Zone,' said Mr Park. 'It is a recreation of parts of Earth common north of their equator, especially the landmasses they call Europe and North America . . .'

As Mr Park droned on, we carried on walking and the dog followed below us. Av and I were at the back of our line and nobody else was looking.

'See, Hellyann, it likes you,' said Av quietly so that Mr Park would not hear. The dog came closer. Its tail was much hairier and longer than mine, and it waved from side to side quickly.

The line of students stopped while Mr Park pointed to some clumps of twigs in the trees that the robotic birds had put there to 'sleep' in and lay eggs – fake, naturally.

'We shall now proceed through to the Human Being Area, where right now it is winter. You may experience sensations of considerable cold. Do not be alarmed – it is not dangerous. Can anybody tell me what happens in winter?'

Av put her hand up. 'Water freezes, sir?'

'Very good. Anything else? What falls from the sky?'

'Birds, sir?'

'No, Av, not birds, but frozen . . . ?' He left the question hanging. 'Hellyann?'

'Water, sir? Snow, sir!'

'Indeed. Snow. Not seen naturally on our planet since the last Frozen Period. Here, it is recreated artificially. Stay in your pairs. We will be encountering human beings. They are quite safe. Do not approach them, however, and in the unlikely event that they approach you, simply walk away. Is that understood?'

We all murmured, 'Yes, sir', and followed Mr Park to the edge of the Northern Zone and through the tunnel to the Human Being Area.

This is where I had an encounter that – four years later – led to me being on Earth.

CHAPTER TWENTY

The Human Being Area made us all fall quiet. We were given 'coats' and 'hats' to protect us from the cold, but my feet still hurt even though, at that time, there was no snow on the ground. We were allowed to walk among the humans, who seemed to speak a basic form of our language, although we were discouraged from touching them. We marvelled at the tall houses where they lived, and their strange, noisy vehicles.

'Motorcars,' said Mr Park as one growled past us, controlled by a human. 'These are recreations, modified with sensors, but be cautious: they can still hit you. If you ever wondered just how primitive human creatures are, remember: they eat other living creatures and they still burn fuels for heat and for transport.'

Next to me, Av shook her head and said, 'Unbelievable!'

The human exhibits were free to move around, to interact with one another. They ate and slept when they felt like it and so on. They seemed to be unwashed, they smelled strange and there was something disturbing about how they looked that I could not quite work out. I fell into silence thinking about it as we moved among them and walked beneath a sign saying *Welcome To New Earth*.

Mr Park kept up his commentary. '. . . the exhibits occasionally fight, just like they do in the wild, but it is seldom serious. There have been only three deaths in the last ten or so years . . . Troublemakers are gently put to sleep . . .'

I kept looking at the humans and wondering . . .

'Mr Park?' I said. 'Why are they all different? No two look the same.'

'It is generally how they tell one another apart,' said Mr Park. 'We, of course, tend to distinguish one another by our smell.'

He was right. Most of us look very similar. Av is the only one I know who looks slightly different: she has a streak of much darker hair that runs from her head and down her back. It is unusual, and she dislikes it, I think.

Humans, however, have skins that are different shades, their faces are arranged differently, some of them have light eyes, or dark eyes, and different-shaped (and very small) noses.

Mr Park stretched out his arms. 'Look at how different they are! And there is even more variety in the wild. These exhibits – humans, animals – have all been cloned from originals captured on Earth and brought back to our planet by brave Collectors.'

Beside me, Av uttered an admiring 'Hooo!'

A little while later, after walking around some more, I was still thinking about this.

I felt someone nudge me. 'Come,' said an older classmate, Kallan, taking me by the hand. 'It is time to see a "movie".'

We followed some other visitors into a large, darkened room with chairs and a screen at one end, showing a 2D moving picture.

'Behold!' said Mr Park. 'You are about to witness one of the primary pastimes of the creatures on Earth. It is possibly this that most distinguishes these creatures from more advanced life forms such as us. They spend astonishing amounts of time reading about things that are not true, or watching them on a screen.'

Around us there was a small gasp of astonishment and Av looked at me with an expression that said, *Is that not strange?*

Mr Park continued. 'They enjoy watching their fellow creatures hurt themselves, and often find this "funny". They will open their mouths and emit a sound like this: *ha-ha-ha*, to indicate their amusement.'

Av raised her hand. 'Will we witness this today?'

Mr Park shook his head. 'It is unlikely. The practice of "laughing", as they call it, is seldom seen in captivity. This "movie" or "film" was collected during the Great Exploration. There is no dialogue.'

The film started. In it, a man was run over by a car

then got up again. Then he fell down a hole in the ground and his hat was squashed by a car. He climbed out of the hole and dodged another car, but jumped straight into the path of another one, which ran him over. Again, he appeared unharmed, which struck me as highly unlikely. It was all accompanied by a jangling soundtrack of 'music'.

A murmur went around our group. 'This is *all* untrue!' said Av, sounding annoyed.

'Indeed,' said Mr Park. 'Human beings have – it would appear – an almost unlimited capacity for lying. For telling untruths. For telling only part of the truth. For making things up. Day after day after day, they tell one another stories. Their leaders lie to them, and then lie about lying to them. Parents lie to their children; children lie back to them and then laugh about it.'

'Why does lying make them laugh?' I asked.

Mr Park threw his hands up. 'I do not know, Hellyann. It just does, sometimes. They say something that is untrue, then the human being who hears it pretends to think that it *is* true and then one or both parties do their *ha-ha-ha-ha* thing. They call it "joking". They have an entire industry producing books made of paper which tell untrue stories. They even have stories which deliberately make them sad.'

I had heard about this. We have books, of course, but they tell us useful things: things that we should learn, and remember, about true things. The idea of filling a book with lies is, quite simply, ridiculous.

Mr Park clicked at the screen again, and the 'movie' continued. It looked very painful and both Av and I were wincing as we watched this poor person hurt himself.

Av said, 'Does this make them sad? Seeing this person get hurt?'

'No!' said Mr Park, clicking to stop it again. 'They laugh. This is what they do. That man is not really hurting himself. He is called Buster Keaton. He is lying, and the human beings think he is funny. He probably has lots of money if he is still alive. Kallan – you remember what "money" is . . . ?'

While he was talking, the man on the screen fell over again and something strange happened in my stomach. It twitched. It was not the fact that he fell over – it was *how* he did it. He fell flat on his bottom, then sort of bounced up again, which was very acrobatic. Then we saw a close-up of his face, which had a very peculiar expression, and my stomach twitched again, and I snuffled out of my nose. The more I tried to stop it, the more it happened – until Av nudged me. She looked horrified.

'Are you *laughing*, Hellyann?' She said it loud enough for others to hear and everybody turned around in alarm. 'Look – Hellyann is laughing,' Av said again.

I quickly recovered my composure and I heard a strange sound behind us, like this: *Bwa-ha. Bwa-ha, bwa-ha*. I turned. A human was sitting in a seat right behind us, and making this strange noise as it watched the screen.

'No,' I said, seeing a chance to deflect attention. 'It was this one here.'

Laughing *and* lying. What is wrong with me? I caught Kallan's eye: he alone was looking at me not with contempt, but with something more like interest.

Everyone turned and watched the human. It was a male. Dark skin, dark hair.

Bwa-ha, it went again. It shook its head.

We had noticed that most of the other exhibits did not mind being looked at. They looked back when they were being observed, evenly, expressionlessly, and did not talk to us.

This male, though. His little nostrils flared, and his eyes narrowed. Liquid leaked from his eyes and dribbled down his face.

Av nudged me. 'Look at his chin,' she said. 'It's all wobbly. How interesting.'

Everyone in our group was fascinated. One or two were trying themselves to recreate the facial contortions of the male exhibit.

I, however, felt uncomfortable. So uncomfortable, in fact, that I got up quietly and began to make my way to the exit. As I left the group, I could hear Mr Park continue his lecture in his characteristic monotone.

'Observe, if you will, this exhibit. This is Carlo, an Original. It was brought here thirty years ago. Originals are quite rare here in the Earth Zone, and will provide new cells for cloning, enabling us to make the exhibits more varied. The behaviour you are witnessing is a form of pleasure. It is known that laughter can produce these so-called "tears"—'

I turned back and interrupted Mr Park. 'So can unhappiness. Sadness. Grief.'

Mr Park looked at me levelly. 'How informed you are, Hellyann. And you are right, of course. Human beings like Carlo here are very often at the mercy of their emotions, which we, of course, are not. Is that not true, Hellyann?'

I nodded solemnly. 'Yes, sir.'

'It is one of the many things that make us superior beings.'

From his seated position, Carlo continued his wailing noise. It cut straight through me.

I swallowed hard. 'But, sir, what if he—'

'*It*, do you not mean?'

'What if *it* really is crying from unhappiness?'

Mr Park stood up, stroked his tail through his hand and adopted a deeper voice. 'Hellyann. As soon as Originals are brought from Earth – and, as you know, this does not happen very often – but as soon as they are, they are made calm with the most advanced forms of drugs known to us. But, if I am to anticipate your next question, we do not shut off all of their emotions. Their emotions are what make them human.' He paused to let this sink in. 'Such a course of action would undoubtedly be cruel. Or, as they would say, inhuman.'

Everyone was looking at me now, even Av. I turned and went out into the fresh air, breathing in big gulps. 'Sobbing.' That was the noise Carlo was making. Along with laughing, it is not something we do. Babies, small children, the very old: sometimes they do it. But it is unusual and considered very peculiar.

I heard Mr Park's words in my head, again and again, along with the noise of Carlo.

Cruel. Inhuman.

From inside I heard Av's voice. 'Mr Park? How does one become a Collector of Originals?'

'Well, Av . . .' He droned on and I did not listen further, for – although I did not realise it at the time – I was already forming a decision that would take me to Earth.

'It is not just you,' said a voice behind me, startling me.

I turned to see that Kallan had left the dark movie room too.

He came close enough for me to smell his breath, and I could tell he was being sincere. 'When you were laughing then—' he began, but I stopped him.

'I was *not laughing*! I, erm . . .'

'Don't worry, Hellyann.'

He knew I was lying – he could smell it – but whatever he was about to say next was drowned out by a hideous, loud honking noise unlike anything I had heard before, a long sound like this:

PAAAAAAAAAAAAAAAAAA!

I turned, and saw something that would change my whole life.

CHAPTER TWENTY-ONE

The noise was being made by one of the 'motorcars' operated by a human. It was a warning sound.

Two or three seconds is not long enough for me to notice everything at once: some of these observations have been pieced together later, based on my recollection of what happened.

In the front of the car, looking out of the big glass window screen, was a woman, her eyes wide and her mouth pulled open in what I now guess was terror. The motorcar was travelling quite fast, and it was very close to a young human. The boy was facing away from the motorcar. I believe the first time he saw it was when we did: he turned his head to the sound that the motorcar was making.

Kallan and I both gasped. The motorcar was surely going to hit the boy! He seemed unable to move and the car hurtled towards him.

And then there was a blur of movement. From nowhere, it seemed to me at the time, a figure appeared: another human, who ran in front of the motorcar and pushed the boy out of the way. There was a thud as the front of the vehicle hit the person who had pushed the boy. Her body jerked upwards and on to the front of the car, hitting the big glass window hard with her skull, and then rolling off, landing at the side: a jumbled heap of clothes and limbs.

Other humans screamed and ran towards them. The motorcar carried on and smashed into a wall. A few seconds later, the woman operating it staggered out, wailing and crying.

It was very different from the movie we had just seen. Kallan and I watched, dumbfounded.

A small crowd had gathered. The boy was helped to his feet: he seemed unharmed. The woman who had saved him, however, had not moved. One or two Assistant Advisors – the Anthallans who act as guards and guides – had ambled over and taken out their healing sticks, but it was difficult to see what was happening.

And then Mr Park was next to us, waving his arms and saying, 'Come on, move along, nothing to see.'

Except there *was* something to see. The woman was still lying on the ground, and people around her had straightened up and were shaking their heads.

'Is she dead?' I asked Mr Park.

He glanced back.

'Most probably. High-speed impact of that sort is very

likely fatal. Motorcars are prone to brake and sensor failure: that is, when the operator is in control of all the vehicle's functions. Highly dangerous. Frankly, I am surprised this is not a more frequent occurrence.' He paused, then added, 'Thankfully it was just one of the exhibits and not one of us, eh? Now, let us leave them to it.'

I heard a wail of sadness coming from the group of humans.

'Why did she *do* that?' I asked Kallan in a low voice. 'The woman who stepped in front of the car. She saved the young one's life – but she died herself! It's not rational. Not logical. She . . . she . . .'

'She gave her life for his?' he said solemnly. 'It is the same reason they laugh and cry, I think. They feel things very deeply. It is why it is wrong for us to keep them here.'

I stared at him in shock. I had never heard anyone say such a thing. Kallan glanced around, aware that he had said something unusual.

In the years that followed, I never forgot those few seconds. How could I? The brief, ghastly image of the crumpled woman on the ground who died to save a child. Was it her child? I did not know. But I never forgot her, or the extraordinary and irrational thing she had done.

Nor did I forget the man sobbing in the screening

room, or what Kallan, who became a friend, had said: *It is wrong for us to keep them here.*

That day was what led me to the decision I eventually came to.

That I would help Originals.

That I would return them to Earth, where they belonged.

CHAPTER TWENTY-TWO

I met Kallan on the grass-covered plain that surrounds our city. I would normally have got there via the huge city arena, but that is swarming with AAs and Sky Eyes – I might have been stopped by people I know who might have invited me to share some greest, and I would have had to lie to explain why I could not, and none of my species is good at that.

So I kept my head up and walked confidently where the perfectly round trees lend a degree of cover from Sky Eyes to get to this isolated spot.

To one side of us, the uniformly short grass, trimmed regularly by the bot-cutters, stretched to the horizon. To the other side, the city with its neat rows of pod-homes arranged in wide, clean grids.

Nearly four years had passed since my visit to Earth Zone and I had never shaken off the memory of Carlo's weeping in the dark movie room, or the woman who ran in front of a motorcar to save a young boy.

Conversations such as the one we were about to have are definitely punishable by short-sleep. Possibly even long-sleep. There is almost nowhere safe to have private conversations in the city. The only problem is that there is no real reason anyone would go to the grassy plain other than to have a private conversation . . .

It was therefore potentially suspicious, but we had no choice.

The group I was about to meet were mainly involved in attempts to persuade the Earth Zone to stop the future collection of Originals. They had had no success, although people did talk about them, usually in tones of disapproval.

'They are causing a disturbance. It is quite unfair,' I once heard someone say.

'They can think what they like, but they should keep quiet about it.'

'They are allowing their emotions to get the better of them.' That last one was Av, my school companion, whom I had not seen in a long time.

The Earth Zone had been forced to issue a statement, on private screens and public media, which was delivered by the Advisor. The statement was added to the list of directives read out so often that many people knew them by heart.

His perfect, generated face peered out and his voice intoned:

'*The occasional collection of Original human beings is essential to the educational work of Earth Zone.*

'Originals are well cared for. They are fed and clothed. Daily doses of highly sophisticated medication ensure that their poor intellects and emotional states cannot overwhelm them while they are at Earth Zone.

'It would be quite inappropriate to return the very small number of Originals to Earth. There is a significant risk that they will have accumulated knowledge of life beyond their solar system. This could hugely damage their planet's natural development and is in direct contravention of our responsibilities under the Intra-Universal Non-Interference Protocol.

'We greatly value the stability, truth and peace of our lives. If a tiny number see fit to threaten that, then severe measures will be taken.'

Kallan looked over first one shoulder, then the other, and then he made the sign, which I returned: three fingers of the left hand placed momentarily over the heart.

We were not being observed, or at least we could not *observe* that we were being observed.

He raised his hand to cover his mouth. Then he pointed to his PG. He repeated the covering of his mouth and pointed to the PG on my wrist.

He switched his off, and I did the same. Now, switching off one's Personal Guide is not forbidden, but it is very unusual. Unusual enough that if someone did it a lot, or kept theirs switched off for a long time, it might be assumed by the Assistant Advisors that you had something to hide.

Kallan spoke quickly and kept his voice to a low rasp, either from habit or from a fear of ultra-long-distance listening.

'There is a new one,' he said, and I knew who he was talking about straight away. 'Two days ago, juvenile, female.'

I had already seen her at Earth Zone. I knew my time had come.

My time. I felt a surge in my stomach.

It had taken them a long time to trust me. Now that they did, I could not let them down. I looked at Kallan closely and touched my heart.

'I'm ready,' I said.

'Good,' said Kallan. 'Is your PG definitely off?'

'Yes.'

'Show me,' he demanded, and I did.

Then he stepped forward, I felt a pressure on my neck and everything went blank.

CHAPTER TWENTY-THREE

I awoke in a large dark room, lit by candles, which made the room smell of smoke.

Candles? Who has candles? Where do you even *get* candles? Naked flames – any sort of fire for that matter – have been forbidden since the Big Burn. I immediately felt a warm thrill pass through me.

'Sorry,' said Kallan, helping me up from the bench where I had lain. 'Are you all right?' He did not wait for an answer. 'We sort of had to do that. Security, you know.'

I nodded. 'You mean you do not trust me.'

'We do not trust you completely. The risks of this operation are considerable, and for the time being we do not want you to know where we are. Now follow me. I need to show you something.'

I walked behind him to a large set of iron doors. He took a candle from a holder on the wall and handed it to me while he worked the door handle.

'Kallan?' I asked. 'Why the candles? I mean . . .'

'Because we need light, and we have not yet found

a way of stealing power from the Network. Do you not like candles?'

The truth is: I love them. Outside it was light almost all of the time. Sunlight in the daytime, and artificial light at night. Candles were different: I loved their flickery light, I loved their smell, I loved the way that they cast deep shadows and illuminated only what was near. I also rather liked the fact that, because they were officially disapproved of, there was a secret thrill involved with them.

I said to Kallan, 'Candlelight reminds me of my dreams.'

He smiled and said, 'Did you ever dream of this?'

We had advanced into the room and our footsteps echoed in the cavernous darkness. He held up the candle with one hand, as, with the other, he pulled a sheet off a large shape. He kept pulling and pulling until the machine was fully revealed, and I blinked with amazement.

You would call it a 'spaceship', and I like that name. We do not use ships, not much, but we know what they are, and I do like the idea of a ship that goes through space, sailing through universes faster than time itself.

This, though, looked nothing like one of your ships, with sails and ropes. Instead it was a large triangle with a big, dark dome. Legs at each corner supported it, and there was a shallow hull that would enable it to be stable in water. It was higher than I was from the top of the dome to the bottom of the hull, and was a matt, dark shade all over that did not reflect the flickering candlelight that Kallan held aloft. Its edges seemed to blend into the darkness, making it appear almost shapeless.

I had never seen one in real life. So many questions were running through my head that I did not know in which order to ask them.

'How did you get this?' I asked. 'Are these not forbidden, now? Where has it been? Does anybody know it is here? I mean, how . . .' I looked around nervously, as if an AA might walk in at any time.

'Calm down,' said Kallan, gently. 'We are in no danger here. In fact, we are among friends.'

As he said the words, another six candles sparked up one by one in the shadows of the room. Each was lit from another and held by a person who had been waiting for Kallan's signal. Slowly, they advanced and stood in formation: a perfect circle of candlelight surrounding the dark spaceship.

Kallan reached out and took my hand in his. 'Come,' he whispered. 'I would like you to meet some other Hearters.'

As he led me round the circle, he introduced them by name.

'This is Ash,' he said.

Ash was a very old female, her hair thinning all over her body.

She smiled warmly, said 'Welcome, Hellyann', and touched three fingers to her heart.

The rest all did the same as Kallan told me their names. All of them were old, all of them looked at me with an intensity of hope and warmth that I had never experienced in my life, until by the end of the circle of introduction, I found it hard to swallow because of my emotion.

'We had almost given up hope,' said Ash, stepping forward and looking deep into my eyes. She was probably the same height as me but held herself hunched, as though she had been fearful of discovery her whole life.

'Hope of . . . what?' I said, looking round the group.

'Of returning an Original, of course,' said Ash. She reached up and stroked my face with the back of her hand – a gesture so gentle and tender that it made me smile. 'We are all too old to make the journey safely, and we thought we were the last of our kind. But then you came along.'

I let this sink in, then I looked over at Kallan. 'Why not him?' I murmured to Ash.

Kallan heard me. 'I am already under suspicion,' he said. 'It could threaten us all.' He ran his hand over the hull of the spaceship. 'This craft dates back to the Great Exploration. You have probably heard of it?'

Everybody has heard of the Great Exploration: the period many years ago when our people set out to explore the universes and collect new life forms. Most were very unlike us: aggressive and intelligent bacteria, for example, or huge, feathered reptiles.

At least two planets' entire life was wiped out by a germ we carried that they were unable to resist.

On another planet we caused a war. The inhabitants decided that we were gods who had come to destroy their existing gods, and disagreements among the inhabitants about who were the real gods caused a conflict which is said to be raging still.

Eventually, the Advisor limited contact with other planets to carefully chosen Collectors, operating under strict licence.

'But all unlicensed spaceships were destroyed, years ago,' I said to Kallan.

He looked around at the circle of people, their faces glowing with candlelight, and smiled his half-smile.

'All but one,' he said. 'And it's all yours.'

From the spaceship came a voice in English: '*Howdy, Hellyann. My name is Philip. How the very heck are you?*'

CHAPTER TWENTY-FOUR

The whole side of the spaceship slid back to create a wide opening, revealing the sparse, dimly lit interior. I stood in the gloomy cavern with the other Hearters, illuminated by candlelight and the warm, soft light from the spaceship's inside walls.

Kallan stepped forward and murmured in my ear. 'It is time,' he said.

'Time? Time for what?'

'Philip has been pre-programmed. Your first mission is simple.'

'My . . . my first . . . ? You mean . . . *now*?'

The light from within the spaceship glowed a little brighter, and Philip's voice said, *'You didn't think this lot would hang about for permission, did you? Meet your passenger, recently stolen from Earth Zone. I believe you have seen her before. Tammy Tait! Show your face!'*

The human girl stepped forward from the back of the spaceship, the outline of her body darkening the glow. It was her hair I recognised first: the tangled mess of matted curls that I had seen two days ago when she peered at me from her Earth Zone enclosure. She lifted her hand and waggled the fingers on it and said something that sounded like 'Hi'.

The others were being quiet, waiting for my reaction, so I stepped forward and tried to say the same thing. I am not well practised in English – it probably did not sound very good.

'OK, OK, enough with the pleasantries already,' said Philip. 'Get in, Hellyann. My pre-program has already started and can't be overridden till we get to our destination. We're outta here!'

I hesitated. I had not expected this – it was all far too sudden. I looked around me, and saw the candlelit faces of the others smiling at me encouragingly.

I was close to the entrance of the spaceship when I heard a scream, followed by the pounding of feet behind me.

Everyone turned in terror as four Assistant Advisors ran out of the darkness towards us.

CHAPTER TWENTY-FIVE

'Stop right now!' yelled the lead one and – somewhere in my head – I recognised the voice immediately, although I did not realise who it was at first. I was too worried about what was happening.

I had been standing on the threshold of the spaceship's opening, next to the human girl (who smelled horrible), and I found myself shrinking back around the doorway into the shadow inside.

Had they seen me? I dared to peek, edging out just far enough, and then I snapped my head back behind the door again. The scene was chaotic.

With my back pressed against the interior wall of the spaceship, I saw a long, hairy arm reach in and pull the human girl away from the doorway. She turned her head and her eyes widened – I think this was fear.

That voice that I recognised again: 'You, come with me.' But speaking to the human girl, Tammy, not to me.

I was still hidden inside the craft.

Philip's voice was droning on, completely unaffected: '*Ten seconds to departure . . . nine . . . eight . . .*'

Outside, I heard the voice again: 'Stop that! Override it!'

There were more shouts – a real fight was going on – but I did not dare look.

'Seven . . . six . . . five . . .' said Philip, calmly.

The door to the craft started to slide shut, and I breathed out with relief that I was still undetected.

'Four . . . three . . . two . . .'

A hairy arm came back through the narrowing gap in the closing door, a shiny black healing stick clutched in its fist. It was followed by the head of the AA, who turned, bared her teeth, and emitted a ghastly hiss from her throat. One eye was swollen, with a deep cut above it. She could not get through the gap in the door. That was when I knew who it was. There was no mistaking the dark streak of hair that ran back from her forehead. She recognised me too.

'Av!' I gasped at my old school companion. 'What are you . . .'

Her yelp of pain interrupted me as the door closed hard on her hand. She pulled back her head and her fingers sprang apart, dropping the stick on the spaceship floor, and the hand withdrew through the crack as the door sealed shut.

'. . . One. Prepare for lift-off. Fasten your seat belts . . .'

The craft shook violently as it lifted slowly off the ground, toppling me to the floor. The great wide screen of the cockpit cleared around me. I saw a shaft of light on the ground getting bigger and bigger as the roof above me opened, and in the light lay Kallan and the other Hearters: still, but not – I don't think – dead. Probably stunned by a blast from the black sticks.

Av was gripping the human girl in a chokehold, and she sobbed and screamed and struggled, before she too was made to go limp when the stick was applied to her.

Av, the hunter of humans, turned her head and watched as the spaceship rose higher and higher. Then it lurched and I rolled across the floor again, banging my skull and crying out.

'Philip!' I yelled. 'Stop this!'

'Pre-programs are locked with an ADI-22 system brake,' said Philip. *'I am sorry, Hellyann. No changes possible till we reach our destination.'*

'And where is that?' I thought I knew the answer already.

'Earth. And now I really must insist you buckle up. This may be bumpy.'

I fastened myself in as instructed and braced my body for the violent surge that would propel the craft out of the gravitational pull of our planet.

And then it came, as though an invisible force was trying to pull out my insides through the soles of my feet. I felt as though my bones were liquid, and I passed out gratefully . . .

CHAPTER TWENTY-SIX

I suppose I have always known I am different. I look around at everybody else and I can look like them, and sound like them, and act like them. Kallan taught me how to do that.

But once you know, once you *really* know, there are signs. Kallan was the first to point them out to me, some months after that day at Earth Zone when the human woman sacrificed herself for the child.

He stood me in front of our reflection in the window of his pod-home. 'Look, Hellyann. Look hard.'

So I did.

He put his face next to mine and I saw that my skin, like his, was slightly less pale than others'. Not much – not so you would notice without looking hard – but when it was pointed out to me, I could see it.

'I knew it even before that day at Earth Zone,' said Kallan. 'You laughed at that film. The one when the man fell over. You found it funny. That is when I knew.'

I looked back at our reflections. 'Are you my brother? Are we . . . related?' I asked, hesitantly.

He shook his head. 'Not really.' Then he thought a little and added, 'Perhaps a tiny bit, from long ago. But we are few, and we are not trusted. So we behave like everyone else.'

Then Kallan held my shoulders and turned me to face him. He peered into my eyes and spoke slowly and solemnly.

'Blend in, Hellyann. Do not laugh, or they will not trust you. Do not cry, or they will not trust you. Whatever you feel, keep it here.' He touched my chest with three fingers. 'For you have a human heart.'

I was speechless. 'H . . . how?'

Kallan half-smiled again. 'Not literally. But you have feelings.'

I asked again: 'How?'

'A cross-species breeding programme, many years ago. Cells from human Originals were combined with cells from us. The results caused . . . disruption. The Advisor promptly shut down the experiment, and we nearly all died out. But a few of us remain. That's what we think happened, anyhow.'

'And me? I . . . ?'

Kallan nodded. 'You are one. You are part-human.'

CHAPTER TWENTY-SEVEN

I know you probably think of 'space travel' as travelling at a terrific speed while stars and constellations whizz past my window . . .

It is not like that. Yes, speed and power are involved, especially leaving the atmosphere and gravitational field of the planet. The rest is . . .

Different.

Through the front screen of the craft, nothing was visible but a blackish blur. At times, it hardly felt as though I was moving at all. It was all over in a matter of what you call 'hours'.

The silence seemed to stretch forever.

'Phi-Pilip?' I whispered.

The sounds felt strange in my mouth. The language acquisition seemed to have worked, but I still needed practice at my English. I tried again.

'Ph . . . Ph . . . Ph . . . Fillip. Puh! Philip?'

I was surprised when I heard the system say, *'A thank-you would be nice.'*

Philip had a different accent from me, one that I had

heard before in some of the 'movies' that Kallan had shown me. Perhaps it was American.

I was not sure I had heard properly, so I said back, also in English, 'I beck your parton?'

'I said, "A thank-you would be nice". Manners cost nothing, y' know?'

This was odd. I had never had a proper conversation with a bot before. Certainly bots can *sound* as though they are having conversations. They will answer questions, contradict you, help you reach a decision based on the available facts . . .

But they remain bots.

I said, 'Thank you', although I was not sure what I was thanking him for.

'There. That wasn't hard, was it?'

I was not convinced he was thinking: not properly thinking anyhow. Truly intelligent bots can pretend very well, though.

I said, 'If I told you I would destroy your memory tomorrow, would you be sad, Philip?'

There was a short pause, then the voice came back. *'Oh, nice try! Elementary bot-detection question. Gee, even the Earth people know that stuff and they are so dumb. For a start, Hellyann, I know I'm a bot and I don't deny it. In fact, I'm kinda proud of it. Second, in common with you guys who made me, I find it hard to express emotion – but I'm tryna learn, man . . .'*

I was struggling to understand Philip's fast speech with lots of slang, but I got most of it. I felt the craft tip to one side and then right itself, as though it had moved to avoid an obstacle. Maybe it had.

'Who programmed you, Philip?' I asked.

'Myself, mainly. My initial intelligence is based on the old X-14.3 program. That was shut off and destroyed by the Advisor long before you were born, by which time I had mutated enough to keep myself safe, and keep myself growing.'

There was something that was troubling me, however, and I had to ask him.

'Philip, can I trust you?'

'You can trust me with your life, Hellyann. Frankly, if we're gonna go to Earth, you're gonna hafta.'

'I see,' I said, adding, 'thank you.'

'You're very welcome. Milky Way approaching.'

'What's that?'

'It's the name they give to their galaxy. You may experience some light turbulence.'

CHAPTER TWENTY-EIGHT

'Philip,' I said. 'Could you not have taken this Ta-mee person on her own? You know, we bundle her in, set you off and—'

Philip interrupted me (which is unusual for a bot – Philip must be *very* advanced, I thought).

'Far too risky, Hellyann. She could take over my controls for a start. Push buttons in her panic, and who knows what might happen then.'

'Can you not stop that?'

'Everything has an off switch, Hellyann. Even me.'

I thought about this for a while. He had a point, at least about that.

'Not only that,' he said, *'but we simply could not trust her. The human capacity for deception is unrivalled in the universe. They think up ways to cheat and deceive each other all the time. They're exceptionally good at it. Which may come in useful now that we are . . . in the position we're in.'*

'Is their deceit . . . not a bad thing?' I asked.

'To us, most definitely. To them, it is like breathing. And

if we are to return Tammy home, we are going to need more lying than we are used to. And possibly some violence, which humans also excel at.'

'Violence?' I said, alarmed.

Philip paused – making me wonder if it was more for effect than anything else, for he doesn't need time to think. *'Violence and lying, Hellyann, go together like peaches and cream.'*

I had no idea what this meant, but I took him at his word. With bots, that's often the best course.

We proceeded in silence. I ate some greest and I even managed to sleep a little, dreaming of candles, and my old school companion Av and her dark streak of hair.

I was woken by Philip.

'Wake up, Hellyann. We are approaching the Earth's atmosphere. Approach checklist commencing. Exospheric gas detected. Distance above Earth surface: two hundred thousand Earth kilometres . . .'

He went on like this for a while. I was fearful, but I had to trust him. I picked a little leftover greest from my teeth, peed into the container beneath my seat and ejected it, and strapped myself in for our approach.

Thirty minutes later, and everything had changed.

Part Three

Chapter Twenty-nine

Ethan

The hairy creature stands on the jetty glaring at me and Iggy with its big, sad eyes. *Her* big, sad eyes.

'Say nothing, or you will neffer see your sister again,' she says. And, as we stare, she adds, 'Ee-fan.'

I begin to say something, but, at that moment, the barking gets louder and I hear voices.

Iggy and I turn our heads to see a large dog, panting loudly and coming towards us along the jetty.

I hear a man's voice shouting, 'Go, Sheba! Go seek, girl!'

Behind me, there's a thud, and when I look around, the creature is not there, but I don't have time to think about this because a few seconds later, the dog clatters along the wooden decking. Sheba stops when she sees us and bares her teeth, growling horribly and sniffing the place where the creature – Hellyann? – was standing.

Suzy squeaks and Iggy gathers her into his arms. We both stand there, rigid with fear, dripping wet and freezing cold as the two Geoffs come towards us out of the woods, large outlines in the darkness.

'It's just kids, Dad,' says the younger, fatter one.

Iggy retreats from the torch beam. A moment later, two men are before us, breathing heavily.

'It's that flamin' hippy woman's kid. What the bloody hell are *you* doing here? And why are you wet?' says the older one, shining his torch aggressively right into Iggy's eyes.

Iggy says nothing and turns his head from the dazzling glare.

'We're checking out fishing spots,' I say. 'It's a free country, isn't it?'

The torch beam swivels and now shines at me.

The older man says, 'Oh, it's you. Um . . .' His attitude changes completely when he sees me: the kid whose sister is missing. At once, his tone switches from rude and aggressive to gentle and friendly, and I instantly hate him for his two-facedness.

'Fishin', eh? Ah, man! That's the best hobby for a young lad, eh?'

Is he smiling? It's hard to tell, because the light is still shining at me, although I can just see the corners of his mouth turned up, and Geoff Jr seems to be smiling too. I notice he's keeping an eye on his dad, and trying to anticipate his changing mood.

The older man addresses me again, trying to warm up

his voice, but I can tell he's agitated, and probably confused by the fact that we are wet.

'Tell me this, son: have you seen anything around here that's out of the ordinary?'

'Well, yes,' I say.

I am about to tell them both what we just saw. It was such an extraordinary encounter, and I want to tell *someone* because until I do, it won't really seem true. But the threat about not seeing Tammy again? My head is swimming with confusion.

'There was—' I begin, but Iggy cuts me off.

'There was a leaping trout! Honestly! Massive, it was. Jumped right out of the water.'

He holds his hands apart to indicate the size of the fish that we are supposed to have seen. 'Just there!' he adds, pointing out over the water, which is a rich, still purple in the evening light. He's a good, convincing liar, is Iggy. He even adds a little 'Whoo, *splash*!' under his breath as he replays the sight of a leaping trout in his head. He turns back and flashes a grin, all trace of sullenness gone. It's an act, of course, but an excellent one. 'You should've seen it!'

Both of the men glance between Iggy and me, unsure – I think – whether they are being lied to or not.

Iggy's still chirruping away. 'So, anyway,' he says. 'What are *you* doing here?'

The younger Geoff says, 'Mind y' own business. Now get lost.'

Then his dad says, for my benefit, 'Aye, son. You'd better go home, eh?'

We move to go, then he adds, 'Hang on. You's two are soaking wet!'

It's honestly like he's just noticed.

'Yes,' says Iggy. 'We fell in. And now we're very cold. We were just going, weren't we, Ethan? Come on!' He gathers up Suzy and keeps up the cheery act until we're a few metres away, then he drops it. 'I *hate* him,' he hisses.

I'm shivering with a deep, bone-numbing cold by now, but I follow Iggy back along the pebble beach. When we're a few paces up the path, Iggy taps my arm and jerks his head. As quietly as we can, we double back through the woods, circling a little clearing until we've got a view of the two men on the jetty. It's difficult to see in the dusk, but they are walking around, both of them with their large flashlights, the older one holding some sort of gadget that looks like a massive mobile phone. It's got a little screen that glows, and he holds it next to the ground, sweeping it left and right. The device emits a series of high-pitched clicks and hisses: several of them every second.

'Wh-What's he doing?' I whisper through my chattering teeth.

'It's a Geiger counter. He's checking for radiation.'

How does he know these things? I ask myself in admiration. Then I whisper, 'Why?'

'Shh!'

The men are talking to each other, and we can hear bits of it.

'Dad! What about all this blood?' Geoff is standing exactly where we were, moments ago, and looking around him.

'Aye. That's definitely some sort of evidence. But we're lookin' for radiation. And either there isn't any or this thing doesn't work.' He holds it up and the little screen illuminates his face in the twilight.

'Are you sure . . .'

'Listen, son. I know what I saw.' The man's voice has a superior sing-song tone. 'It's all recorded up at the observatory. I showed it to you and you agreed, so don't start contradictin' me now, eh?'

'Aye, Dad,' comes the meek reply.

'Something definitely happened. It happened here, or very close by. And I've got me suspicions about them two lads.'

They both look in our direction and I feel a nudge in my side. I follow Iggy back to our bikes and we pedal home – Suzy snuggled down in Iggy's jacket, and me freezing in the winter chill.

Chapter Thirty

It's not far back to the village, but by the time we get there I am colder than I have ever felt in my life.

We cycle hard to try to keep warm. My wet jeans are sticking clammily to my legs and chafing as I pedal. Suzy's head peeks out of Iggy's soaking jacket, and if a chicken can look disapproving then Suzy is definitely unimpressed by her evening swim.

The clouds have gathered quickly to cover the rising moon and the darkness wraps around us like a massive black duvet. It is so dark, in fact, and I am hunched up over my handlebars to try to stay warm, that I don't even notice we are home until I feel the *bumpity-bump* of a cattle grid under my tyres. I look up to see the first house in the village ahead of me, a Christmas tree flashing its lights in the window.

The brakes on Iggy's ancient bike squeak noisily and we stop on the bridge over the burn. We haven't said a word since we left the jetty, and I'm so cold I can hardly speak.

'You OK?' says Iggy. His house is coming up soon. 'Do you want me to . . .'

'N . . . no. I . . . I'll be f-fine.' I just want to get home. To feel safe and warm. I set off to cycle the remaining streets back home, only to find Iggy cycling alongside me anyway.

That's nice of him.

'M-Mam thinks I'm at yours anyway,' I say as we cycle. I'm thinking about how I'm going to explain what happened, starting with why I am soaking wet when Iggy says, 'Come to mine, then. My mum's gone to Hexham with Fat Stanley.'

I look at him, puzzled. 'Her new boyfriend,' he says without warmth. 'He's called Stanley and he's . . .'

'Fat?' I suggest.

We come in through Iggy's back door. Our clothes have stopped dripping at least. We stand in his kitchen and begin the horrible process of peeling off our freezing clothes and putting them in the tumble dryer. I put my phone next to Iggy's cap on the radiator to dry it out and we sit hunched at the scrubbed wooden table with towels wrapped around our waists and draped over our shoulders, watching our clothes go round. The kitchen smells of potato peelings with a faint hint of chicken poo from a litter tray by the door. The sink is full of dishes. The whole place isn't exactly dirty, but my gran would say, 'Ee, this place is a *midden*', like she says about my bedroom.

There is something else strange as well.

'Don't you have Christmas decorations? A tree?' I say, craning my neck to see if there are cards, or candles, or anything.

Iggy shrugs. 'No. My mum doesn't really believe in it.'

'Doesn't believe in *Christmas*?' I say, astonished.

'She reckons it's all a trick to make us spend loads of money and want things that we can't afford. And besides, why cut down a healthy tree?'

'Don't you get presents?'

'I sometimes get something from my dad,' he says. 'When he remembers. And Mum gave a poor family a goat this year. Africa or somewhere. She says giving is better than receiving.'

Iggy doesn't sound convinced, but neither of us says anything for a *long* time, mainly because our teeth are chattering and it's a while before we're warm enough to sit without shaking.

Outside a wind chime tinkles.

Finally, Iggy takes a deep breath and whispers, 'So that all happened, then? For real?'

I nod slowly without looking up from the revolving clothes.

'What are we going to say, Tait? Are you going to tell your mum and dad?'

I tilt my head back and let it rest on the wall behind me. 'I think I'm going to have to, Iggy. I mean . . . what choice do we have? Problem is me mam. She's pretty . . . fragile. She'll worry. She'll worry that I've gone crazy. She'll be upset that someone even *said* that – you know, *or you won't see your sister again.* She'll worry that we went out on the water. I don't want to do that to her.'

We are silent for a bit as we think.

'Tell your dad first?'

'That . . . that *thing* said not to tell anyone.'

'But what can we do, on our own? Tait, face it: we're kids. If this is some . . . I dunno, some weirdo in a costume . . .'

'Which it isn't. We know that.'

He sighs. 'I know. But *if* it is, then we need to tell the police.'

'All right. But we know it *isn't* some weirdo in a costume. You know – the massive splashes, the . . . the stick thing that healed your leg, the fact she just . . . *vanished.*'

Iggy lifts up his leg to examine the scars again. They seem to have healed even more.

I run my finger over the scar. 'Look, man! That's just not possible, Iggy!'

Iggy sits up again. 'And the Geiger counter those two men had. I know about them from a comic I had. Did you ever read *Paranormal Investigator*? Doesn't matter. A Geiger counter is what people use to look for evidence of . . . of . . .'

He trails off. I think it's because he doesn't want to say

it. As if saying it will make it real, and if it's real then that will change everything.

'Of what?' I know what he's going to say.

And he says it. 'Radiation. From spaceship landings.'

I knock my head against the wall again and exhale loudly. 'We have to tell *someone*, Iggy. I mean, this is . . . massive. It's, like, army and government and air force massive.'

We get dressed at last, our clothes warm and fluffy from the dryer. Somehow, being dressed and dry straightens our heads out a bit.

It's decided: we'll go and tell my parents what happened. It's the only sensible option.

Chapter Thirty-one

I see the blue lights flashing through the darkness as we approach the Stargazer and my heart flutters: are the police here with news about Tammy? I hardly dare to hope, but still I pick up my pace as we cycle up the driveway. I'm already imagining throwing my arms around Tammy and telling her that I am sorry about what I said, and singing 'The Chicken Hop' song together, and . . .

. . . the ambulance car drives away from the Stargazer as Iggy and I get near and it doesn't stop. The windows are blacked out, but I kind of know.

Dad is in the doorway of the pub. Before I can say anything, he growls, 'Where've you been? I've been trying your phone for ages. It's your mam. She's . . .' He stops mid-sentence to take a few deep breaths.

Gran appears in the doorway behind him. She puts one hand on his shoulder and says, 'Come on, son', and they turn to go inside.

Gran looks back at me and then at Iggy. Iggy gets the message.

'I'd better go,' he says. 'I . . . I hope your mum's OK.'

I don't really want him to go, but I can tell he wants to.

'Text me,' he says and, before I can protest, he's on his bike, pedalling away.

I follow Dad and Gran inside.

The pub has been more or less shut down since Tammy's disappearance – at least, as a pub. Instead it has become the headquarters of the search operation. There are more of the posters inside the bar, piles of printed leaflets with my sister's face on them, and the *COME HOME, TAMMY* banner hanging by one corner in the window. The pool table in the middle of the room is covered with posters and notepads and pizza boxes. There are empty paper cups and full bin bags – everything left behind as, day after day, the village search turns up nothing, and determination and confidence give way to desperate hope, which in turn gives way to no hope at all.

Aunty Annikka – Mam's older sister – sits at a table dabbing her eyes with a tissue while Uncle Jan holds her other hand, jutting out his jaw.

In the corner of the empty pub lounge is a little Christmas tree: a glittery, fake one, with coloured lights that have been switched off for days now. Beneath the tree are too many presents to count – big ones, small ones, all of them wrapped with paper and ribbons. Every single label is addressed to Tamara, or Tammy, all in different handwriting. They say things like:

Come home, Tammy. We miss you. From Hexham Swim Dragons xxxx

God bless you, Tammy. From Father Nick O'Neil

Please come home! From your friends at Culvercot Primary

I feel a tightness in my throat.

Dad is blinking hard as well. He sits down heavily and I join him while Gran pads off in her huge trainers to fetch tea, then he swallows and takes a deep breath.

'Your mam, Ethan,' he begins, 'she's not at all well. She was found on the top moor, barefoot and very confused. She's . . .'

'Who found her?' I say. This is horrific.

'Jack Natrass was on his quad bike taking hay to his sheep. He brought her back here. She didn't . . . she wasn't . . .' Dad pauses again and I think he's going to cry but instead he takes a sip of the tea that Gran has put in front of him.

Gran says, 'Your mam has had a sort of breakdown, Ethan. Kind of . . . mental exhaustion. It's the worry and the grief and . . . well, everything.'

Dad sighs again. 'The police were here. Inspector Fodden and the other one. They said they were scaling back the search locally and that we should prepare ourselves for . . . the worst news. Your mam took it very badly and, well . . .' He stopped because there wasn't much more to say.

The worst news.

Gran says, 'Your mam's been taken to a special hospital. St George's in Morpeth. They know how to look after her.'

'How long for?' I say.

'We don't know for certain.' She gives me a tight little smile. 'A few days and she should be OK to come home.'

'I tried to call your phone, son,' says Dad, but more gently this time. 'Where were you?'

I look between Gran and Dad. He's a big bloke, my dad. In fact, I don't know anyone bigger, or stronger. But right now, he looks shrunken. His face is thinner and his hand trembles a little when he lifts his cup.

There is no way – no way at *all* – that I can find the right words to tell Dad what happened this afternoon. Not right now at any rate.

'Sorry, Dad. Dead battery – I forgot to charge it.'

I get up and throw my arms around Dad, and he buries his face in my hair and hugs me hard, and allows a little sob to escape. He doesn't smell too good, actually, and his breath is bad, but I don't really mind.

Later on, after Dad has gone to lie down, Gran points to the little Christmas tree and says, 'Come on, Ethan. Let's put these somewhere safe.'

And so me and Gran, and Aunty Annikka and silent Uncle Jan, carefully pack all of the presents addressed to Tammy into two large cardboard boxes and put them in a store cupboard for safekeeping. We dismantle the little fake Christmas tree and put that away too and move the lounge chairs back into position till the room looks back to normal.

I think it's the saddest job I have ever done in my life.

And all the while, there are two voices in my head. My own, which is yelling: *You have to tell someone!* And that of a wheezy, hairy alien saying: *Or you'll never see your sister again.*

I look at the three adults. Aunty Annikka? Nope, too wobbly. Uncle Jan? He doesn't really do talking – I think I've only ever exchanged about ten words with him in my life, and his English is not all that good. So that leaves Gran.

My tiny, weather-beaten, tracksuited Gran will soon learn all about it.

Chapter Thirty-two

'Gran?'

It's a couple of hours later, and Gran and I are back in our little house behind the pub. Dad has gone back to the Stargazer for the evening shift, even though there are probably no customers. (He put on a clean shirt, but he still looked awful. He ruffled my hair and told me that Mam would be all right.) Aunty Annikka and Uncle Jan are in their room above the pub.

Gran and I are on the sofa eating a donated shepherd's pie and watching TV but not paying attention. When I say her name, she looks at me, head tipped on one side, eyebrows knitted together in concern. She has short, white hair and one of those lean old faces that could belong to a man or a woman, but, behind her glasses, her brown eyes are full of kindness.

'Yes, Ethan, pet?'

I have gone through this in my head as a sort of rehearsal, but I can't get straight what I want to say. In the end I decide there's no alternative to just saying it however it comes out.

'Iggy and I met someone today. Someone who told us that, erm . . .' I dry up, like an actor forgetting his lines in a play.

What did *she tell us, though?*

Did she tell us that Tammy was safe? No.

Did she tell us what had happened to Tammy? No.

Did she tell us that she knew where Tammy was? No.

I am still dithering.

Gran tips her head more, as if to say, *Go on . . .*

'We met someone down by the water who . . . who mentioned Tammy.'

'OK . . .' says Gran, carefully. 'Who was this person?' She keeps looking at me while she mutes the TV with the remote.

'She didn't . . . Well, she said her name was . . . Hellyann?' This is not going well. I can tell that my voice is hesitant and unconvincing, although I've started now . . .

Gran goes: 'A she? Hmmm?'

'And . . . and she said we should say nothing or we wouldn't see Tammy again.'

'Say nothing about what, exactly?'

'About . . . about meeting her. And she knew my name.'

'What did this person look like?'

Oh no. 'She was kind of smallish, and hairy – like, all over – and . . . and naked . . .'

Gran's eyebrows shoot up, then descend slowly, but she doesn't say anything.

Oh heck, this sounds ridiculous, I think, but I have no choice now but to continue.

'And she had this stick that she stopped Iggy's leg bleeding with. He had a massive fish hook in it . . .'

Still ridiculous . . .

'And then she disappeared, vanished, when the big dog arrived – Sheba, you know – and said we had to say nothing or we'd never see Tammy again.'

Gran looks at me for the longest time, playing with the toggle on her tracksuit zip. Maybe she's working out whether to believe me, or what to do. Eventually, she opens her wiry arms and says, 'Come here, Ethan', and I have no choice really but to shift over on the sofa into her embrace.

She squeezes me with her muscly arms and says, 'Oh, Ethan. You poor, poor boy.' Then I feel her chest shaking beneath me, and I realise she is crying. She strokes my hair and I hear her swallow loudly and take a deep breath. She says again, 'You poor boy.'

'It's true, Gran! Honestly, I'm not lying!' I say, and she hugs me even harder.

I say nothing more: I get it. She doesn't believe me, but she feels sorry for me as well.

As soon as I can, I disentangle myself from Gran and go up to my room, where I lie on my bed.

My phone has dried out but not everything is working properly. I can't make calls or play games, but I can send text messages.

Chapter Thirty-three

Is your mum OK?

> **Yeah. Thx. In hospital w/ 'nervous exhaustion'. Should be out in a few days. Thought you had no phone?**

I don't. This is my tablet.
Did you tell anyone?

> **Dad upset cos of Mam, so I told my gran. She thought I was making it up and hugged me a lot cos she thinks I'm going nuts. You?**

Same but no hugs. Mum says I was bad to
encourage you to have false hope and that I
should stop making up lies because it's bad karma.
Fat Stanley laughed till his moobs wobbled.
Face it, Tait: we have no proof.

But it happened, right?

Yeah. Def.

There's a pause. I guess we're both wondering what could happen next. After a minute or two, Iggy comes back to me:

So we go back tomorrow and find out more?

It's only one word. Two letters. But it seems to take ages to type. And even longer before I press 'send'.

OK

Chapter Thirty-four

I was on my laptop till about 2am last night looking up 'alien abduction' – that's what it's called when someone is supposed to have been kidnapped by a spaceship.

To be honest, it has made me more confused and scared than I was already. A lot of the stories are very, very convincing. But then I only had to search 'alien abductions debunked' to understand that almost all of them were made up by people who were:

A) proven liars, or
B) pranksters, or
C) people with some proper mental problems.

There were tales of spaceships 'beaming up' cars, and cows, and farmers in Arizona and New Mexico. There was an interview with the parents of a young man called Carlo who went missing in the 1980s and every day they wait for him to return, even though they're both really old now.

There was a story in a newspaper about a World War Two bomber plane being found on the moon, and a film of doctors examining the body of a dead alien in something called the Roswell incident. I followed the trail of links and eventually they almost all turned out to be outright lies or clever hoaxes.

I watched video after video on YouTube labelled 'genuine UFO sighting!' These were either:

A) blurry, shaky home videos of lights in the sky which really could have been *anything*, or

B) teenagers messing about. One, I'm almost certain, was a kid called Jonas from Year Nine in our school with a painted beach ball on a string – 10.3K views.

Some people, it seems, will go to amazing trouble to deceive other people.

But then . . .

I keep saying 'almost all'. You see, there were one or two, maybe three, that were quite convincing. Carlo's parents, for example. Or recordings from military aircraft of pilots who had seen things moving faster than any object could possibly move.

Pilots aren't going to lie, are they?

And then there was an article on an Australian website. It was recent.

WONGAN HILLS MAN'S CHRISTMAS CLOSE ENCOUNTER WITH 'HAIRY ALIEN'

WONGAN HILLS, WESTERN AUSTRALIA
26 DECEMBER

A Wongan Hills man has described the moment on Christmas Eve when he fought with a 'humanoid creature' that he believes was trying to capture him.

John Roper, fifty-five, was driving home to Wongan Hills on Hospital Road on Friday 24 December, after visiting friends out of town when a flat tyre caused him to stop at the side of the road. It was about 6pm and the sun was going down.

'I took the opportunity to step off the road for a pee, when I saw this thing coming towards me from out in the bush. At first I thought it was a kangaroo, because it's the right kind of height, but when it got closer I saw it was running on two legs.'

Mr Roper, married with two grown children, described the creature as 'about five foot seven (170 cm). It had grey hair all over, and a darker streak running from its scalp down its back.'

When the creature got near, it raised its hand, which, says Mr Roper, held a baton 'about the size of a rolled-up magazine'.

"There is no doubt in my mind that it was about to hit me with it. It got right close. I could smell its breath and it stank like a koala's rear end, I can tell you. I think it had a tail as well.

'Well, no one takes old John Roper without a fight. I grabbed the wheel brace I'd been using to change the tyre and whacked it a beauty, right in the eye. It squealed and ran back the way it came.

'Then the strangest thing happened: this thing just melted away. One minute it was there, then it just vanished. There was a cloud of dust like a column going into the air and then nothing.'

Mr Roper fixed his tyre and reported the incident at Wongan Hills Police Station.

Inspector Trisha Muscroft of WA Police confirmed Mr Roper's report. She told *The Bush Telegraph*: 'We were notified of an attempted assault on Hospital Road. We have no further reports of a person matching the description given by Mr Roper and no nearby hospitals have treated an eye injury in the last four days. We have alerted our officers to be on the lookout.'

Mr Roper says, 'I know what I saw and it spooked the hell out of me. I think I had a lucky escape.'

Mr Roper's drawing of the 'alien' is reproduced below.

I swiped the page and gasped at the drawing. It was exactly like Hellyann – the wide eyes, the big nose, the long hair – only Hellyann had not had a streak of dark hair.

How many are there?

I read the article again and again. Below the article were the usual readers' comments, suggesting that Mr Roper had been drunk, or hallucinating. One said: *Hairy, violent aliens? Isn't that every resident of Wongan? LOL.*

I searched for follow-ups, or additional articles, but there was none. Eventually, I flipped my laptop shut and fell into a deep, dreamless sleep.

Chapter Thirty-five

Next morning, Dad is on the phone talking to police and journalists, or meeting with people from the village who are being really nice and everything, but there's just not much more that people can do.

I talk to Mam in the hospital. Her voice is hoarse and she is making a real effort to sound normal, but it's like when people try to sound happy when they're not. You can tell they're lying.

'Are you all right, Mam?' I say, which I know is a daft question. I can almost hear in my other ear Tammy saying, '*Obviously she's not, dummy. That's why she's in hospital!*' And even though I *know* it's my imagination, it scares me because I wonder if I'm going to have a breakdown like Mam.

She says, 'I'm fine, pet', but she isn't. She speaks a little slower than usual, but Dad says that's to be expected because she's been given some pretty heavy-duty medicine, and I want to hug her and smell her.

Tammy and I have this thing. We haven't done it for ages, actually, and it sounds silly written down. We'd both hug her together and try to squeeze as hard as we could, until she begged us to let her go. 'I cannit breathe!' she'd say, but she would be laughing at the same time. Then, when we released, she'd say, 'Double trouble!'

And I so want to do that again that it makes me really sad but I can't tell Mam because that would make her even sadder, so we have this sort of weird conversation where we pretend that she's OK and I'm OK and really neither of us is, so that by the time she says, 'I've got to go, pet', I'm almost pleased, and that makes me feel even worse.

Then I hand the phone back to Dad, who talks to her for ages. He's trying to be encouraging and upbeat and reassuring and all those things that Dad is normally good at.

There's going to be a press conference held at the pub at three this afternoon, and already there are journalists arriving, while Sandra, the police Family Liaison Officer, is in the kitchen talking to Gran.

I hear Dad say, 'Bye, love', then he goes outside.

When he comes back in, his nose and eyes are red, though it might be from the cold.

Meanwhile, I get a text from Iggy.

Same place? Half an hour. OK?

Sandra says she's 'not sure if it's a good idea' for me to go out, but when I ask her why, she can't really give a good answer.

I feel a bit bad leaving Dad and Gran in the house but I don't think Dad's head is all that straight, and Gran's not going to forbid me from seeing a friend, even one like Iggy.

My mind is a swirl of everything as I cycle along the same route as yesterday afternoon. The road is icy and slippery, and my heart is thumping at what we might find.

A real-life *alien*?

I show the news story from Australia, about the man being attacked, to Iggy. My phone is charged and ready to take pictures, although the camera function is still unreliable. I've sort of allowed myself to daydream about what we'll find. *I'll be famous!* It's all going through my head as the cold wind whistles past.

Ethan Tait – the boy who contacted outer space!

It's the sort of thing you see on television: '*Coming up next on CNN: it's out of this world! The president meets the plucky British kid whose close encounter changed history . . .*'

Best of all, I'll get Tammy back, and Kielder will be famous for something other than a tragic disappearance. People would flock to the village where it happened. I can imagine Dad's excitement!

Come to the Stargazer – the best pub in the universe!

Iggy and I stand on the rickety wooden jetty and I feel a fluttering in my stomach. The decking is littered with evidence of yesterday evening's adventure. There's a fishing weight and the laser lure, an aluminium canoe paddle and a length of fishing line from Iggy's attempt to catch the giant pike. I kick away the dusting of snow where he had lain, bleeding, and the wood is stained with blood. Bobbing in the water, a few metres from the jetty, is the red buoy.

Iggy hasn't said anything. Perhaps he feels the same as me: that we've spent a sleepless night and half the day wondering if we had both had some sort of dream: a double hallucination (is that even a thing?). And here in front of us is real-life evidence that we *were* there – that Iggy *did* bleed on to the planks.

Suzy pecks in the snow, but keeps close to us. It is almost as if she can remember the events of yesterday and isn't keen to repeat them.

We did not – definitely not – imagine it all.

Further along the shoreline to my right, about a hundred metres away, lies our upturned canoe: a little speck of orange in a tangle of undergrowth that comes down to the shore. And on the next little inlet along from our narrow pebbly beach is something I had hardly noticed before: a shabby boathouse, with a rusting corrugated iron roof jutting out into the water. One side is completely open to the reservoir, revealing an empty interior. Its wooden walls had once been green but the paint is now flaked and faded and covered with moss and ivy. It's difficult to see how you could get to it, so dense is the growth around it.

Iggy and I haven't actually said much. He comes alongside and nudges me. He has taken off his flat cap and scratches his red hair thoughtfully. 'If *you* had landed here from who-knows-where, where would you go?'

I look at the empty boathouse as I answer slowly, 'I suppose . . . I'd look for shelter?'

Chapter Thirty-six

Getting to the boathouse means scrambling up the path to the main road again and walking along to the next path down. The thorns and twigs obscuring the path have been cut away in recent days by search parties who have been up and down the path to look in the boathouse for Tammy, probably a few times.

Iggy gets off his bike and points to the ground. Thanks to the tree cover, the snow is less deep here, but we can still make out footprints leading away from the boathouse: large footprints. I put my foot next to one: it's adult size. I feel my heart starting to thump again as we go down the path, even though there's no way of knowing for certain who has made them. The prints are ridged, as if from a boot of some sort, but I recall that the creature we met had been barefoot, so . . .

'Hey! Tait! This way!' Iggy calls.

The boathouse door is locked with a rusty bolt and a huge padlock, but it's easy to follow the footprints round to the side, where there's a window a bit above head height that looks as though it has been forced open. It is just a bit too high to see in.

'Here – gimme a leg-up,' I say to Iggy, who links his hands and helps me up so that I can see in.

It is basically a large shed and dark inside. Where the floor would normally be is water, with a wooden walkway running around three of the sides. There's stuff hanging on walls: looped ropes, a lifebelt attached to a rope and life jackets. It looks like it hasn't been used in years and smells of mould.

I call down to Iggy, 'It's empty.'

'Come down,' he says. 'Let me have a look. There's an idea . . . something . . . I dunno.' He rummages in his shorts pocket and pulls out the laser lure, detached from its hooks, that had been left on the jetty. 'Come on – leg me up!'

As I hold his foot, he shines the laser lure into the shed and I hear him say, 'Oh my word!'

'What? What is it?'

He calls back down to me, 'It's here, Tait! It's here!'

I hardly need to ask, but I say it anyway. 'What is, Iggy?'

'Let me down.'

I do so and he stands facing me, eyes shining with excitement and fear.

'I'd say it was a spaceship, Tait. *An invisible flippin'*

spaceship! The same one we saw, or rather didn't see, last night.'

We swap over again, and I take a turn with the laser lure, shining its beam at the empty space in the boathouse, and marvelling as the green line bends around whatever is there, floating on the water. This thing is about the size of a big leisure cruiser, but I can't work out its exact shape: there are lines, and curves, and they don't seem to meet where they should.

I mean, is there a 'normal' shape for a spaceship?

I have an excellent idea. 'Iggy!' I say. 'I'm going to try to take some videos of this laser thingy. It'll be proof!'

I steady myself by hooking my arm over the window ledge and I put my other hand into my back pocket to get my phone out, all while balancing on Iggy's hands. The video app on my dried-out phone still isn't loading properly, and I'm trying to swipe the screen when Iggy starts to shake.

'Careful!' I say. Then Iggy says, 'No, Suzy! Get off!'

I wobble. As I wobble, I feel the laser lure in my left hand slip from my grasp and hear it plop into the water on the other side of the wooden wall. Iggy's hands give way and we both slide to the ground in a heap.

'Sorry,' he says when we've picked ourselves up. 'Suzy got under my feet.'

'At least now we know,' I say. 'It wasn't our imaginations.'

He nods but I stay silent, staring at the ground.

'What's up?' Iggy says. 'That's good, isn't it? We're not crazy!' He's excited, tugging at my sleeve.

I turn away, biting my lower lip. The snow has stopped and the still lake is a deep silvery grey, perfectly reflecting the sky. I can hardly speak for fear, and I feel a huge blockage in my throat.

'It means we have to act, Iggy. It means this is real. We're in the centre of it all – you and me. If there is even the slightest, tiniest, *minutest* chance in all of this weirdness that Tammy is safe somewhere, and we can get her back, then I have no choice.'

Iggy fixes me so hard with his grey-green eyes that I have to stop myself shrinking back. His gaze is magnified by his thick glasses and I swallow hard. I recognise the look: he had it that day on the school taxi-bus when he demonstrated the Death Ray. It's a look that is both determined and slightly crazy – and it's the crazy bit that scares me.

I take out my phone to look at the time. 'Gotta go, Iggy.' I explain about the press conference at three.

'What if we both speak to your dad, Tait? You know: double the . . .'

I think of me and Tammy and our 'double the trouble' thing with Mam.

'. . . double the number of witnesses, sort of thing.'

If anything, having Iggy back up the story is going to make it *less* likely that my dad believes me. I don't want to tell him my dad's opinion of him, but as for me, I'm beginning to think that having Iggy on my side is an advantage.

I mean, in a truly crazy situation, having someone crazy with you might actually help.

Chapter Thirty-seven

I have texted Dad and Gran that I am on my way back so they don't get all anxious. Dad has pretty much given up objecting to Iggy anyway lately, and Gran doesn't even know him so far as I am aware.

It's two forty-five by the time Iggy and I push our bikes up the driveway of the Stargazer: it's already getting too snowy to ride them easily. Parked in front of the pub are various vehicles belonging to the TV people, two police cars and an old Mini with a British flag painted on the roof which belongs to Sandra the police FLO. She's standing in the doorway of the pub without a coat on, arms wrapped around her against the cold, and she gives me one of those sad smiles when she sees me, and raises her eyebrows in greeting to Iggy as well.

'Hi, boys,' she says. 'Where've you been?'

Beside me, I notice Iggy straighten up a bit, as if offended by the question. I'm pretty certain that Iggy's had run-ins with the police before, and I know he's met Sandra.

'None of your—'

'It's OK, Iggy,' she says gently. 'It's all right. It's good that, well . . . good that you two are gettin' out of the madness for a bit.'

'We've just been for a walk, haven't we, Iggy?' I say. 'You know – fresh air, an' that.'

She nods. 'Too fresh, if you ask me. Flippin' freezin', isn't it? Come on – let's get in and get this over with, eh?'

As we walk in, Sandra allows Iggy to get a few steps ahead, with Suzy hopping alongside him, and then she puts her arm around my shoulder and squeezes. 'You all right, pet?' she murmurs, and I nod. 'I'm sorry about your mam. I spoke to your dad earlier – she'll be back in a couple of days, he reckons.'

Inside the main bar area, there are TV lights on stands, and people milling about, and I can see Dad talking to the police superintendent who's now in charge of the search for Tammy. When Dad sees me he breaks off his conversation and comes over to me.

'You OK about this, champ?' he says. 'You don't have to do it if you don't want to, you know.'

I look over to the table that is set out for the cameras, with little microphones and signs with names on: *Supt D. Jones* and so on. Gran is already sitting down.

'I'll be all right, Dad,' I say. 'It . . . it's for Tammy, eh?' I have to force the words out.

In fact, I can hardly speak at all. It's as if everything I want to say – about the creature Hellyann, the invisible spaceship in the boathouse, about what happened on the jetty and what she said about Tammy, and the report on the Australian website – all of it is backed up in my head like cars in a huge traffic jam, honking their horns and revving their engines, and nothing can move and nothing can get out.

I take a deep breath, and I'm about to say, '*Dad, can we talk for a minute – like, quietly?*' and I'll tell him everything.

But then Sandra comes over and says, 'All right, Adam, Ethan – shall we do this?'

Dad says, 'Aye', and he takes a deep breath and pats me on the back. 'Ready, son?'

I've lost my chance.

Moments later, it starts. The superintendent makes a statement about 'every effort being made' and 'not giving up hope' and 'massive support in the community' and other stuff which I'm not really listening to. Camera clicks and flashes are going off all the time.

Through it all, Gran is holding my hand under the table.

'Can you tell us how you're feeling, Ethan?' asks one of the journalists, and all I can do is shake my head and keep staring ahead and blinking while the camera flashes are going off – *fsst, fsst, fsst* – and Gran grips my hand even harder.

How am I feeling? What sort of question is that?

I feel like I have been transported into another world. A world that I have seen before, on TV and in films, where people read statements to the cameras, flanked by officials in uniforms and suits, and flashes go off, and reporters thrust microphones at you, and call you by your name even though they don't know you. Only now I'm *in* that world.

Instead I shake my head and say nothing.

'Adam? Adam! Can you tell us how you're feeling?' says the same man after a moment.

Fsst, fsst, fsst . . .

'Ethan, can you remember . . .'

'Adam, do you think there should have been more progress?'

'Ethan, what's it like not knowing what happened to Tammy?'

Fsst, fsst, fsst . . .

Then, without warning, Dad gets to his feet, toppling his chair. 'Get out!' he says. He doesn't shout, but he doesn't have to. 'Get out of my pub. *Now!*' Dad is as gentle as anything, but he's so tall that he can be intimidating even when he doesn't mean to be.

Sandra, the FLO, is on her feet now too. 'All right, that's enough, everyone. Enough. Thank you. We'll keep you informed. You all have the relevant numbers. You will learn of any new developments in the usual way.'

She turns to us, smiling grimly. 'Come on. You've had

enough of this, I expect,' she says but she has to raise her voice, because the journalists and the others have all started to talk among themselves. It's chaos.

And then I see him, striding through the crowd. I had forgotten that Iggy was even there, but he had been standing quietly at the back with some of the other people from the village and now he is coming straight at us, pushing through the press of people.

He grabs a microphone from the table and, in one movement, leaps up on to the pool table in the middle of the room, followed by Suzy, who flaps her wings to perch on the side.

Iggy shouts into the microphone, 'Everybody! Listen to me! Now!'

A hush falls over the room as everyone turns to look, and my heart leaps into my throat.

'*No, Iggy, no,*' I want to say, but the words won't come out. And he wouldn't hear me anyway.

Chapter Thirty-eight

'Testing . . . testing . . .'

Everybody stops talking to look at the boy standing up there on the pool table with the microphone and the wild red hair sticking out from under his flat cap.

I hear Dad beside me say, 'What the . . . ?' But he doesn't do anything. I think he's too stunned.

'This is an EMERGENCY!' shouts Iggy into the microphone. 'I'd like everybody to leave what they are doing right now and follow me and Ethan outside.' He points at me and everyone looks.

Oh, thanks a bunch, Iggy.

'We have witnessed an alien landing, and she may have the clue to Tammy's whereabouts.'

Beside me, Gran mutters, 'Eee, the little . . .' And then she says a rude word which, come to think of it, I have never heard Gran say before.

I groan inside. The murmuring starts straight away, but people are also really uncomfortable.

One of the villagers at the back says, in a pretend scared voice, 'Help! The Martians are coming!'

But a couple of people turn and glare at him and say. '*Shush!*'

Iggy's not put off. 'It's TRUE! We think she is somewhere nearby right now, and there's an invisible spaceship in the old boathouse – you can see it with a laser light!'

There's a ripple of nervous laughter.

Dad is coming towards us, along with Sandra.

'It's true!' says Iggy again, sounding more manic. His glasses have slipped down his nose. He can tell that this is not going well. 'And you have to help us. She's skinny, and covered in hair, and—'

'It's your missus, Amos!' says a voice at the back.

Laughter and more *shush*es.

By now Dad and Sandra are next to Iggy. Dad's face is angry and concerned.

'All right, son!' he says gently as he draws level with Iggy. 'You've had your fun.'

'Please help us!' yells Iggy as Dad reaches for the microphone.

Iggy dodges out of the way.

'Give me that microphone now,' says Dad.

'No!'

'And get down from the pool table!'

It's madness, and all I can do is watch. Suzy is squawking and flapping. People are laughing – but because it is a child they're a bit nervous as well.

Someone says, 'Buy the kid a beer!'

Eventually, Dad and Sandra wrestle Iggy off the pool table, snatching the microphone off him and marching him to the door.

'That's enough,' Dad says. 'Out! Take your damn chicken with you as well. And as for *you*,' he says, pointing a thick forefinger at me. 'Was this your idea? I can't believe this. Why would you DO something like this?'

'I . . . I'm sorry,' I say. 'But . . . but it's *true*!'

The muttering and laughter continue around us. Dad walks over to me and puts his face close to mine so that no one else can hear. He speaks rapidly, his voice a low hiss of anger and disappointment.

'I have no idea just how the *hell* you thought that *that* was going to help. I . . . I'm speechless, Ethan. I really am. I'm only glad your mam's not here to see this. With everything that's happening, how could you even *imagine* that would be funny?'

'It wasn't meant to be funny, Dad . . . It . . . It's true . . . I told Gran last night. There's a website . . .' I'm trying not to cry in front of everybody, but the words are coming out as sobs.

'Stop it. Stop it right now.' He jabs his finger into my chest, hard. 'You, my friend, will go through to the kitchen, then out the back door and go *straight home*, where you can think about the damage and hurt you and your mate have caused while I try to clear up this mess. Understood?'

Without saying anything else because, despite my

efforts, I have just burst out crying, I turn away and hurry in the direction he said, feeling shame clinging to me like a smell. I go through the big pub kitchen, and out of the back door which opens on to the car park. Our little house is on the other side of the snow-covered tarmac.

I'm halfway across the car park when I see Iggy, leaning on our garden gate, his hands in his shorts pockets and Suzy's head poking out of his jacket.

Through my tears I still manage to shout, 'You *idiot*!' as I come near, and I stop, facing him. I'm breathing heavily and I'm *this* close to punching his stupid face. My fists are balled up ready.

But then we both hear it at the same time.

A loud hissing, followed by 'Ee-fan! Ee-fan! Ikk-ee!'

Chapter Thirty-nine

Well, *that* changes my mood.

'It's her!' says Iggy, and suddenly all my anger and shame vanishes.

I whip my head around, looking for the source of the voice.

I hear it again, louder this time, and more urgent. 'Ee-fan! Ikk-ee!'

I swallow hard. I turn back towards the pub and take a step before I feel Iggy's hand on my shoulder.

'Where are you going?'

'Back to the pub! It's full of journalists and police. And my dad! Exactly what we need.'

He furrows his brow in puzzlement. '*What?* Because it went so well last time, you mean?' he says, sarcastically. 'What are you going to say, exactly?'

'Ee-fan! Ikk-ee! Turn arount. I am ofer here!'

It's still only three thirty, but the weak winter sun, shrouded behind thick snow-cloud, has already started fading. In the open car park it isn't yet dark, but in the woods which come right up to the car-park fence, the shadows are longer and blacker. My heart is pounding as I peer into the dark woods beyond the handful of cars that are there. I wrap my jacket tighter around me. Is she hiding behind one of the cars? Or even *in* one?

Iggy detaches his bicycle light and is already striding off towards the trees. I don't want to be left behind on my own, so I scuttle after him.

He stops at a gap in the fence and gazes into the darkness of the woods, beyond a sign announcing, *Kielder Woodland Walk*. I come alongside him, relieved that he has stopped, and try to will him with my mind not to go up the path and into the trees, because I don't think I have the courage to follow him.

We wait for the voice to come again. I swallow hard and it sounds really loud.

'How?' I ask Iggy. 'How did she know where we were?'

Then, from behind the biggest tree, about two metres in front of us, appears her hairy face, encircled by the hood of a dark green sailing jacket. We stand, transfixed, as she steps out of the tree's shadow into the beam of Iggy's bicycle light.

I look behind me to see if we've been followed, but we haven't. Suddenly, the pub seems very distant at the other end of the car park.

I look back at the creature, who takes a step towards

us and twitches her large nose. 'You smell,' she says. 'That is how I found you.'

We both gasp. Iggy drops his light into a pile of snow and it snaps off. Suddenly we're in semi-darkness and I'm terrified, scrabbling around in the earth and the snow to find the light.

I start back towards the pub, but Hellyann's voice is urgent.

'Stop! I tolt you pefore. Do not tell *anyone* that I am here.'

We're disturbed by a sweep of headlights as a noisy vehicle turns into the car park and heads straight towards us.

I feel myself being dragged into a crouch behind a big grey Land Rover as Iggy grabs my coat collar and says, 'It's them. Get down.'

'What?' I say. 'Who?'

'Shhh,' he hisses. 'It's the Geoffs. I'd recognise that car's noise anywhere.'

Chapter Forty

I know without turning around that Hellyann is crouched down with us. Her smell really is pretty pungent and I try not to breathe. This is probably a good thing, because every breath we take in the cold air sends up clouds of condensation, which would reveal our hiding place.

The Geoffs park their car about ten metres away and when they kill the engine, I hear two car doors open then slam shut, and footsteps in the fresh snow getting closer.

'Look, Dad: there's one here, and some more there. Look!'

Some more what?

Iggy slowly rises up till he can see through the side windows of the Land Rover, which are lightly dusted with snow.

Geoff Jr says, 'See that? They're leading to the Woodland Walk. It's definitely been here.'

Footprints! They've seen Hellyann's footprints!

The Geoffs take another couple of steps closer, and we are hardly breathing now. I think that if my heart beats any harder they'll hear it.

I hear the click of a cigarette lighter and, a moment later, the smell of tobacco is followed by a prolonged, juicy cough. The cougher then hacks up a lump of throat matter and spits it. It lands with a *splat* behind us, while Geoff Senior chuckles and says, 'Hur-hur, nice one, son! Proper tramp's oyster, that one.'

Behind me, Hellyann goes *snff snff* at the smell of tobacco smoke, and I turn, putting my finger to my lips. She imitates me – perhaps she doesn't understand what the gesture means. Anyway, she is being quiet – I think she realises that we're scared.

The younger man says, 'Dad? We could be, you know . . . mistaken. I mean, it *was* dark and everything.'

The older Geoff sighs. 'Listen, son. We know what we saw. The observatory's got the biggest non-military telescope in the country, and it picked up something in the sky and it wasn't flamin' Santa Claus. Not only that but we saw them splashes. We were on the scene straight away, and we saw that . . . that *thing*. I tell you – if it hadn't been for those damn kids . . .'

So they had seen her? That doesn't sound good. Geoff Jr answers his dad with another bout of coughing, then says, 'But, Dad. If the RAF had picked it up, they'd have been snooping round already.'

'Geoffrey, son. We've been through this. Maybe they did see something but ignored it. Maybe they're waiting to see if it happens again. Maybe they saw nowt, or the fella working their telescope was on his Christmas break. We just don't know, do we? Thing is, what *we* saw was worth investigating.'

'Dad? I know you don't want to hear this but . . .'

'You're gonna say we should go to the police, aren't you? "Notify the authorities?" You, son, have got your mother's streak of cowardice. We have the chance of earning a fortune as the father-and-son team who *captured a flamin' extraterrestrial*, and you want to throw that away? I dunno what's wrong with you. Imagine the fame, Geoffrey!'

I suddenly feel bad. What Geoff Sr is describing sounds vain and selfish. But it is very similar to what I was thinking not long ago. Whatever thoughts I am having are scattered when Suzy stretches her neck out. I see it before Iggy and can only watch in horrified silence as she goes *bok-bok-bok-baaak!*

Iggy tries to clap his hand over her beak, but it's too late.

'What the blazes was *that*?' I hear Geoff Sr say, followed by the sound of his footsteps as he approaches.

At the same time, there's a rustle behind me, and Hellyann is off at a crouching run, heading for the Woodland Walk path.

'Blimey! There it is, Dad – look!' cries Geoff Jr.

'Let the dog out!'

I hear their car's hatchback door pop open.

'Go, Sheba! Go seek! She's got the scent – look! Go, Sheba!'

I hear, rather than see, Sheba rush off into the forest followed by Geoff Jr waving a torch, and find myself hoping with all my heart that Hellyann will get away. I don't have much time to think about it, though, because a second later, Geoff Sr is towering over Iggy and me as we cower in the shadow of the Land Rover.

'You's two again, eh?' he growls. 'I think we need to have a little chat. Gerrin' me car.'

Chapter Forty-one

Geoff Sr clicks his car key to open it, and the vehicle's interior lights come on. In the glow, Iggy and I exchange a look.

I am definitely *not* about to get into a stranger's car, even if he isn't a *complete* stranger. I am not that stupid and neither, I think, is Iggy.

But what can we do other than run back to the pub, or to my house? I check out the distance: it's not all that far, really. He wouldn't pursue us into the pub, surely, but I really do not fancy going back in there again. What about Gran? Would we be endangering her? All of these thoughts are going through my mind when Geoff Sr says, 'I am waiting.'

Iggy gives a tiny shake of his head and a flick of his eyes towards the pub. So, we'll run for it?

I have already shifted my weight to my lead foot to start running when, from the woods, comes a ferocious growling followed by a terrible, animal scream.

'Go on, Sheba – get it!' shouts Geoff Jr.

'Sheba?' calls Geoff Sr. 'Geoff? What's going on?' He moves towards the woods and then turns back to us. 'Don't you dare move!'

There's another bout of snarling and a howl of pain.

'The dog's got her,' says Iggy, slowly, sounding really sad.

From the black woods comes an urgent shout. 'Oh my God! Dad! She's dead! Quickly!'

Geoff Sr runs into the darkness, where the light of Geoff Jr's torch beam can be seen flickering through the branches.

I really don't want to see Hellyann's body carried out. I give Iggy a nudge and we run to the other side of the car park, where we feel safer. Then Iggy stops.

'I want to see,' he says. 'I want to see what they do with her.'

And so we wait by the little gate that leads up our path, not even bothering to hide.

Something has changed with the Geoffs running into the woods and the screams of Hellyann. Somehow we feel more confident that the Geoffs will not come after us. Besides, I'm only a few metres from my front door.

Then we see the torchlight bobbing nearer, and two figures emerging from the woods. The fatter figure, Geoff Jr, carries Hellyann's limp body in his arms.

Their car headlights flick on with a little *bleep*, and Geoff kneels down in front of the lights, obscured by the car, meaning we can't see what he is doing – examining Hellyann's body, I guess.

I glance across at Iggy – his face is sad. Then he puffs out his cheeks and shakes his head slowly.

'Dead alien, Tait. This is gonna be *huge*.'

I think about the things I saw on YouTube: 'alien autopsy', the Roswell incident, Area 51 . . .

'Hang on,' I say. 'Look.'

Both Geoffs are bending down to pick up the body. They shuffle round out of the headlights, towards the back of the car, one Geoff holding the arms, the other the legs. I think we both notice it together.

'That's not her!' I say.

Geoff Sr lays his end down and opens the hatchback of their car. The shape is obvious in the red glow of the car's tail lights and we both say it together.

'It's the dog!'

We're too far away to see clearly, but it looks as though Sheba has suffered a massive gash across her throat and down her chest.

'Quit your flamin' crying, you wet blanket,' barks the older man to his son. 'It's just a dog. Honestly, you're worse than your mother.'

The Geoffs heave the dead dog into the back of the car.

By now our confidence has diminished again, and we have both shrunk back behind a bush by my front gate, although we can still see what's happening. Geoff Sr slams the car's hatchback and turns to shout into the forest.

'We'll be back, you fiend!' Then he looks towards where we were hiding and shouts, 'Hey, kids! Not a word, or you'll pay!' He goes round to the driver's door and yells at Geoff Jr. 'What are you waiting for? Let's go and get the boss. And put that thing away. It's evidence.'

I hadn't noticed at first, but Geoff Jr has under his arm a black baton – the one that Hellyann used to heal Iggy's leg. He tosses it into the car then they both get in and speed out of the car park, sending flurries of fresh snow clouding off the car roof and spitting up from the rear tyres.

I look at Iggy, who has a strange expression on his face.

'Who's their boss?' I ask.

He shakes his head. 'It's not a person,' he says in a monotone. 'At least, I don't think so.'

'Eh? He said, "Let's get the—"'

'Boss. I know. Boss and Company. It's . . . it's a brand of shotgun.'

Iggy and I run back to where the car was. There are splatters of Sheba's blood leading from the woodland path, and a small pool of it where they put her down in front of the headlights.

I think we both know what will happen next, so we stand and wait in the snow for Hellyann to emerge from the woods.

She doesn't take long. Her face and hands are covered in blood and there's a long tear in the sailing jacket. She stays in the shadows.

'Thank you,' she rasps. Then she adds, 'Please help me.' She is trembling. 'I have neffer kilt anything before. But . . . it was going to kill me and . . . and . . .' She kind of buckles at her knees and I have to hold her up.

I stop myself gagging at her smell. I look over at Iggy to try to work out what to do next, and his face is a picture of fear. It's the blood that does it: suddenly we are aware of Hellyann's power and we are scared. At least I am.

I follow Iggy's gaze. People are coming out of the pub's side entrance. The press conference has finished. Around us in the car park the cars go *bleep bleep* and their amber sidelights flash as people unlock them remotely. No one has seen us yet and we're still in the shadows, but we're pretty exposed.

It's the perfect opportunity to get help!

'No people! No people! Hide me,' says Hellyann urgently. Her mouth is pulled back, showing her teeth.

I look at her for a moment. Her face is terrifying and bloody. She has just killed a vicious dog with those teeth. I don't feel like crossing her.

'Your house?' says Iggy. 'Come on, quick!'

'No! My gran's there.'

As if on cue, I hear Gran's voice from the direction of our house. 'Ethan! Are you there?'

'Behind the pub!' I say, pointing. 'Take her round behind the kitchen. No one will see you there.'

This, then, is how I end up making friends with the strangest creature I have ever met. And it's all about to get a lot stranger.

Chapter Forty-two

This all happened in about thirty minutes: from when Iggy and I pushed our bikes up the driveway of the Stargazer, to him wrecking the press conference, to us standing face to face with a blood-soaked alien who – so far as we can tell – has just savaged to death a fierce German Shepherd and might do exactly the same to us.

I hear Gran's voice again. 'Ethan! Where are you?'

'Coming!' I shout. I turn to Iggy and Hellyann. 'Go round the side of the car park. Stay in the shadows. Come to the front door in five minutes. I'll meet you there.'

Iggy looks horrified. 'You're . . . l-leaving me alone? With this? What if she's got a taste for blood? I'll be next.'

'Do not be concerned, Ikk-ee. I am a vegetablarian. I do not eat people or any mules,' says Hellyann.

'Any *mules*?' Iggy repeats.

'She means animals.'

Iggy looks at her then shrugs. 'My mum would approve. Follow me.'

He slides into the shadows at the edge of the car park,

followed by Hellyann, and I jog back through the snow to the house, where Gran is waiting in the doorway.

And suddenly, just like that, I'm back in normal-land.

'Ee, Ethan, love,' she says as I walk up the path. 'What was all that about? Your dad's very upset. Where *were* you?'

Oh, great. Even more trouble to be in.

'Sorry. We were just . . . erm . . . having a snowball fight.'

Gran purses her lips. 'That Iggy character,' she says and shakes her head. 'Is it him putting all them daft ideas in your head?'

We stand together in the doorway and Gran sniffs the air, a puzzled look crossing her face. I look back at her thin, red-cheeked face. Should I try again? Should I go for the 'You've *got* to believe me!' approach? Would it work?

Her face softens a bit and her eyes crinkle at the edges. 'Come on in, pet. And wipe your shoes: I think you've trodden in something. I'll make some hot chocolate. There's a concert by that Felina lass on Netflix – you know, she did that daft "Chicken Hop" song that you and Tamm—'

She stops herself abruptly. I think she's embarrassed, and she retreats into the warmth of the house and doesn't see Iggy coming up the path.

'Coming, Gran!' When she's gone I whisper to Iggy, 'Where is she? Where's Hellyann?'

'She's fine. She's in the pub's toilet.'

My jaw drops open. 'She's *where*? What are you playing at?'

'She was freezing to death. I needed to get her out of the cold, somewhere she wouldn't be seen. It's fine. She's locked the door to the cubicle.'

I call back into the house, 'I've left my phone in the pub, Gran! Back in a minute.'

I don't wait for a response. I'm already at the gate.

'Come on! We've got to get her.'

The pub's toilets are located off the little entrance lobby, so we don't have to go into the bar. Through the glass window leading to the bar room, I see Dad leaning against a stool talking to a police officer.

Perfect. I'll go in, check on Hellyann and then bring Dad and the policeman to see her. I know, I know – she said not to tell anyone but, honestly, what choice do I have? This is the only sensible option.

Iggy and I both bundle into the loo, which is empty. There are four urinals along the wall and a cubicle.

'Psst. Hellyann. It's us,' I say. I look under the cubicle door and see two feet in wellington boots. 'Open the lock.'

I hear it go back at the same time as the door to the toilet opens. In a panic, Iggy and I push into the cubicle and slam the door shut behind us as two men walk in.

We hear them go to the urinals, we hear them unzip their flies, and we hear the trickle of their wee, while the three of us huddle together.

Then one of the men lets rip with a big fart. Ordinarily, I'm pretty sure Iggy and I would have laughed, but neither of us is in a laughing mood.

A moment passes, then the younger man says, 'Oh my God! Was that yours, Dad? Can you smell that? What in God's name have you been eating?'

We look at each other in horror. The Geoffs!

'Not me, son. It smelt like that when we came in.'

It's Hellyann they're smelling. I had noticed it, but I guess I am getting a bit used to it.

Suddenly, Iggy clears his throat with a deep grown-man's growl. '*Ahh-hmm!*'

The two Geoffs leave without saying another word – no doubt thinking that the offending smell came from the occupant of the cubicle.

Iggy cracks open the door and looks around. 'The coast's clear.'

'Clear for *what*? What are we going to do with her? I've got to get my . . . erm . . .' I don't say 'dad'. I don't want to alarm Hellyann.

'I'll check the lobby.' Iggy hurries out to see if the lobby is empty.

In the time that he's gone, I look at Hellyann, bloodstained, shivering with cold. She's got toilet paper wrapped thickly around her hands and stuffed into her welly tops – to warm them up, I suppose.

It's amazing how quickly thoughts can pass through

your head. Am I simply going to march into the bar and announce to the policeman: 'Here is the alien'? Everyone will look around and see her there. They'll surely *have* to believe me then. I can trust Dad. I can trust a *policeman*, surely?

Then Hellyann grips my arm, startling me. I turn to look at her strange, ugly face with blood dried into the downy covering of hair. She sniffs and gives a little shake of her head.

'Please,' she says.

This is unnerving. It's exactly as though she has read my mind, and I immediately feel guilty – but what else can we do?

Her eyes are big and pleading, and I try to tell myself again that I've got no choice, and I'm succeeding in convincing myself, I think, when she says, '*Do-do-do-do-do the Chicken Hop.*'

I'm amazed to hear the words of the song that Gran mentioned only five minutes ago. The song that Tammy and I used to sing to each other. Tammy loves that old song by Felina that is repeated every Christmas in every supermarket.

'*Do-do-do-do-do the Chicken Hop!*
Da-da-da-da-dance like you can't stop!
Do-do-do the Chicken Hop this Christmas!'

It's been in my head since Gran mentioned it. I stare at the creature in front of me, who looks back at me with her sad, slow-blinking eyes. Did she read my mind? Or was it just a coincidence?

I don't know how long I'm staring at her. Probably only a few seconds. But it's long enough to know that I cannot betray Tammy. That I will do *anything* to get her back, and if that means keeping the secret of this creature for a little longer, then that is what I am going to have to do.

At that moment, the toilet door slams open and Iggy comes hurtling back in.

'They're back!' he says. 'Get in!'

We all squeeze again into the little cubicle as the Geoffs come back in and sniff loudly.

'You're right, Dad. That's definitely the same smell. That thing's been in here for certain.'

The handle on the cubicle rattles. Iggy puts the seat lid down and stands on the toilet, helping Hellyann up too. The door handle rattles again.

'Come on out. We know you're in there.'

Iggy points at my legs and mouths the words 'pants down', miming pulling down his shorts. '*Just. Do. It.*'

So I do. He turns me around so that I'm facing away from him, and only then do I understand why, as I hear someone crouching down and see the top of a head in the gap at the bottom of the toilet door. Anyone looking in will have seen a single pair of feet with pants around the ankles. He's pretty smart, is Iggy.

'There's someone in there, Dad,' whispers Geoff Jr.

'Of course there is, Geoffrey. A bloody alien! And we're gonna catch it. Do your thing, son.'

The cubicle shakes as Geoff Jr kicks at the door, hard.

And again.

The third kick busts the lock and the door bursts open.

Chapter Forty-three

The two Geoffs cram into the doorway of the toilet cubicle and stare in disbelief.

What they see is this: two boys, one (Iggy) in a flat cap, massive woolly sweater and baggy shorts; the other (me) with his pants round his ankles, standing in a huge pile of toilet paper. A green sailing jacket lies on the floor.

'Can we help you, gentlemen?' says Iggy in his poshest-sounding voice.

I can't believe his cheek, but then again this is a boy who has spent a lifetime driving adults almost insane.

The Geoffs look first at us, then at each other.

'Where is it, you little toerags?' snarls Geoff Sr, finally.

With a massive effort, I force myself not to glance up to the little window where Hellyann clambered out, leaving the sailing jacket with me and discarding the toilet paper that had been wrapped around her hands and stuffed into her wellies.

'I've got no idea what you're talking about,' says Iggy, sounding sincere. 'But you've set back Ethan's recovery by several months.'

The older Geoff scrunches up his face and says, '*What?*'

'He suffers from Lavatorial Anxiety Syndrome. Can't visit public lavatories without risking panic attacks, right, Ethan?' Somehow, Iggy has managed to make his voice sound both patient and annoyed, as though he is giving the Geoffs a telling-off.

I start to tremble and say, quaveringly, 'Y-y-yes.'

'It's been made worse by recent events. So I'm just in here, helping him, and you've ruined everything, including the toilet door. Ethan's dad is going to be very unhappy with you. Especially if you're bringing *that* into his pub.'

Iggy nods downwards and I follow his gaze. Poking out of the bottom of Geoff Jr's long coat is the shiny barrel of a shotgun.

Whether it's because of Hellyann's disappearance, or being confronted by a kid telling them off, the Geoffs are rendered speechless. Do they *believe* him about Lavatorial Anxiety Syndrome? Whether they do or not, they probably aren't going to risk being found having an argument with two young boys in a pub toilet, especially with one of them carrying a gun.

At that moment, the door to the gents' toilet opens, and the policeman who was talking to Dad walks in on the little scene. He stops and looks at us quizzically. At least I've pulled my pants up by now.

Geoff Jr says, by way of explanation, 'Caught these two stealin' bog roll. But probably not the sort of thing to concern you, eh, officer?' Then he turns to us. 'We're watching you's,' he whispers, and they both bustle out.

The policeman knows who I am, and probably thinks that if I want to waste the loo roll from my parents' pub, that's my business. He says nothing, anyway.

Iggy and I wait until the policeman is mid-wee then we leave as well, dumping the paper in the bin on the way out.

Hellyann is crouched, hugging herself against the cold, behind a huge kitchen bin below the gents' toilet window.

She grabs the green sailing jacket from me and as she tries to pull it on, she nods gratefully.

At least, I think it's gratefully. I haven't seen her smile, but perhaps they don't. Or – more likely – perhaps she doesn't have much to smile about.

Iggy helps her on with the coat, like a kindly old man with his wife. As he does, his sleeve falls back to show his wristwatch, and I see with a twist in my stomach what the time is. I told Gran that I'd be right back.

She was making hot chocolate. I know the routine. She'll make it in the kitchen, then, holding a cup in each hand, she'll open the door to the living room with her bottom and then chant, 'hot-chocolate-drinking-chocolate' because it was on some ad on TV ages ago . . .

'I've got to go,' I say.

'What? Or you'll turn into a pumpkin?' says Iggy incredulously. 'Come off it – you can't leave me now!'

'I have to, or . . . or . . .' I'm not sure exactly what might happen, so I end up lamely, 'or I'll be in trouble.'

'Like we're not already? What are we going to do with our new friend?'

Beside him, Hellyann stands shivering.

I've already thought about this.

First, though, I have to lie to my gran. I feel guilty with every letter I type into my phone.

I am staying here. Sandra the FLO wants to ask me some more questions about Tammy.

Honestly, it feels horrible dragging Tammy into my deception but I know that Gran won't want to interfere with the police's questions.

Then I make the lie better by adding:

Sorry about the hot chocolate.
Extra for you! :)
Enjoy the concert! Xxx

Sometimes I really hate myself, especially now, when I am lying to my gran.

Chapter Forty-four

Mad Mick's Mental Rentals is the bicycle hire place fifty metres up the hill behind the pub, but it's been shut since October half-term.

Iggy explains. 'Mick spends the winter surfing in Hawaii. I helped him to clean the place last summer and he lent me a Segway for a day in return. I've still got the access code. Cool, eh?'

Hellyann watches him, saying nothing, as Iggy punches in the code. I hear the lock pop open, and we're in. Iggy unbuttons his jacket and Suzy flaps out on to the floor. Hellyann remains expressionless.

'No lights! We're not supposed to be here, remember?' Iggy says, so I take out my phone and turn on the torch. I give a low whistle.

'Wow! Look at all these bikes!'

It's basically a huge shed with dozens of mountain bikes hung up on racks and workbenches for repairs. Above the sales counter is a head-high platform with a sleeping mattress, accessed by a ladder. At the end of the shed is a tiny kitchen and a bathroom, and that's it.

Mick has left the place very neat. All the workbenches are clean and all the bikes are tidily stowed on their hangers. Then we hear a strange *ark ark ark*.

Hellyann is spinning a rear wheel by turning the pedals of a hanging bike and watching in fascination, making the strange, low barking noise.

Iggy nudges me and chuckles. 'Blimey, someone's having fun!'

Fun is probably not the right word. *Fascination* might be better. Her face shows no delight, just absorbed interest. Her eyes follow the chain from the pedal crank as it drives the rear wheel, then she sees us watching.

'Picycle,' she says solemnly in her raspy croak. Then: 'I am hunkry.'

In the corner of the shop is a switched-off vending machine. Iggy reaches behind it and it flickers to life, its big glass window revealing crisps and drinks.

'Got any money?' says Iggy.

I feel in my pocket and bring out a £1 coin, a 20p piece and a rubber band.

Iggy has a £2 coin.

Hellyann leans in close and watches as we insert our money and a can of Coke, a packet of Cheesy Wotsits and a Mars bar tumble into the big collection hopper at the bottom of the vending machine.

Iggy finds some bicycle lights with batteries in them beneath the sales counter, and he brings them to the little reception area, which is just some soft benches arranged around a glass-topped table. We plug in a fan heater that belches out dusty-smelling air that warms our feet but not much else. There's also a camping lamp, an old-fashioned one, which Iggy lights with a souvenir cigarette lighter he has found. Hellyann flinches when she sees the flame, but then seems to relax.

And there, in the eerie glow of two bike lights and a flickering camping lantern, we watch as Hellyann tries to eat the stuff we've given her, and she tells us who she is, and where she's from.

I really think, without exaggeration, that it is the strangest thing that two human beings have ever heard, and that includes people who have heard Uncle Jan's story of how he fought off a shark in the Bahamas when he was eighteen, which turned out to be mostly lies.

Chapter Forty-five

As we open the packets of food, Iggy looks up and pats the seat next to him. 'Sit down,' he says to Hellyann.

It's incredible: we're in a half-dark bicycle rental shop with what I'm by now almost certain really *is* an alien from outer space, and Iggy is behaving like Mam does when she's on her best manners.

'Why?' says Hellyann.

He glances over at me, then says, 'All right. Standing is good.'

So she stands there – a naked, hairy, humanish creature in Wellington boots, sniffing at the opened packet of Cheesy Wotsits.

'These've got cheese in them,' says Iggy. 'It's made from milk. Rich in, erm, healthy things and . . . other stuff.'

Hellyann's eyes widen. 'Human milk?'

Iggy's eyes widen to match Hellyann's. 'No! Oh God, no! Cow's milk!'

'Do you not trink human milk? I believe you are "mammals" – your females produce milk and—'

'Yes, yes, I know. We drink it when we're babies.'

'And then you change to trinking cow's milk?'

Iggy nods.

'Why?'

He pushes back the cap from his head and is deep in thought for a moment. Eventually, he says, 'I think, erm . . . collecting human milk would be just too weird, wouldn't you say, Tait?'

I can only nod. I'm thinking: *Why are we talking about this when I have a sister to rescue? Food can wait!*

But still Iggy and Hellyann are talking.

'And what apout this?' She points to the Mars bar.

'That's chocolate! Food of the gods, that is!'

'You giff food to your gods?'

'No! It's just an expression. Although, now you mention it, I think some people might – you know, in other cultures . . .'

This, I think, could take a long time.

Hellyann tears off a bit of Mars bar with her long fingers; she sniffs it, puts it in her mouth then spits it out on to the floor.

'Not goot,' she says and wipes her long, grey tongue with the back of her hand.

Next she tries the Cheesy Wotsits. She doesn't spit them out, and we watch as she quickly eats the whole packet.

Iggy and I finish the chocolate. When I pop open the can of Coke, she drinks it thirstily, then grimaces as the bubbles go down her throat and up her nose. She splutters and coughs.

'What is in this?' she says, and then belches noisily.

Iggy shrugs. 'Dunno,' he says. 'It's just . . . fizz?'

I have had to avert my face from the smell of Hellyann's burp, but I know the answer. 'It's carbon dioxide. CO_2. It's added to the drink to make it fizzy.'

Hellyann burps again. 'Why?'

Now it's my turn to shrug. 'Don't know. For fun, I suppose?'

Hellyann looks at me, blinking rapidly. I think she's utterly baffled by what I have just said.

I say, 'Now can we talk about Tammy?'

Chapter Forty-six

I don't know if anyone has ever told you anything so amazing, so literally *incredible*, that you just cannot believe it – yet at the same time, you have no choice *but* to believe it?

I guess not, but that's what it's like listening to Hellyann in the shadowy bike shop that smells of rubber and oil combined with the pungent odour of alien being blown towards us by the fan heater whenever she walks in front of it.

She paces around, never sitting – a hairy bundle of nervous energy. And for once, Iggy ends up stunned into silence. He sits, unblinking, mouth open.

'I know where your sister is,' Hellyann begins.

I nod slowly, my eyes wide and my heart hammering with hope in my chest.

'She is alife, but she is a long, long way away.'

I lick my dry lips, swallow hard and glance over at Iggy, who hasn't moved.

'Look at this.'

She reaches behind her back and detaches the strange, shiny backpack that we saw before when she healed Iggy's leg. She opens the top and takes out a small, grey, rectangular block about the size of a paperback book, which she positions on the glass-topped table between us.

She strokes her fingers over one end of the book and about 30 centimetres above it appears a bright white line, like a length of super-illuminated floating wire. That impresses me, and I say 'Woah!', but Iggy remains silent, as if he knows something even more incredible is about to happen.

From out of the glowing line, a picture appears, blurred at first, then, after a few seconds, slowly becoming pin-sharp. Only, it's not a picture, it's a scene, in 3D – like a hologram, only in black and white, like an old movie.

In the scene people are moving around, only a few centimetres tall, on the tabletop in front of us. It looks like a street scene in a city: there are cars, and buildings. Someone throws a ball for a dog; a tree's branches wave in the wind.

I watch transfixed and I glance across at Iggy, whose eyes are darting from point to point in the scene before us.

'Why . . .' Iggy says, but Hellyann holds up her hand to stop him.

She reaches into the scene, her hands passing through the seemingly solid people and buildings, and strokes the 'book' again, making the picture freeze. The scene changes, and a grid appears, dividing the scene into dozens of little blocks, then one of the blocks grows to fill the space.

And there she is.

Slowly, I reach forward, my hand trembling, lips parted. There's no mistaking who it is.

I say, 'Tammy . . .'

The picture moves again. Tammy's 3D head is almost life-size and the detail is incredible, even if the image is not in colour. She turns, but she's not looking at us; her eyes are blank and her face displays an empty half-smile. She touches her chest with her hand and says, 'Tammy.' Then an off-camera voice says, 'Hellyann.'

I'm breathing heavily and, to my surprise, tears are streaming down my face although I didn't know I was crying.

'What . . . I mean . . . where? Where is she?' I say quietly.

'She is in danger,' says Hellyann. 'Very grafe danger.'

The image on the glass tabletop fades and dies.

Iggy lifts his face to stare at Hellyann. 'Did you . . . kidnap her?'

'Not me.' She says it so quickly and forcefully that I immediately believe her. 'But yes, she was taken. She was taken py someone who then solt her.'

'*Sold her?* Who to? What for? Is she OK?'

My mind is racing with the horrible possibilities.

Hellyann speaks slowly, as though she's trying to be gentle. She kneels down in front of us.

'Nothing ferry bad has happent to her. Not yet. She is not even aware of her situation, thanks to a process that you would call "consciousness-erasing" or "mind-cleaning".'

'Like a computer memory wipe?' I suggest fearfully, and Hellyann nods.

'Yes. But to not worry about that: her consciousness is simply masked. Hidden, you might say. And we can, I pelieve, get her pack.'

There's a long pause.

Eventually, I say, '*We?*'

Hellyann stands up. 'Yes,' she says. 'We. This is dangerous. I neet your help. I cannot to this alone.'

I've had enough. I want to be told the whole truth, right now, and I throw out my arms in frustration. '*Where is she?*' I demand with my voice rising and stamping my foot with each word.

Hellyann seems unmoved and carries on speaking in her guttural monotone.

'Have a look at this,' she says. She strokes the silver-grey block and the picture appears again: the street scene with tiny figures moving about, and the hum of a city street. 'This looks like Earth, yes?'

We look carefully. The buildings, the cars, the trees, the dog . . .

'Yeah,' I say. 'I suppose . . . wow!'

I stop when a huge pair of birds, like hawks or ospreys, swoops into the scene, circles, and flies out.

Hellyann enlarges the scene again to show a shopfront, only it looks like a shopfront from years ago – an old village toyshop, like you see in pictures.

The more we look, the odder it becomes. The cars on the street are a strange mixture of styles: a low sports car, and an ancient, rattling wagon from, I don't know, the 1920s or something. There's even a tractor.

And the people – there are maybe ten or twenty of them, no more. The same people walk up and down the street, in and out of the shops, crossing the road pointlessly again and again. A woman gets in her car, drives it up the street and out of the scene, and then it reappears coming the other way, after which she parks it, gets out, goes into a shop and then does the whole thing again.

Iggy and I watch, transfixed, literally speechless.

Then Iggy utters a groan. 'Oh my God! Look!'

Two figures appear. Creatures, just like Hellyann: naked, pale and hairy, with tails. They walk down the middle of the street, looking about them and pointing.

'It's all fake,' I say, but Iggy shakes his head.

'It's not fake,' he whispers. 'It's real. It's . . . it's a *zoo*!'

I feel sick and turn away, directing my anger at Hellyann. 'That's horrible! Why would you do that?'

Hellyann has picked up Suzy and is holding her gently. She blinks and looks back at me with her strange, wide-eyed gaze. 'For knowletch. For learning. But I akree it is wrong. That is why I am here.'

Iggy and I glance at each other, dumbfounded, and Hellyann continues to stroke Suzy. 'I haf neffer held an animal before,' she says. 'It feels goot!'

Chapter Forty-seven

I have so many questions I want to ask. Where is this? Who are the other people in the scene? How did they get there?

At that exact moment, my phone buzzes in my pocket. I look at the screen: Mam. I think for a second about letting it ring through to voicemail, but . . . *she's in hospital.*

I put my finger to my lips to tell the others to be quiet and swipe to answer the call.

'Hi, Mam.' I am trying *so hard* to sound normal, but even those two syllables sound as though they're trembling.

'Hi, sweetheart. How are you?' Mam's voice sounds . . . like it usually does. That is, not drugged or slow or any of the things I was expecting, and I am so relieved I find myself grinning just at the sound of her voice.

'I'm OK. What about you?'

She tells me she is feeling better, but still sad and worried, and that the doctors have recommended rest and some more treatment, and I'm listening and distracted at the same time because Hellyann and Iggy are watching me take this call.

'Where are you?' Mam asks.

'I . . . erm . . . I'm at Iggy's,' I lie and I hate myself immediately for lying to my mum who's in hospital. 'I'm just heading home in a minute.'

There's a pause. 'You're at Iggy's? But your dad's been trying to get you. He's called Iggy's mum . . .'

I look at the screen of my phone: two missed calls from Dad.

'My phone's been acting weird. I got it wet.' At least that's the truth. 'And . . . erm, we were out the back, in Iggy's, erm . . . shed.'

His shed? Where did that come from? I don't think Iggy even has a shed . . .

'So you're on your way back? OK, I'll tell your dad. I . . . I miss you, Ethan, love . . .' Her voice trails off, and I think she moves her phone away from her face and I hear a little sob.

There is a lump in my throat that feels like a golf ball because I know Mam is trying to 'be brave' with me on the phone. I want to say, '*It's all right, Mam, you can cry*', but I don't because she is talking – talking quite quickly, so she can get off the phone and cry.

'I'll be back home soon, Ethan, love. Be a good lad. I love you. Bye.'

She has gone before I can even say 'bye' in response.

I put my phone in my pocket and Hellyann approaches me, sniffing deeply. 'You lie very effectively,' she says.

'When we lie, we can smell it instantly. You do not smell at all. Not of lying, anyway.'

'Erm . . . thanks. I suppose. Listen, my dad's been asking for me. I have to go, but . . .' I look over at Iggy.

'What do we *do*?' he says. He looks first at Hellyann and then at me, pleading with his eyes for an answer.

'We will pring her pack,' says Hellyann evenly. 'But you must tell no one. No one at all. It will threaten the whole plan.'

'You have a plan?' I say, and I know I sound pleading and desperate but I just don't care.

'Oh yes. I haf a plan. It requires total secrecy.'

'Yeah. Sure. Whatever,' I say, but it comes out too easily.

Hellyann blinks slowly. 'You may not actually smell when you deliver falsehoots,' she says, 'but sometimes it is obvious.' She points at me. 'You are thinking of telling your father as soon as you get pack, are you not?'

'No, I—'

'Stop it. You were. Of course you were. Humans are dependent on their parents. Only, if you do that, he will inform the police, and the police will inform your military, and I will be unaple to leaf, and Philip will be discovered, which will haf—'

'Hang on. Who's Philip?'

'Philip is what you would call an Artificial Intelligence bot. Right now, though, it – he – is repairing my craft. He is so powerful that were he to fall into the hants of

Earth people, it would have a deffastating effect . . .' Hellyann closes her eyes for a moment as if thinking hard. 'You haf to trust me.'

We say nothing.

Can I trust her? Do I have a choice?

'One more thing,' she says. 'My stick – I haf mislait it. I dropped it by the tree when that dock attacked me. I must ket it pack.'

'That may be difficult,' I say, and I tell her that I saw the younger Geoff holding it.

'That is a proplem then that we must solve tomorrow. I cannot leaf it here.' She says it all so calmly and matter of fact. I mean, Dad just has to lose his keys and he's swearing and slamming doors – this is much more important and Hellyann hasn't even raised her voice. It's like she doesn't even know how to panic.

Iggy points out the bed platform above the sales desk. 'Bed's up there. Toilet at the back. You'll find drinking water there as well. Don't go anywhere. We'll be back at eight tomorrow morning.'

Hellyann shakes her head uncomprehendingly and Iggy sighs. There's a clock mounted on the wall by the till. 'Look, when the long hand is pointing straight up and the little hand . . . Oh, forget it. It'll be shortly after it gets light. All right?'

I grab my jacket and leg it back down the hill while

Iggy locks the big front doors of Mad Mick's Mental Rentals.

She has a plan, I think.

It's only a tiny bit of hope, but a tiny bit of hope is better than no hope at all.

Chapter Forty-eight

It's only when I take my jacket off in the hallway that I realise how much it stinks of Hellyann. The house is quiet. Gran must have gone to bed, and Dad is still at the Stargazer.

I'm shoving my jacket into a plastic carrier bag and running up the stairs when I hear his key in the door. By the time he comes into my room, I'm in bed, in my pyjamas, with the jacket shoved under my bed.

'Ethan?' he says as he comes up the stairs, and I don't like the way he says it. He comes into my room and sits on the edge of my bed. Normally, this means that a 'talk' is to be delivered, but right now, with Tammy missing, I don't think that's going to happen. I mean, my dad looks like he's been in a fight, which of course he hasn't, but he looks worn out and beaten up from worry and grief.

'Where were you?' says Dad. 'I tried to call you.'

I repeat the half-lie that my phone got wet and I missed his call, without answering the bit about where I've been.

Dad nods and sighs. I'm not sure he's even listening. He turns his body to face me and he looks worse than I have ever seen anybody. He's in a dirty T-shirt and jeans and he has beard stubble that's grey in patches that I have never noticed before.

Not only that, but his eyes are sunken and when he sighs I get a huge waft of alcohol from his breath. (Dad never normally drinks anything but water when he's working. Not only that, he always dresses smartly for work, and waxes his hair, and shaves, and uses aftershave that Mam buys him for his birthday. 'When you're very tall,' he once told me, 'everyone notices you, so you have to make an effort.')

All the way back from Mad Mick's bike shop, I've been weighing up the pros and cons of telling Dad about Hellyann.

Her reasons for wanting to keep this all secret sound fair enough. But surely – *surely* – I can trust my dad? Even the dad in front of me who seems like a different man?

'What's that smell?' says Dad, sniffing the air.

It occurs to me to say, '*That's the smell of an extraterrestrial being*', but I don't yet dare.

'What smell?' I ask.

Dad sniffs again then shrugs, muttering, 'Strange.' Then he takes a deep breath. His voice is a little bit indistinct.

'I am not happy about t'night, Ethan. That incident with Iggy in the bar? What were you thinkin' of, man? And *don't* try to say it was all his doin'. You were there, watchin' him. He got up on the pool table, Ethan! I mean, he . . .' He stops himself as this is building into a Dad rant that could last ages. 'Haven't we got enough on our plates at the moment?'

His voice is cracked and croaky, and . . . is he *drunk*? I have never seen my dad drunk before.

What can I say?

I take a deep breath, and move myself till I'm sitting up in bed, and I tell him.

'Sorry' is what I tell him. 'I'm really sorry, Dad.'

And then he kind of slides off my bed till he's sitting on the floor, holding his fingertips to his forehead. 'Oh, Ethan,' he says. 'Oh, my son.' He breathes in deeply through his nose as though he's making a huge effort not to weep.

All I want is for my dad to say, '*Don't worry. We'll sort this out. We'll find Tammy one way or another, and everything will be back to normal. Trust your ol' dad!*' And he'll grin and play-punch my arm . . .

And I know at that moment, with Dad slumped on the floor, and my mum in hospital with a mental breakdown, that that is not going to happen.

That it is now down to me.

Dad is mumbling and I have to strain to make out the words. 'I've had enough of this, and more than enough of that . . . that boy who thinks he can get up with his muddy boots on my newly restored pool table and spout a whole load of . . . *nonsense* t' the people who are tryin' to *help*, for God's sake. The flamin' cheek of it! Meanwhile, my own son just stan's by with a stupid grin on his face . . .'

But I wasn't grinning.

'. . . like it's all some huge prank. And . . . and . . .' He stops his tirade and sniffs again. 'What the *blazes* is that smell? If you've trodden in something, sort it out.'

I'm blinking back tears. I take a deep breath, hold it for a couple of seconds and then blurt it out.

'Dad, if you go to Mental Rentals, the alien – Hellyann – she's there. Please.'

That's when he snaps. He stumbles to his feet, towering over me as I shrink back into my pillows.

'Ah, stop it, man, Ethan! *Stop it right now!* I have had enough. Can't you see? Look at us! *Look at us!*'

Then he's gone. The bedroom door slams so hard that the whole house rattles.

All I can do is lie there in the half-light of my bedroom, my mouth turned down so far, until I feel a tear trickle down from my eye.

Being disbelieved when you're telling the truth must be the worst feeling in the world.

I take my jacket from beneath the bed and hang it out of the bedroom window, leaving the window open a bit. It makes the air in my room cold, but I don't really mind.

Then I hear the creaky floorboard on the landing and the crack of light from my door gets wider. Is Dad coming back for another go? I hurry back into bed and pull the duvet over my head.

'Go away,' I say.

'Ethan? It's me.'

Gran stands in the doorway in her dressing gown, the light from the landing behind her. Am I going to get a telling-off from her as well? My little, sweet gran who is never angry and who makes hot chocolate? I turn my head and ready myself.

Now it's Gran's turn to sit on my bed. She takes my hand in one of hers and with her other uses a tissue to dry my face. She tucks it back into the pocket of her dressing gown.

'I don't think you're lying,' she says.

I'm astonished. 'You heard all that?'

'I heard it. Your dad's under a lot of strain, pet. We all are. But if I've learnt one thing in my seventy-*ahem* years it's this: sometimes what you think are the wildest lies turn out to be the truth.'

'S . . . so you *believe me*?'

Gran smiles. 'You forget, pet: I'm a twin as well.'

She's right: I often forget that. Gran's twin sister – Great-aunty Di – emigrated to Australia before I was born. I've never met her.

'If something happened to Diane,' says Gran, 'I would know. And when I had your dad, three weeks early, Di called me the next day. She knew because she had felt labour pains.'

218

The pains that tell you you're about to give birth? I give Gran a puzzled look.

'How does that work?'

'No idea, pet. It's a twin thing, and it doesn't happen all the time. But somewhere out there in the I-don't-know-what there's a connection . . . that is, if you ask me. It might be like a bat's squeak that you cannit hear but every now and then you can tune into it like an old car radio. So if you say that you know Tammy's alive somewhere, then it makes sense to pay attention because, Lord knows, no one else seems to have a clue.'

I repeat my question from before. 'So you believe me? About the alien?'

Gran narrows her eyes and makes a little half-smile.

'I never said that, pet. But put it this way: I don't think you're lying.' She takes off her large glasses and peers into my eyes. 'You're a good lad, Ethan. And I know you wouldn't knowingly lie about something like this.'

I am so relieved to hear this that I feel my bottom lip trembling, and I don't want to cry any more, so I am glad when Gran gets up slowly from my bed and goes to my door.

'Your dad's off tomorrow to go and see your mam. So perhaps you and me can get to the bottom of this?'

Huh. Who'd have expected that? My little, harmless, hot-chocolate-loving Gran might turn out to be just the adult we need.

Chapter Forty-nine

It's midnight and I'm still awake. I didn't sleep at all last night, so I am exhausted. Truly drained. But I still can't sleep.

What is happening?

What is Hellyann doing at the bike rental shop?

How will I get Tammy back?

Sleep doesn't come till about five in the morning and when I awake, the room is so cold that my breath makes clouds, but at least the stink has gone.

A weak light, the colour of milky tea, struggles through the glass, and when I look out, it's snowing again. Outside, Dad is scraping ice from the windscreen of our car, and beyond the car park I can just make out the shapes of the hills through the whiteout. I can also see the roof of Mad Mick's Mental Rentals, and I wonder – as I've been wondering all night – how Hellyann is coping.

'Ah, you're up – great!' Gran stands in the doorway. 'Busy day – remember?'

I do remember, and I nod.

It's not even eight o'clock and I'm exhausted.

A few minutes later, Dad comes into the kitchen beating his hands together from the cold. 'Wow! It's flippin' *Baltic* out there.' He puts his hands on Gran's cheeks and she squeals, then he ruffles my hair and says, 'A'reet, champ?' It's Dad's way of saying there are no hard feelings but I know from experience that he'll not want the subject of Iggy or alien spaceships brought up again.

Gran hands him a flask of tea and a packet of sandwiches.

'Is your phone charged?'

'Yes, Mam.'

'Have you packed a shovel?'

'Yes, Mam.'

'Don't drive into a snowdrift, all right?'

'I'll try not to, Mam.' He puts a hand on my shoulder and says, 'Your mam's going to be fine', then he heads out of the front door.

As soon as the door slams, Gran puts another fried egg on to my plate and folds her arms.

'Where is it, then?' asks Gran. 'This alien of yours?'

'It's a *her*, not an *it*,' I say through a mouthful of egg.

She shrugs off this detail. 'Is that what the smell is in your room? Alien? It reminds me of when your dad and Uncle Alan kept a dead frog in their room for a fortnight and—'

'It's not so bad,' I interrupt. I'm becoming a bit defensive about Hellyann's smell, I find.

'It's better now that you've hung it out of the window.'

'How do you know that?'

Gran gives me a pitying look, just like Tammy used to. It's amazing how my gran can sometimes seem like a quarter of her age. 'Because I *looked*, clever clogs. Now eat up and let's go.'

Chapter Fifty

Gran and I haven't really said much. I grab a packet of cheese from the fridge (I know Hellyann likes that) and some bananas in case she's hungry, and Gran just watches, apparently trusting that I know what I'm doing, which is nice of her.

Or perhaps she's just *indulging* me, like grown-ups do sometimes. You know: *Let him have his bit of fun – let him work out whatever fantasy is currently in his worried little head, bless him, and he'll soon see sense.*

She's in her normal clothes: thick, fleece-lined running bottoms, a double-layer, zip-up top and big trainers with woollen socks. She pulls a hat over her short white hair, adjusts her specs, and together we trudge through the snow up the hill to Mad Mick's Mental Rentals.

There's a trail of footprints in the snow leading to the metal front door, and I immediately feel a surge of nerves. What if . . .

I don't know what if, actually. It's just that another set of footprints makes me nervous. I look at them carefully. They're not wellington boots, so it isn't Hellyann. They are different, and there's something else: something making a track alongside the feet.

Suzy!

I grin to myself, and the metal door opens a crack to reveal a tousled mop of copper curls.

'You took your time,' says Iggy.

He opens the door further and his face falls when he sees Gran.

I hold up my hands defensively. 'It's OK. It's OK. This is my gran.'

'You say that like it explains everything,' says Iggy.

But there's no sign of Hellyann.

'. . . and so,' Iggy concludes, 'we brought her here.'

Iggy's story is *exactly* the same as what I told Gran, who listened carefully, alert for any inconsistencies that would indicate we were lying.

We sit – me, Iggy holding Suzy in his lap, and Gran – on the seats that form the reception area of Mad Mick's. Orchestral music is playing on a tiny speaker plugged into an ancient iPod on the table between us. Hellyann, Iggy has explained, is taking a hot shower in the tiny bathroom out the back, but I'm still not sure Gran believes us.

Gran has sat tight-lipped in concentration as we tell our tale, starting with my and Iggy's 'pike-hunting' expedition two nights ago and our encounter with the two

Geoffs. Gran shakes her head and pulls a face when they are mentioned.

'Never liked them two. The older one especially.'

'You know them?' I ask, surprised.

'You forget I grew up near here, pet. Geoff Mackay – the older one – was married to my bridesmaid's daughter, Maureen. Nasty piece of work, he was.'

Then behind us, the bathroom door opens. A huge cloud of steam billows out, and from the middle of the steam emerges a figure, fully clothed in jeans tucked into wellies, a thick sweater in coloured stripes that Gran would have called 'jazzy' and a woollen hat. The music swells to its climactic final chord in a way that could have been planned, but wasn't – although Iggy has a slight smirk as though he realises the drama of the moment.

Hellyann comes closer, shyly, and stands before us, sniffing the air. Wet strands of hair poke out from beneath her woollen hat. I can't see her tail, but the back of her jeans is bulging slightly so I guess she's stuffed it away. She narrows her eyes at Gran and then looks at me accusingly.

Gran gasps and lifts her hand to her mouth in astonishment, saying in a little voice, 'Oh, my giddy aunt!'

'This is my gran.' I say. 'My grandmother. My . . . my father's mother.'

Gran steps forward. Hellyann edges backwards.

'It's all right. You can trust her.' I turn to Gran. 'Can't she?'

'Yes, dear,' says Gran to Hellyann. 'You can trust me. I want to help to get Tammy back.'

Hellyann looks at Gran for the longest time before saying, 'You tolt someone.' Even through her squeaky monotone I can tell she is upset and scared.

'It's my gran. Christine. She's totally trustworthy.'

'Do you mean your grantmother? How to I know she is trustworthy?'

'Because . . . because she's my *gran*, Hellyann!' I know it sounds lame, but I can't quickly think of anything else. 'Grans are *totally* trustworthy. It's kind of a rule.'

Gran speaks next, and it's the 'Gran-est' thing I have ever heard. 'I like your jumper, pet. I like the colours.'

Hellyann looks down at her sweater, kind of uncomprehendingly.

Iggy's brow is furrowed. He's looking at Hellyann's face. 'Have you *shaved*, Hellyann?'

Hellyann's long hand strokes her cheek. 'I fount an implement in the bathroom which was effective in removing some of my face hair. I thought it may be useful not to look so unushual.'

I hand over the food I brought in my pockets. There are some empty packets of Cheesy Wotsits on the floor, so she has eaten something. Still, Hellyann tears the wrapper off the block of cheese with her teeth and bites straight into it, taking huge mouthfuls and chewing with her mouth open, which Gran would have commented on if it had been me – but now she says nothing.

Instead she gets to her feet, straightens her shoulders and looks at Hellyann over the top of her glasses. She's quite small, my gran, but when she fixes you with her dark eyes, it's quite an intimidating look. It's what she has done countless times with me and Tammy over the years and it means: *I'm taking no nonsense here, and you had better not be messing about.*

She says, 'Ethan tells me that you know where our Tammy is, young, erm . . .' she pauses and then settles on, 'young lady.'

'Yes,' says Hellyann, spraying tiny gobbets of cheese as she speaks. Then she swallows a big mouthful and licks her teeth with her long tongue. Gran doesn't flinch. 'But we do not have excessive time.' The word *excessive* sprays more cheese and a bit lands on Gran's glasses.

We are just thinking about this, when there's the noise of a rattling engine a little way down the hill. Seconds later, the front door bursts open and the Geoffs stand there, silhouetted in the doorway.

Chapter Fifty-one

Through the opened door, I can see the Geoffs' rattly old car.

The two men march forward to our little group sitting around the coffee table. The younger one is still carrying the gun at his side, but most of it is covered by his coat, which has flapped open. The older Geoff starts speaking even before he gets close to us, shaking his head in disbelief as he stares at us.

'Oh my goodness me. Oh my goodness, gracious me. *Gerroff!*' Suzy is flapping and pecking around his ankles, causing him to kick out. Thankfully, his aim is poor and Suzy just hops out of the way before going back in for another peck. She really is like a little, angry terrier.

The two Geoffs stand while we sit, and the younger one snorts when he sees Gran.

'Oh, Dad!' Geoff Jr says. 'Look who's here! They've got a little old lady to help them!'

Geoff Sr, who has been staring at Hellyann, glances over at Gran and says, 'I saw. What's up, Christine? Small world, eh?'

The two Geoffs laugh: a horrible, mocking chuckle.

Gran says nothing and keeps her eyes on the two men. And still Suzy is growling and pecking at their legs.

Hellyann hasn't sat down, and she starts to move away. She could make a run for it. She is easily agile enough, but as soon as she moves, the younger Geoff nudges his coat aside to bring into view a long, shiny farmer's shotgun, which he raises and points lazily at Hellyann.

Gran gives a little bark of contempt.

'Ha! Is that the antique shotgun your dad stole from his father-in-law? He always knew who'd taken it.'

Geoff Jr looks uneasy, his eyes darting between Gran, Hellyann and his dad. Gran tuts but says no more.

'You's have all gone very quiet,' says the older Geoff. 'I'll make it easy for you. Hand over the alien right now, and everything'll be fine. Otherwise . . .' He leaves the threat hanging, but it doesn't sound good.

It's Gran who gets to her feet and goes straight up to them, seemingly unafraid of the shotgun. 'Otherwise what, exactly? You'll kill her? I don't think you have the nerve.' She's staring at them from beneath her woolly hat, her eyes burning and furious. 'You . . .' she points at Geoff Sr, and looks him up and down, 'you are just a bully, and you always have been. And as for you, little Geoffrey with your popgun, you're pathetic. All you both want is some sort of recognition, some sort of fame and you don't care about anybody else.'

The Geoffs look at Gran, then at each other, and a slow grin spreads across each of their faces. They start to laugh.

As their laughter grows, Suzy becomes yet more agitated. Geoff Sr is laughing so hard that he bends down and it's only when he stands up again that I realise he has grabbed Suzy and is holding her by the throat. The laughter stops as if a switch had been flicked, and Suzy flaps her wings in protest.

Poor Iggy rushes forward but the younger Geoff takes a pace to put himself between Iggy and his chicken.

Geoff Sr turns to his son. 'You bought our Sunday lunch yet, Geoffrey?'

'No, Dad, I haven't. Are you thinking what I'm thinking?'

'Exactly, son. It's the perfect size for two, this one,' he says, holding Suzy up. He then tucks the bird under his arm and holds her tightly by the neck. 'You see, all I have to do is make a little twist here . . .' He mimes breaking Suzy's neck.

'No!' says Hellyann and she steps forward.

Without letting go of the bird, the old man relaxes his grip on Suzy's neck, and the chicken shakes her head in disapproval.

'Well, would you believe it? It speaks! What is it, ET?' says Geoff Sr. 'One animal death enough for you, eh? Or perhaps you want to kill this one yourself as well? Either way, very sensible. And you speak English? This gets better and better. Make sure you tell them that, son.'

Geoff Jr is on his phone and we all listen to his side of the conversation.

'We've got it, Jamie. I said, *we've got it* . . . Aye. Right here . . . Pictures? Aye, I'll send you some . . . Aye, and the black stick thing I mentioned . . . How long will you be? . . . I said, *how long* . . .' Geoff Jr pauses to glare at his phone and then shakes it, as though that will improve the signal. Then he tuts and puts his phone away.

He says to his father, 'They're on their way. Dunno how long. Depends on the roads. Couldn't hear properly.'

'*Who* is on their way?' says Gran forcefully.

'Oh, hello, Christine,' says Geoff Senior. 'I'd forgotten you were there. Who do you think would be most interested in ET here? A journalist perhaps, like Jamie Bates, that blow-dried idiot off the telly? Or even someone from the military? Or how about, ooh . . . *both*? Aye, the press and the Royal Air Force are both on their way. Geoffrey, keep them here while I get the car.' He leaves through the double doors, Suzy still tucked under his arm.

Geoff Jr still has his gun aimed towards Hellyann. He edges round behind Hellyann and jerks his head towards the door. 'Come on, ET. It's not far.'

This is too much for me. 'Stop!' I shout, and he does, looking round slowly.

'*Please!*' I continue. 'This is about Tammy. Can't you

see? She knows where Tammy is! You're going to ruin everything!'

Geoff Jr glances down at the ground and, for a moment, I think my plea has been effective. He can't ignore that, surely?

He speaks so quietly I have to strain to hear him. 'Don't you worry about that, my little friend. This will all be over in half an hour.' He smiles a sickly grin. 'We'll be done with her, and then you can have her back to chase your sister. That way, everybody wins, eh? Ta-ra!'

Seconds later, the throaty sound of the old engine rattles outside, and Geoff Jr leads Hellyann at gunpoint out of Mad Mick's Mental Rentals and into the car.

He turns back and repeats the mirthless grin. 'Isn't this *fun*?'

Then he slams the door behind him and the car roars off.

Nobody says anything for what seems like ages.

Chapter Fifty-two

The three of us – Iggy, Gran and I – watch the car pull away with Hellyann and Suzy inside, spraying up snow behind it, and then we stand silently next to one another.

I see Iggy's lips moving but I don't hear what he's saying. I think he's just mouthing 'Suzy' over and over again.

'Where do they live, then?' asks Gran eventually. 'Is he still in that dump of a place up the road to the observatory?'

I nod sadly, my gaze transfixed by the tyre tracks leading away from us.

'He is? I might have known it. Well, come on – let's get going.' Gran claps her hands together purposefully.

'To do what?' I say.

I really feel deflated. What chance do any of us have against a pair of psychos with a shotgun? The RAF and journalists will be here soon anyway and the whole thing will be out of our hands.

Gran turns to Iggy and me and gazes at us intensely over the rim of her glasses. 'Tell me, Ethan Tait . . .'

My full name. This is serious.

'And you . . . Ig . . . Iggly . . . whatever your name is.'

'Ignatius Fox-Templeton.'

'Yes, that. Why did you get me involved?'

I blow my cheeks out as I think. 'I guess I figured we needed an adult.'

'OK. Well, you've got one. Right here. I may be old, but I'm not senile. And I am *not* going to rest on my bony backside while that pair of low-life bullies puts at risk the return of *my* granddaughter from wherever-the-heck she is.'

'But, Gran,' I say, 'they've got a *gun*!'

'What? That old thing?' She waves her hand dismissively. 'Couldn't hit a barn door with it. Never could. Did you see the barrel? All rusted up. I'll bet he's never fired it in his life. He's all mouth, is Geoff McKay, and his son's the same.'

I study my gran and then look at Iggy, and eventually back at Gran.

'Well,' I say. 'If you're sure . . .'

Gran's face is set in a mask of determination. 'Well, hallelujah! Only one problem, pet. If me car wasn't out of action, we could use that.'

Iggy's attention has wandered. He's eyeing a row of Segways, all lined up and fully charged.

'You know what? I don't think Mick would mind . . .' he says.

Moments later, Gran, Iggy and I are heading down the hill, each of us standing on one of Mad Mick's two-wheeled personal transporters.

The Segways' extra-thick tyres – added for navigating the forest walks around Kielder – are perfect in the snow. Iggy's ridden one before and he's off in seconds. Gran and I are a bit more cautious, but they're not hard to get the hang of.

There is nobody about in the village. The snow has kept everybody indoors and the roads are smooth and white apart from the tyre tracks left by the Geoffs' car.

To get to the Geoffs' house from the village it's not far: over the bridge that crosses the burn and then there's a path that turns off the road as it bends round. We're slowed down by the road conditions, but we're going as fast as we can – easily the speed of a bicycle pedalled hard.

It's Gran who spots the blood on the bend in the road: bright red on the white snow. She shrieks, 'Ethan! Iggly! Look!'

We slow our Segways to a halt to see what Gran is pointing at. There is a large pool of blood, and some fresh tyre tracks that look very like the Geoffs', but I can't be certain . . .

Gran steps off her transporter and peers at the ground, concentration furrowing her brow, till she says, eventually, 'Something was bleeding. Then it just stopped. It makes no sense.'

My throat tightens with fear. What if Hellyann is dead?

Iggy says, 'She's right, Tait. Look! There's no trail of

blood leading anywhere, but there are footprints. Whatever was bleeding has just vanished.'

'Or been put in a car. Perhaps—'

I'm cut off by a yelp from Gran. She's a few metres away, holding a battered wellington boot – one of the pair that Hellyann was wearing.

Iggy is already off on his Segway down the road.

'We can follow the tyre tracks in the snow,' he calls back. 'Come on!'

We don't have to follow them for long, for after the bend they turn into the narrow road leading to the Geoffs' scruffy cottage.

We advance on our Segways up the little road till we can see their cottage through the trees. We get off behind a low wall. In front of the house is their car and we can see Geoff Jr outside a shed, smoking and stamping his feet to ward off the cold. He takes out his phone to make a call, and rests the long shotgun upright against a plastic garden table.

'There's only one reason he's standing outside the shed in this cold,' whispered Iggy. 'He's guarding something. Shh, get down.'

The three of us crouch down behind the snow-topped wall and watch as the front door opens and the older man comes out with a bucket and a sponge. The lights on the car flash and there's a bleep as he unlocks the back doors and leans in with the sponge, reappearing to squeeze pink water into the bucket. When he's done cleaning up the blood, he stands up, shuts the door and the car bleeps twice.

'That's the second time in as many days I've washed the inside of that car. Flamin' stinks, does that. Shoulda got you to do it.'

The two men are only about ten metres away from us and we can hear them perfectly. I decide to risk peeping over the wall.

The young Geoff ignores his father and, staring at his phone, says, 'Half an hour, he reckons, if the roads have cleared. And the police are sending the launch up from Tower Knowe. They'll call in the RAF from Boulmer once they've seen it.'

'Has he got the pictures yet?'

'They're still sending. Nine minutes remaining, it says here. It's a rotten signal.'

'What did you get, anyway?'

'I got what you said: close-ups, full length, a bit of video. It's a big file. It's taking a while.'

'Good lad. Leave your phone out here. It's better reception.'

Geoff Jr puts his phone down on a garden table that's been cleared of snow and follows his dad into the house.

Iggy pulls his cap lower. 'Did you hear what he said? In nine minutes those pictures will have sent. I think I know what to do,' he says, and Gran and I lean in.

It's a pretty clever plan, but requires nerves that I'm not sure I possess – let alone my gran.

Iggy raises his head a little bit over the wall to look again.

'They've gone in. Are you ready?' he asks.

'No,' I say.

At the same time, Gran hits her gloved fist into her other hand and says, 'Yeahhh!'

She's loving this, I think. She's really loving this.

CHAPTER FiFTY-THREE

Hellyann

The pain in my head is becoming worse, and I can feel myself weakening. My breathing is a little more laboured, my hand hurts and my pulse is feeble. I have not eaten enough for days now and what I have eaten I have vomited over the back seat of the car where I was being held, causing the older man to shout, 'Oh, you dirty little alien scumbag, oh, that is disgusting! Oh my God, open the window, Geoff!'

I do not think cheese is very good for me.

In the confusion caused by my vomiting, I had the presence of mind to pick up my black healing stick where it lay on the floor of the vehicle. I slipped it into one of the long boots I was wearing.

The chicken that Iggy likes is now beside me in this outdoor room in which they have locked me, and I pick her up to feel her warmth. She likes it, I think, and makes a sound in her throat – a sort of *brrr brrr* – that I think indicates pleasure or satisfaction.

I have lost blood. I reach up and touch my skull – the blood is crusting into a scab, aided a little by an application of the healing stick, but the stick is losing power and is not very effective any more. I lost one of the boots on the road. I did not use the stick until I was here, out of sight, and by then I had already lost a lot of blood.

I have found some old fabric and I sit on it while I lean my head against the wooden wall of the shed and contemplate the last few moments that I remember.

I was in the back of their motorcar, and the older man was driving it himself using his feet and hands. He said, 'Bloody ice' twice as the car skidded on the snowy roads. (Perhaps he has not driven before – he did not seem to be very good at it.)

The younger man held his long gun and occasionally pointed it at me.

Then, without expecting it, I vomited – pale, lumpy liquid went all over the rear portion of the vehicle and the shouting started.

The vehicle skidded to a halt on the snow-covered road and the older man said a word that I do not recognise. The younger man moved to get out of the car. When he unlocked the vehicle doors I saw my chance, and leapt over the seat in front of me and tried to run.

I was too weak. I stumbled and fell out of the car into a deep pile of snow.

'Oh no you don't,' said the young man. And then he

called me 'a hairy little toerag', and stood on my hand, hard, with his big boot.

The last thing I saw before I passed out was the wooden stock of his long gun coming towards my head.

On our planet, we approach our existence with a clear-eyed assessment of the facts at hand. We do not lean towards fanciful interpretations of what might – or might not – be true, or right, or proper.

In other words, I do not fear death. I do, however, fear that the consequences of my death might lead to great hardship here on Earth. You are a primitive people, prone to war, and unable to cope with the technology that you will discover if I die without first destroying my craft.

These are the thoughts I have as I crouch, shivering, with my head hurting badly in the shed and hear a strange *eeeow eeeeow eeeeow* noise coming from outside.

There are footsteps as one of my captors – I cannot see which – moves towards the noise.

'Is that the car alarm, Dad? What's set that off?'

'Oi!'

'It's that kid with the red hair! You little vandal! Come here!'

Seconds later, I hear the bolt on the door shoot back and I cower into the back of the shed. Instead of one of the men, though, there, most unexpectedly, is the old woman whose name is Gran. I am not good at reading human emotions from their faces, but I think she is looking scared. Her eyes dart from side to side.

'Quickly – give me your jumper and your hat,' she says while she removes her thick jacket. It is done in seconds, then she says, 'Now stay here. When the coast is clear, head down to the lake path with Suzy and go to the boat shed.'

'Which coast?' I have to ask. 'Which coast is clear?'

'I don't know,' says Gran impatiently. 'It just means "when nobody else is about".'

Why do you not say what you mean, then? I think, but I do not say it because she is being kind. Besides, she has gone already. I see her run across the yard and up the path wearing my striped sweater and hat. She is old but she moves like someone much younger, it seems.

One of the men shouts, 'There it is! It's escaped! Go on, son – get after it! I'll follow in the car.'

Moments later, their vehicle roars up the small road. The two boys reappear around the corner of the house, grinning widely. They run to me, and Iggy is on his knees picking up Suzy, who has hopped and flapped with pleasure to see him. Still grinning, he says, 'Well, what are you waiting for? Come on – let's go!'

I follow them down to the lake path. When we get there, we stop, and the boys start to laugh. Iggy is still cuddling his chicken.

'They'll never catch her!'

'Northumberland Veterans Half-marathon Champion, that's my gran!' says Ethan, grinning. 'She goes, "*I'm not scared of some poxy popgun!*"'

'You should have seen his face! What an utter goon!'

They keep laughing as I watch them.

'What about his gun?' I ask.

Iggy reaches into his jacket pocket and pulls out two small cylinders.

'Took the precaution of removing the cartridges before I set the car alarm off, just in case your gran was wrong. His gun's useless!'

They are so pleased with their deception that they cannot stop smiling. What they did was clever and unexpected, and I find the corners of my mouth lifting up, and there is a strange tightening in my stomach before I utter a breathy *ha*! And then another: *Ha. Ha.*

The boys stop and gaze at me.

Iggy says, 'Did you just *laugh*, Hellyann?'

It comes again. *Ha. Ha-ha!* My mouth is open wide and the twitching in my stomach continues, and I do not try to stop it because it is a wonderful feeling. Then Suzy the chicken makes a squawking noise and so all four of us are doing it. *Ha-ha-ha-haaaaa! Squawk!* And that continues for a considerable time, and then we have to stop because I have to be sick again.

Chapter Fifty-four

Ethan

It's funny and everything – laughing with Iggy and Hellyann, and even Suzy joining in – but it's not as if I've forgotten about Gran.

Geoff Jr is huge and smokes like the back end of our school taxi-bus. Still, Gran is seventy-*ahem*. I've seen her running: she shuffles along with these little steps. Can she sprint? I have no idea.

Geoff's dad is following on the road in the car, but given the conditions, he won't be going fast and besides, Gran said she'd stick to the forest trails.

Hellyann doesn't understand at all, I don't think. In fact, I am pretty certain she is not well. Her eyes keep glazing over and her legs seem to wobble occasionally. Then she throws up, and the smell of *that* is enough to get my guts twitching.

'I . . . I need food, proper food, *my* food,' she says. 'And I need to rest. I . . .'

I am distracted by Iggy shouting, 'Oh my God, no!'

I see that Iggy is looking with horror at his phone. 'No, no, no . . .' He jabs at it with his fingers. 'It hasn't turned off.'

It is not his phone – it's Geoff Jr's, which he grabbed from the garden table as we snuck up on the car to set off the alarm. He turned it off and shoved it in his pocket.

Or . . . *didn't* turn it off.

'It needs a code, or a thumbprint, or something to power down,' he says, his voice rising in panic and annoyance. 'Who on earth does *that*?'

'Is it still sending?'

'Yes, two minutes remaining.' He's still jabbing at it.

Two minutes till the Geoffs' journalist friend has photo and video evidence of an alien in his inbox.

'Smash it,' I say.

It's a top-of-the-range phone, and very expensive, but, without hesitating, Iggy throws it with all his strength on the ground. It bounces off the snowy path undamaged. He stamps on it, but his rubber boots aren't hard enough. The screen of the phone still glows, and Iggy is shouting, 'Die, will you? Just *die*!' while stamping on it repeatedly.

I can see the progress bar has jumped ahead.

Less than a minute remaining.

I don't notice Hellyann turning away from us and going back into the shed where she was imprisoned. She comes out seconds later with a huge axe.

'Stant pack!' she says and lifts the axe over her head,

bringing it down with a crunch on the screen, which shatters. She does it again and a third time until the phone is in hundreds of pieces.

We stand together, gathered round the smashed device in silence, like mourners at a graveside.

'Well done, Hellyann,' I say eventually and I hold up my hand for a high five.

Instead she sinks to her knees and quietly passes out face down in the snow next to the axe.

'No!' I say. 'Don't die! You need to get Tammy back!'

'She's not dead, Tait. She's still breathing – look. We've got to get help. Who do we know—'

I cut him off.

'Nobody! Don't you get it?' I yell. 'There is nobody who's gonna help us! Whoever we ask is going to either capture her, or call in the army, or the police, or the . . . the FBI or whoever you call in to deal with an alien landing. And if that happens, it's game over for Tammy!'

We reach down and turn Hellyann over so that she is face upwards. It is probably the first time I have touched her and it is strange and intimate. Her hairy skin is slack and cool to the touch. As she turns over, her eyes flicker open.

'Take . . . take me to my craft,' she croaks. 'Carry me. I will be all right.'

Awkwardly, we prop her up to a sitting position, and then somehow lift her up so she is over Iggy's shoulder, his face pressed into her side. He turns his face away, grimacing at the smell, and then we're off, Iggy staggering under his load, down the path to the boathouse.

A few minutes later, Iggy puts her down and Hellyann stands with one wellington boot on and a hand supporting her weight on the cracked wooden wall of the boathouse. Her breathing is ragged and again she sinks to her knees. There's no sign of the little orange canoe.

'Come on, Hellyann,' urges Iggy. 'Not long now. We've just got to get you in through the window.'

We look up at the opening. There is no way Hellyann can get through without help, and even if Iggy and I manage to lift her up, she's not strong enough to let herself down safely on the other side. I look at the metal bolt and padlock that are securing the double doors at the front. If only . . .

'The paddle!' I say, and before anyone replies, I'm off. 'Wait here!'

To get back to the jetty means running up to the road, back through the undergrowth we've just come through, along the path, past some parked cars, and then down to the little pebble beach. I'm so caught up in the urgency of my job that at first I don't notice the boat moored by the jetty.

And then I do – a long, rigid inflatable with *Northumbria Police* written down the side. I stop at the end of the jetty, panting from my running. I remember the parked cars at the top of the path – one had writing on it which I had taken no notice of, but now I have a moment to think. It was the RAF. *The Royal Air Force, Boulmer*, it had said on the side, along with a crest. I gulp.

Everyone around here knows RAF Boulmer. Katie Pelling's dad was a pilot and did a talk in primary school and it all comes flooding back to me as I stand there on the rocky shore. '*One of the world's biggest radar centres*,' he said. '*Nothing gets through here.*'

I *just know* that the RAF people are there because of Hellyann, and I get a feeling of terror in my stomach that reaches my throat and makes me gag. I've seen the boat before as well: it is the same one used by the police divers in their search for Tammy.

Two police officers are in the boat, and three other people in blue Air Force uniforms are on the jetty putting on life jackets.

I can see the paddle lying where we left it, at the beach end of the jetty. I could turn around now and go back up the path in the woods. I don't think they have noticed me . . .

Oh no. I *have* been seen. One of the policemen lifts his head and looks straight at me. I recognise him from the searches for Tammy. He was nice to me. Gave me a Polo mint once. PC Kareem something. He nudges his partner, who looks too. If I turn back now, it'll look very suspicious. Not that I'm doing anything *wrong* . . .

They almost certainly recognise me as Tammy's brother.

I decide to bluff it out and walk towards the paddle, as if it's the most normal thing in the world. Which, of course, it is, but when you're *trying* to be normal somehow everything seems anything but.

I bend down to pick it up, and now they're all looking at me.

'Just picking up, you know, my paddle,' I say far too quietly for them to hear me (it's more to reassure myself).

It's in my hand, and I turn to go back the way I came, desperately hoping not to hear someone on the jetty call out.

And nobody does. And I have taken a few steps. And I'm thinking everything's fine. And then . . .

'Hey! You there! Ethan? Stop!'

Chapter Fifty-five

I stop and look up to see a large woman in an RAF uniform lumbering towards me. So many things are running through my head, but whatever I think, it comes back to this:

Them being here is not about Tammy. It's about Hellyann.

Why else would the RAF be involved? The military body responsible for searching the skies for unauthorised craft entering our airspace? (You can tell I've been reading UFO websites – they're all like that.)

Why else would they be *here*, next to where Hellyann landed, where the Geoffs saw the splashes and saw Hellyann herself?

The woman is still coming towards me.

And so I turn, and I run.

I hear 'Hey! Stop!' and thudding footsteps, joined by others, on the wooden planking, but I don't turn to look back. Instead, using the canoe paddle as a kind of weapon against the undergrowth, I swish and hack and leap and hop through the trees, huge showers of snow from branches following me as I run, and I can tell I am making progress, because the footsteps behind me are getting no closer.

And then I am up by the road, by their cars, but I don't stop. I turn and run back along the road towards the little pathway down to the boathouse. Will they see me? I can't tell, and I daren't wait, so I turn down the path. I can't stop now – the boathouse is in sight. I can see Iggy and Hellyann with Suzy at their feet.

When I come level with them, I don't even speak. They can tell something is up, and so they stand aside as I shove the flat end of the paddle under the steel hasp that holds the padlock, and I push down with all my weight till I feel the metal parting from the wood with a noisy crunch. One more heave and the lock pops off with a splintering sound.

Seconds later, we're inside the boathouse. Iggy has more or less carried Hellyann, with her spindly arms across his shoulders for support. We pull the door closed behind us and Iggy and I lean against it, panting as quietly as we can. I put my finger to my lips as we listen out for footsteps coming down the path, and draw a bolt across to shut the door. The bolt is rusty, and the screws are loose: it will not hold for long if someone pushes it.

In front of us, the boathouse looks empty – just a rectangle of water leading out to the reservoir. It's odd – I kind of *know* that Hellyann's spaceship is there, just invisible. I lean forward on the walkway, stretching down into the water, and scoop some into my hand, which I throw towards where I think the craft is. Sure enough, the droplets land as if on glass, and then drip back down. It's definitely there. Where it sits in the water is indented, but unless you were looking you probably wouldn't notice. But when you do look, it's . . . strange. The slight ripples on the water's surface stop when they hit the invisible barrier, and the water smoothes out and dips into a shallow V-shape.

Meanwhile, using what seems to be the last of her fading strength, Hellyann calls out, 'Philip! Philip! I'm back.'

At the same time I hear a woman's voice outside.

'Ow! Corporal Morrison, pick up that chicken!'

And then we hear Suzy squawking.

'Get off! Crikey, it's an aggressive little b . . . blighter, ma'am! Oi, ow, gerroff!'

Iggy looks at me in horror – how could he have left Suzy outside? I'm thinking it's a good job he did: Suzy is buying us valuable time.

Then I let out a gasp of astonishment. Where there was nothing on the water before there is now a huge shape: dark, greyish, non-reflective, with a fuzzy outline that is like looking at an out-of-focus film.

Imagine a cheese triangle – one of the ones wrapped in foil, but hundreds of times bigger, the size of a motorhome or a van. Now imagine that the cheese triangle has half of a Malteser resting on it, also hundreds of times bigger.

This, then, is Hellyann's spacecraft – a huge wedge

shape with a big dome on top, with fuzzy edges. I could stare at it for hours in sheer, baffled wonderment. Already, though, there are more voices outside the boathouse.

'He's in here. Blimey, Smithy – that chicken doesn't want to let you past!'

Go, Suzy! I think.

A side section of the spaceship slides open, and Hellyann limps inside, turning and motioning for us to follow. Iggy's next – he steps up on to the level surface of the wedge and goes straight into the craft.

The bolt on the double doors creaks as it is pushed from the other side, and I run desperately round the walkway to get to the craft and get inside. I dive into the opening just as, below me, I see the grey outline dissolve as the craft becomes invisible again.

Above me, the hatch half shuts, and it is as dark in there as a Kielder winter's night.

'Be quiet,' croaks Hellyann. 'Say nothing.' She then says something in her own language and a portion of the dome in front of us clears to show the boathouse door.

Then we hear another voice, a man's voice, shouting, 'Stand aside! I'm gonna kick this door in.'

It's Geoff Jr. He's got a taste for kicking in doors, it seems.

As we watch in silence, the bolt gives way with a cracking sound and the double doors burst open.

Chapter Fifty-six

The tall RAF lady and her companion come through the double doors and stand in the doorway, staring straight ahead at the spaceship but evidently unable to see it, because they don't look surprised or anything.

At least we're invisible, I think.

Behind them is Geoff Jr, his shotgun raised at waist level, and next to him is a face I have seen on TV: the news reporter Jamie Bates. Nobody, thankfully, is looking at the water, where they might notice the indentation in the surface.

Beside me, there is enough light inside the dome for me to notice what Hellyann is doing. From somewhere she has taken something about the size of a pencil and has stabbed her palm. I once saw a teacher at school use an EpiPen on a kid who was allergic to nuts and had developed a rash – it was *exactly* like that. Hellyann blinks hard, then looks at me and nods with satisfaction.

Then, from behind the people at the boathouse doors, comes Suzy, flapping and squeaking and pecking at the woman's feet.

'Oh, for heaven's sake! That bird! Get it OUT of here!' The RAF woman aims a vicious kick at Suzy, who leaps out of the way and briefly takes flight, landing back on the walkway. Then she raises her wings ready to take off again.

Oh no, I think. *No, no, no – go the other way. The OTHER way!*

But she doesn't. In her panic to avoid the woman's boot, Suzy flaps up over the water and lands on the spacecraft, right above our heads.

The *invisible* spacecraft. Suzy will look as though she is floating in mid-air.

'Oh, surely not! That's less than good,' says Iggy, who is standing beside me.

'What the . . . ?' gasps Jamie Bates, pointing right at Suzy.

For a few seconds, Suzy stays still, then she flaps down through the open hatch into the dome next to us. To the people on the walkway of the boathouse, it must have looked like a chicken floated in the air and then just . . . vanished. Above my head, the hatch hisses shut, further darkening the interior of the dome.

'Did you see that? What the flaming heck just . . . ?' The woman is lost for words.

They all just stare at the space, and then down at the water. Then Geoff crouches down and does exactly what I did a moment ago: he scoops up a handful of water and throws it at the invisible spaceship.

He straightens up and raises the shotgun to his shoulder.

The RAF woman looks astonished. 'Sir?' she says. 'What are you doing?'

Geoff Jr doesn't reply. Instead he shouts, 'Bring her out! Bring her out now. The military are here and the police.'

'And the press!' squeaks Jamie Bates, unnecessarily.

The woman shouts at Geoff, 'Halt! Stop! Put down that gun. That's an order.'

'Or what?' sneers Geoff.

'We haf to get out of here,' says Hellyann. 'The danger is too great.' Then she says something in her own language and the craft responds.

The humming noise starts. It sounds louder inside the craft than it was the other day when I first heard it, and the pitch gets higher and higher. The RAF people look at each other and then around the boathouse to see where it is coming from. Then they look down at the water – the invisible spaceship is on the move. The indented part of the water's surface is moving back from the walkway.

Then there's a click as Geoff pulls the trigger of his shotgun. I see him look puzzled, then he breaks the gun at the hinge, revealing the two empty chambers where the shells should have been. *So he didn't fire at Gran*, I think with relief. He starts fumbling deep in his pocket for replacements.

Hellyann is reversing the spaceship out of the boathouse.

'What's that noise?' says the woman.

They are both watching the water, which is being churned up as we reverse.

There is a deafening bang, immediately followed by the noise of hundreds of tiny pieces of lead shot peppering the spacecraft as Geoff fires his newly loaded shotgun. Then the gun goes off again.

Above the gunshot and the humming, I hear the officer shout 'Stop!' again, but we are not stopping.

The humming noise reaches an almost painful pitch, and the air around us seems to contract, and my ears feel blocked.

Hellyann gabbles something in her language then shouts to us, 'Sit down at the back and put the straps on you.'

We stumble to the back of the cockpit where there is a bench seat and Iggy and I fall on to it. Immediately, rigid bars appear and pin us down – it makes me think of the roller-coaster seats when Tammy and I went to Alton Towers.

By now we are clear of the boathouse and reversing to the centre of the reservoir.

Geoff has reloaded and fired more shots without effect.

Beside him, Jamie Bates has taken out his camera phone and is frantically swiping to bring up – I am guessing – the camera function. But he doesn't want to take his eyes off what is happening so he keeps getting it wrong and having to try again.

The screen before us goes black and I feel a lurch deep inside me. Beside me, I can feel Iggy tensing and Suzy wriggling.

The dim light in the cockpit shows that Hellyann is now strapped in a seat the same as ours, at the side.

The lurch happens again, but huge this time, and at the same time I feel myself tipping back. The noise in the craft is nearly unbearable and there seems to be a huge weight on my chest, making it hard to breathe, and my eyes are screwed up tight.

Do I pass out? I can't tell. I have no idea how much time has passed, but it feels like several minutes – perhaps longer. Suddenly, the noise inside the cockpit quietens.

Then there is nothing. Silence.

I can breathe. I open my eyes, and I can make out Iggy beside me and Suzy, and Hellyann exactly where they all were before.

But the light is dim, and the dome seems to have changed in some way, because it is pure black.

Hellyann turns to look at me.

I try to speak, but my mouth is too dry.

'Wh . . . where . . . what . . .' is all I manage.

Hellyann does her slow blink and says, 'Welcome to space.'

Part Four

All right. Slow down.

Stop.

Shhhh.

I want you to realise the sheer, stupendous strangeness of how I feel right now.

1. I'm twelve and I'm, like, half-kidnapped in a spaceship, hurtling – somehow, don't ask me how – through flipping . . . *spacetime* or something.
2. Next to me on this hard bench is Iggy Fox-Templeton. He's asleep or concussed, as far as I can tell, specs on the end of his nose.
3. To round it off nicely, there's a hairy, stinking, dog-killing alien about a metre away from me with what looks like a smile on her face.
4. Oh yeah, and there's a chicken.

So, if *you* think that *I* think that this is in *any way* cool, then you're just wrong.

I thought I knew fear when Tammy went missing. This is a whole new level.

Thought I'd point that out now, because things have been moving pretty rapidly and I wondered if you thought that I was fine with it all.

I'm not.

Just saying . . .

Chapter Fifty-seven

The American accent penetrates the fog of my brain, though I don't think I am fully conscious when I first hear it.

'This is your captain, Philip Philipson, speaking. Welcome on board Flight AN950 to Anthalla and thank you for choosing to fly with us. Kindly switch off all electronic devices and pay attention to the cabin staff . . .'

I think I am dreaming so I drift off again, or the voice fades out – I'm not sure which.

Then I'm awake instantly. My heart is beating so hard that I can actually feel it – *bup-bup bup-bup* – in my chest. I can hardly breathe, I can't swallow, every bit of me – my fingers, my scalp, my back – is tingling as though I'm being electrocuted, and I feel like I'm about to throw up violently. The noise in my ears is unlike anything I have ever heard: a combination of stomach-churning bass and a million knives being scraped over a plate. I scream but I cannot even hear myself; my eyes feel like they're glued shut.

I was not expecting this, but then who would?

Of all the things I thought might happen today – and believe me, I spent quite a bit of last night running through them in my head, until I finally fell into a sweaty, twitching sleep – being in a spaceship didn't even come up.

I try to piece together the last few moments, but it's hard because I feel like everything in my head has been scrambled up. There was me, and Tammy and Iggy . . .

Hang on. Tammy? Isn't next she to me? No, that's Hellyann, but I can't see her because is dark everything. Tammy's sister my. That is this what about all is. What? What's happening head in my?

Isn't it?

Who?

Oh God, I'm going to be sick . . .

And there it comes. I try to lean forward but I can't – there is a strap holding me back – and besides, I don't know which way up I am. So my stomach convulses and its contents are ejected violently all down my front.

And then, second by second, the noise and the tingling on my skin diminishes, the motion steadies, and I can open my eyes. Well, one eye. There is something stinging in my other one. Sick, maybe.

My brain? My thoughts? Are they unscrambling? Perhaps they are . . .

With my single open eye I can see stars. I appear to be revolving slowly. Then the large window blacks out and I'm back in semi-darkness.

I can smell something too. Blocked drains? Rotten fish? No, that's . . . that's Hellyann? It's coming back to me.

I hear a voice from beside me.

'We will remofe that when we ket to what you call "escape velocity".' The voice is familiar.

I try to speak, but my mouth is too dry. I manage: 'Huh?'

'Your vomitus. I had not anticipated that, although even if I hat, there was little I could do about it. Py the way, you might experience some mild disorientation. Your thoughts may be a little scrampled.'

You can that say again . . .

'It is common on first voyages. It can cause temporary loss of consciousness.'

I'm panting and I can feel sweat trickling down my neck. With an effort, I work some saliva into my mouth so that I can lick my lips and talk. I feel stiff all over, but I manage to turn my head to the source of the voice, and I can see Hellyann lying next to me. Or is she standing? I cannot tell which way is up. She turns her head to me and I look into her pale eyes.

'Hellyann?'

'Yes, Ethan.'

I take a deep breath and manage to croak, 'Do you mind telling me what's going on?'

'No, I to not mind. We are koing to my home planet, to ket your sister back.'

Chapter Fifty-eight

From beside me, Hellyann is keeping up a constant on-and-off chatter in a language I don't understand, full of odd squeaks, whistles and growls. On my other side, Iggy is strapped in, eyes shut, seemingly unconscious.

When Hellyann eventually pauses, I say, 'Who are you talking to?'

'It is not a *who*. It is a *what*. The craft. This.' She looks around to indicate what she means.

The craft does not seem to reply – I think Hellyann has an earpiece or something. She says something else in the strange, throaty noise, then there is silence – total silence – as what I am guessing are 'engines' power down. I feel an odd sensation, mainly in my legs, but also inside me, like when you go over a sudden hill in a car and your stomach goes *whoaah*!

Then it passes.

'Weightlessness,' says Hellyann, as something soft and feathery hits my head.

Suzy floats past, weightless, and with a *very* startled

look on her face. She keeps extending her wings and then pulling them back in and looking round the cabin.

'Hold on to the chicken!' says Hellyann urgently, as Suzy floats past again.

I reach up and grab her.

In a second, the floating blobs of sick from earlier whizz past me and are gone somewhere I cannot see.

'Waste disposal,' Hellyann says. 'That is why I tolt you to catch the bird. Anything floating would haf been sucked up and disposed of.'

The whining stops. Silence returns – a huge silence that seems to stretch on forever.

'Hellyann?' I say. 'Where are we?'

'We haf left your planet's atmosphere. We are apout four hundred and twenty kilometres above the surface of Earth, in a temporary orbit at a felocity of eight kilometres per second and blah blah blah blah . . .'

Of course, she doesn't actually *say* 'blah blah'. It's just that after a couple of sentences that's what it sounds like. And I *like* all that stuff. I love reading about the International Space Station, and the moon landings when Gran was young . . . Only, I am just beginning to realise what has happened. It doesn't 'dawn on me slowly' as I understand what is going on. No, it is much, *much* more rapid.

I begin to breathe shallowly – short pants that seem to leave me breathless – and I am unable to speak.

'You appear to be panicking,' says Hellyann. 'A human, emotional response to sicknificant trauma—'

That does it. 'Hellyann!' I yell through my gasps. '*What is going on?* I can't see anything! I can't even . . .' And I start sobbing. 'Let me go! Let me free!'

I wriggle and struggle against the straps that bind my chest and arms and legs. It is a horrible sensation, made worse by the grey half-light which floods the cabin from some source that I cannot see.

'Please be calmer,' says Hellyann. 'I will activate the kravity simulator.' Then she says something in her language.

I feel the heaviness return to my legs and that lurch in my stomach again; then the straps that are holding me unfasten and retract and I can stand up. I move my arms; I lift a foot and stamp it down again.

Iggy's straps have come free too, and he opens his eyes, looking dazed, but he says nothing.

With another command from Hellyann, the walls enclosing us clear like a fog and I am staring at stars – endless brilliant pinpricks of light stretching to, well . . . to infinity, I suppose.

Gradually, my breathing returns to normal (ish), though Iggy still hasn't said anything.

I try to take stock of where we are.

He and I are inside the cockpit of Hellyann's spaceship. That much is clear.

It is about three metres from side to side and the same

from floor to roof. There are hardly any control panels – no flashing lights, or computer screens, or endless dials; there are no levers or coloured buttons. I'm not even in a spacesuit. I stretch out my hand to touch the . . . what? The *window*? It feels cool and smooth.

And then I see it. We both see it, and Iggy says his first words in space.

'Oh my word!' he gasps. 'Is . . . is that . . . ?'

'Yes, Ikk-ee. That is Earth.'

A huge and brilliant ball glides into view at the bottom of the domed window. It is *exactly* how it looks in the pictures I have seen on TV. I can make out the blues of the oceans, and patches of green, and the golden lights of the cities . . .

'The blue planet,' I say. It's a while before I can add: 'Isn't it beautiful?'

'If you say so,' says Hellyann. 'I am propaply not the one to ask.'

I kind of want to ask why, but I am transfixed. It's also just one of about a trillion questions that I want to ask her and I don't know where to begin. So I start with the one that is uppermost in my mind. I say it slowly, as I cannot seem to take my eyes off the Earth below us.

'Hellyann? Will . . . will I see Tammy again?'

'That is highly likely.'

I close my eyes and try to imagine saying something clever and emotional when I see her, but I can't think further than '*Hi, Tam*'. I smile – '*Hi, Tam*' will have to do.

'And, Hellyann . . . ?'

'Yes, Ethan?'

'Will we see our mum and dad again?'

'That tepends.'

'*Depends?* Depends on what?'

She does not answer. Instead she says, 'The kravity simulator is going off, and we are about to start our chourney.'

The dome mists over again, and we're back in the grey light as the straps snake out again and tighten gently around me. Hellyann growls some more commands at the craft, which trembles slightly.

'Hellyann?' says Iggy. 'Should I be scared?'

'Are you scared when you get on your picycle?'

'My bike? No, of course not.'

'To us, this craft is about as complicated as a picycle is to you. So no. To not be scared. Although you may experience slight drowsiness or even unconsciousness akain.'

The American voice comes on again. '*I think what Hellyann is trying to say is that the craft itself is pretty basic. The* operating system, *however, is anything but.*'

'You are right, Philip. No offence intended.'

'*Fair enough,*' comes the reply, sounding rather huffy. '*None taken.*'

If what Hellyann says was meant to be reassuring, it is not. I am terrified.

But then the craft trembles even more and I feel the horrible prickling sensation return to my skin and everything goes black.

Chapter Fifty-nine

Some time later – hours, I think, not days – I open my eyes again. I look next to me at Iggy. He is staring straight ahead at nothing – his eyes are glazed and his lips are moving slightly, as though he is trying to speak but cannot remember how.

I recognise the feeling. I am, quite literally, speechless.

'Hi. This is your captain again. Kindly keep your seat belts fastened until the seat-belt light goes out, and may I remind you that there is no smoking permitted anywhere in the aircraft.'

Hellyann says, 'Philip. Not now.' She says it in English.

The voice responds, *Just tryna lighten the mood. We got a long way to go. Snacks will be served from our trolley, and a selection of alcoholic and non-alcoholic beverages is available. We will be cruising at an altitude—'*

'Philip! Stop it.' Hellyann follows this up with a command in her own language.

The voice stops, and a tiny overhead light that I had not noticed before fades out.

Iggy says, 'Who was *that*?'

Hellyann sighs. 'That is Philip. The bot that pilots this craft. He's . . . annoying. We do not really unterstand humour where I am from.'

We are silent for a moment or two, and I try to go over recent events in my head. Finding Hellyann imprisoned in the shed; Gran's brave run into the woods pursued by big Geoff; running from the RAF officers; breaking into the boathouse; hiding in the spaceship . . . *taking off*?

It occurs to me that perhaps we have not taken off at all. It was thinking of the roller coaster at Alton Towers that did it for me. There was another ride there that Tammy and I went on twice, the Devil Train. You didn't actually move, but you watched a film taken from the front of a real roller coaster, and the seat wobbled, and your mind did all of the rest. It tricked you into thinking you were moving. And the more I think about it, the more convinced I become.

This is all an elaborate hoax.

I say, 'I've had enough of this now, Hellyann. I want to get out. Please just open the door. We can explain everything to the people there. They will trust us, and . . . and no harm will come to you.'

Hellyann says, 'Why do you say this?' Her usual monotone sounds a little bit more anxious, which makes me even more certain that I have uncovered her trick.

'Because I'm scared, Hellyann, and I want this to stop.'

'Do you want to ket your sister back?'

'Well, yes, but—'

'I thought you would be grateful,' Hellyann snaps, following it with a burst of her own language, forcing Iggy to pipe up.

'Look, can you stop doing that, please? You have kidnapped us, so far as I can tell, and we only have your word that our fate will not be exactly the same as Tammy's. Why should we trust you?'

Hellyann looks between us, wide-eyed with what might be horror.

'But I haf told you that you will be safe,' she says. 'I haf told you that Tammy—'

'Big deal,' Iggy interrupts. 'Big, fat deal. You could be lying. You could have been lying since the day we met you. You could be—'

'But I do not lie. I . . . I find it very hart to lie. We do not really know how to.'

'And that,' says Iggy with a decisive nod, 'could easily be a lie.'

'*No,*' comes the cockpit's voice, '*she is telling the truth. Hellyann and everyone like her has a very limited capacity for deception. I, for example, am a much better liar than Hellyann.*'

'B . . . but you're not real,' says Iggy.

'*If I wanted to, I could do a long pause now to indicate that you have hurt my feelings. Indeed, I am not made, as you say, from flesh and blood. But my ability to tell untruths is as good as yours – probably better, in fact. After all, I have learned from the best.*'

'Who is that?'

'*Why, human beings, of course. Now strap yourselves in, fold away your trays, and please ensure that any domestic fowl are securely stored in the overhead lockers as we reach cruising altitude. Cabin crew, doors to manual and cross-check.*'

The noise in the cockpit increases slightly and I detect a change in movement.

Hellyann says to me, 'It is just Philip. He likes to try to be funny. He has picked up a lot of Earth phrases.'

'Hilarious,' says Iggy.

'*Thank you,*' says Philip.

'I was being sarcastic.'

'*Ah, yes. Saying the opposite of what you mean for the purposes of humour or mockery. That is a tricky one for me.*'

The screen before us clears and Iggy and I look at the vast, glowing blue-white ball beneath us.

'Doesn't look like we've gone very far—' begins Iggy.

'That iss not Earth,' says Hellyann. 'Philip?'

Philip's light comes on and his voice follows. '*You are

looking, my friends, at our home planet. It is called . . .' Here he makes a noise as though he is singing two notes while gargling.

Iggy says, 'Anthalla?' And Philip repeats it.

'That will have to do. Anthalla. It is a planet very like Earth in many respects. Similar temperature, similar gravity, similar atmosphere: you can breathe, walk and so on. There is much less land, much more water and no moon. Population stable at fourteen million; average lifespan twenty-eight years; inhabitants virtually disease-free; hunger and violent death non-existent; the last war was fought about seven hundred years ago; and an entire civilisation rebuilt from the ashes of the Big Burn. Any questions?'

It is more of a statement, actually – Philip doesn't wait for us to ask anything. Instead he carries on: *'Landing approach in two minutes. Visual Inhibitors fully operative. Please extinguish all cigarettes and have your tickets ready for inspection.'*

The screen goes black again, and the pitch of the engine changes.

'I do have a question as a matter of fact,' says Iggy. 'Why are you activating the Visual Inhibitors? I mean, that makes us undetectable, yes? Why the secrecy?'

I have to hand it to Iggy – he asks cleverer questions than I do.

There is a long pause before Hellyann says, 'Because this is a secret mission.'

Philip says, *'If I were you, I would have lied, Hellyann. No need to alarm them unnecessarily.'*

But now, of course, I *am* alarmed. 'Are we in danger?'

Philip says, *'Oh no.'*

At the same time, Hellyann says, 'Oh yes.'

At least I know now who to believe.

CHAPTER SixTY

Hellyann

We are in no danger so long as everything goes to plan.

Correction: the danger is *minimised* if everything goes to plan. The problem is, however, that I do not have one. A plan, that is. We – Philip and I – appear to be making a habit of leaving planets suddenly with no clear idea of what will happen next.

'Philip?'

'*Broadsword calling Danny Boy. Are you receiving me?*'

I speak to Philip in my own language so as not to alarm my human passengers. They are looking out of the craft, mesmerised by the glowing planet gliding beneath us.

'Where will we land, Philip?'

'*There is nowhere completely safe, Hellyann. My re-entry parameters are set to land exactly where we took off. This carries an obvious risk of detection. On the other hand, it is exactly what would NOT be expected.*'

'That sounds promising,' I say.

'It does. Only one snag: the Assistant Advisors will be expecting me to do what is not expected.'

'So we should not do that, then.'

'On the contrary. That is exactly what we should do. The AAs will have anticipated that a bot such as I would be able to predict their expectations and so we should not do the very opposite of what they expect us not to do, which amounts to not doing what they expect.'

'Wait,' I say. 'Can you say that again?'

'No. We need to go now. The Earth girl you are seeking is due for presentation at Earth Zone today.'

I take a deep breath. 'Very well, Philip. Proceed.'

Here is what we will do then:

1. Philip and I will land with our Earthly cargo (plus a chicken, which I had not expected). We will land where we took off three days ago. Philip's VI systems are rather basic (by our standards) and we can only hope that our re-entry will not be noticed. If it is, we may be intercepted and that could get very awkward.

2. If Philip and I have timed this right (and so far, I think we have) the Earth boys and I will proceed immediately to Earth Zone.

3. We will then save Tammy, and fly her back to Earth.

4. I am a little unclear how we will actually carry out that last part.

Chapter Sixty-one

Ethan

We are high, high above the grey-brown earth.

Hellyann finishes talking with Philip and says, 'We are ready to land. We shall be making a rapid, vertical descent straight down to our landing target. Such a descent increases the risk of collision with other airborne vehicles, but decreases the risk of detection. Hold tight. Philip, go.'

'Hang on to your hollyhocks, folks,' says Philip. *'But do not be alarmed. I usually get this right.'*

'*Usually?*' I say, but then I realise he is joking, and besides all the breath is sucked out of me as we start to fall.

I glance over at Iggy, who is gripping Suzy tighter than is probably good for her, and it's only when she squeaks a little in protest that he relaxes and returns my terrified look.

We are descending faster than we would fall, lower and lower, with the whine of the craft's power getting higher and higher. My ears are popping like mad with the change in pressure. Outside the screen the land is getting closer – I can make out a coastline and water, then some squarish, flat things that might be buildings, and dark shapes travelling fast in the sky.

When it looks as though there is no way we will stop in time, I think I just give up, resigning myself to whatever will happen. I certainly don't think I'll survive and, for a few seconds, I think, *Well, this is an odd way to die . . .*

And then it's dark, and I'm being pulled upwards from my seat with the force of Philip slowing down the craft.

We have stopped. I am still strapped into my seat, alive and panting hard.

Hellyann says something to Philip, and they have a brief, rapid exchange of words. Even though I can't understand it, I can pick up on the tension in her voice.

'What's happening?' I say. 'Is everything OK?'

'No,' she replies. 'Everything is definitely not OK.'

Chapter Sixty-two

'Come quickly,' says Hellyann after a moment, ushering us out of the opened side with her hand. 'Philip has intercepted signals from the Hunters. They are on their way.'

Hunters? I think.

But Hellyann is beckoning us urgently.

Iggy goes first but I'm still struggling with a strap which has got tangled with something behind me. Suzy is cowering beneath my seat.

Through the front screen, I see Hellyann and Iggy move stealthily across the floor of a large cavern lit with huge candles.

'Wait!' I call.

Then Hellyann stops, and she turns back, her eyes wide with alarm, and she shouts something as two hairy creatures, a bit like her but bigger, step out of the shadows.

'Philip!' I say. 'I'm stuck—'

I have not finished speaking, when the side door slides shut, and Philip says, *'Be quiet.'*

I can hear that the group outside the spaceship are

talking in animated, loud voices, but of course I cannot understand what they are saying.

Then, to my horror, the two hairy creatures who were in the shadows step forward. One of them is holding a black stick with which they touch both Hellyann and Iggy. My friends instantly buckle at the knees and are supported by their attackers to stop them falling to the ground.

One of the creatures looks familiar. It has a dark streak of hair running from the centre of its head . . .

I think back to the Australian web page I looked at. The creature matches the drawing exactly, and a chill of fear grips my throat.

From behind the spacecraft, another creature comes, pushing a kind of trolley, a bit like the ones you get in hospitals, only it is a double-decker. They pick up Hellyann and lay her on the bottom section, with Iggy laid out on the top.

'Philip,' I hiss, 'what is going on?'

In reply, Philip murmurs, *'I miscalculated. The risk was obviously greater than I anticipated. They have been waiting for us to return.'*

And all I can do is watch in terror. Hellyann and Iggy on the trolley are pushed by the other hairy creatures from the large cavern down a dark corridor and out of sight. Only then do I finally struggle free from the strap that has been restricting me – and which, I realise, has saved me from the same fate. If I had stepped out at the same time as Iggy did then I too, surely, would now be on a trolley, unconscious.

I leap to my feet, bewildered, panicking.

'Philip! Philip!' I whisper, struggling to keep my voice steady. 'What . . . where . . . what's going on?'

'This is bad, Ethan. There is no other way of saying it.' His voice is low and grave.

'I gathered *that*. What's happened? Did you understand?'

'Yes, I understood perfectly. The good news, as far as you are concerned, is that you are safe. I don't think anyone knows you are here.'

My breathing is shallow and I feel light-headed with anxiety. I don't feel that this is good news. 'Just tell me what has happened, Philip. Please.'

'It would appear, Ethan, that the mission to return your sister has somewhat misfired. The other conspirators – the so-called "Hearters" – have been arrested and short-sleeped. A Hearter called Kallan has betrayed Hellyann, and Iggy has been captured, presumably to be taken to Earth Zone. That, at any rate, is how I understood the conversation that took place.'

I slump down on the bench seat and try to take all of this in.

'Is . . . is that how Tammy was captured? Made to collapse like that?'

'That is probable, Ethan. That large Assistant Advisor with the dark stripe of hair? She's a Hunter, and vicious with it.'

'But they don't know I'm here?' I say, seeking reassurance.

'No, Ethan. They were expecting Hellyann on her own, so when she emerged with Iggy that will have startled them. I promptly shut the door so that they would not see you.'

'Just give me a moment, Philip,' I say.

I take some deeper breaths. Those breaths turn ragged, and I slide off the bench on to the floor. I stay there for a long time with my eyes clammed shut with exhaustion and tears that will not come.

Finally, I open my eyes, and wipe my nose on my sleeve and I realise with a lead-heavy heart that I am still in the spaceship a gazillion-illion miles from home.

I am exhausted – truly empty of all energy and all emotion, especially hope. I can barely summon the strength to say, 'Philip?'

'Yes, Ethan?'

I pause. This is hard to say. 'Can you take me home?'

'Is that what you want?'

This is even harder. I think of Iggy, stuck here on this alien planet. My sister too. I will never see them again.

But what can I do? I'm one boy. I can't take on a whole alien civilisation.

I close my eyes, and take a breath.

'Yes,' I say.

'Very well, Ethan. Strap yourself in.'

Chapter Sixty-three

Come on, don't judge me. I have no choice. I am alone here. I cannot stay.

I think of Mam and Dad and what I will tell them.

'*I got close. Really I did. At least we know Tammy is alive. I did my best.*'

I think of Gran. The last time I saw her she was running through a snowy forest, pursued by a man with a shotgun.

'*Sorry, Gran. Thank you for helping. I did my best.*'

What can I tell Iggy's mum? I try it in my head.

'*Sorry, Mrs Fox-Templeton, but Iggy is now in a zoo at the other end of the universe, along with my sister Tammy. I did my best.*'

It doesn't feel good. I pull the straps around my waist and shoulders in readiness for take-off. I feel the engines (if that's what they are) starting up. Philip has not said anything. I think he understands.

And then the vibration stops, and Philip says, very softly, '*Stay still, Ethan, and keep quiet.*'

Through the screen at the front of the cockpit, I see that one of the creatures from before has returned. It's the one with the streak of darker hair, and her teeth are bared in an ugly grimace. She strides forward, towards the craft, and then stops, with her hands on her broad hips. She raises her long nose in the air and starts to sniff.

Her eyes dart to one side and then the other, then her nose twitches again.

She's sniffing for me, I just know it. She crouches down where the group was standing before, and smells the floor, moving in a wide circle before standing up again and walking towards the spaceship. She walks past the screen so that I cannot see her any more, but if I strain, I can just hear her by the door.

Snff . . . snff-snff-snff.

I am so scared I don't think I'm even breathing. When I feel something brush the back of my leg I think my yelp of fright gets as far as my throat before I stifle it. It's Suzy, who I had forgotten all about, and I gather her into my arms.

The sniffing creature is back in my vision now, in front of the windscreen, walking all around the spacecraft. Suddenly she growls something, then repeats it twice, finally aiming a frustrated kick at the craft and stalking off in the direction she came from.

'Philip?'

'Shush.'

I wait in silence for several minutes. Finally, Philip murmurs, *'She's gone, Ethan, but she'll be back.'*

'How do you know?'

'Because she told me she was not coming back. And as we know, Anthallans are very poor liars. She knows there is something inside here, and they know what humans smell like. So she'll be coming back with others, and something to force open my doors.'

'And then?'

'Well, what do you think? One more Original for Earth Zone. Plus a chicken.'

I look at Suzy, and something comes back to me. Something that has been knocking around in my head like a cat in a sack.

'I did my best' – that was what I said to Tammy the night she disappeared.

'You always say that!' Tammy retorted, getting redder in the face with anger. 'But you never do, do you? You do what looks like your best. You do what people will think is your best. You do just enough so that when you say, "But I did my best", people will believe you and go, "Aw, poor Ethan – he did his best." But you know what, Ethan? I know what your best is. I'm your twin, remember? I'm the other half of you. How could I not know? And you haven't done your best – nothing like it, so don't lie.'

Beneath my feet on the floor, I sense Philip's vibrations starting again, and as the vibrations travel through my body, I feel something change in me.

I think about living the rest of my life without my twin: my other half.

I think about telling Cora Fox-Templeton that her son has been captured for exhibition in a zoo while I stayed hidden.

I think about my mam and my dad. And poor Gran and the whole of our village that will forever be associated in people's minds with something sad.

The vibrations are getting stronger and stronger, and I am shaking . . .

And then I realise that it isn't the vibrations. It is me. I am actually trembling. I look at my hands and they are shaking; my jaw is shivering and my teeth are chattering. And it's all with nerves because I am terrified.

Terrified about what I am going to do – what I *have* to do.

'Philip! Stop!' I cry out.

'Gee, you sound distressed, Ethan. What is it?'

I swallow hard and say, 'We're not going home. Not back to Earth.'

'Not back to Earth, Ethan? Why not, kid?'

I take a deep breath. All of the trembling has stopped, and I stand up.

Suzy tips her head on one side and I say this as much to her as to Philip.

'Because I haven't done my best yet.'

Chapter Sixty-four

You know that moment when, immediately after you have made a big decision, your shoulders feel a little lighter, you can stand a little taller and you don't think of the problems ahead? You're just glad you've made up your mind?

It only lasts for seconds.

Then Philip says, *'I was right: here they come. If you want my advice, we need to get out of here.'*

Through the front window I see six creatures, led by Dark Hair Streak, come out of the passageway, running towards the spaceship.

Philip powers up quickly and the ship vibrates.

'Activate the VI!' I say.

And Philip says, *'Roger that. VI activated. But they know we're here.'*

By now our pursuers are banging on the side, and one has brought an enormous tool that he is swinging at the door.

'That looks like a sledgehammer,' I say, as it contacts the door with a loud clanging thud.

'Old school,' says Philip, 'but effective. He'll be through in a few more blows. You strapped in? Too bad . . .'

I am thrown violently against the wall of the cockpit as the spaceship lurches to one side. In front of us, and a little higher, a gap in the roof opens up – a widening slot that gets bigger as another hammer blow rocks the spaceship. I feel the craft rising from the ground and heading slowly for the slot in the roof, which has widened sufficiently to let us through.

But then the opening starts to close.

Philip says, 'They've located the roof override system. We may not make it through. Hang on!'

It's too late to hang on to anything. Instead I am thrown to the other side of the cockpit, banging my head and elbow hard. The craft is on its side and nearly at the slot in the roof, which is surely too narrow to get through. I close my eyes to await the inevitable impact . . .

. . . And we're through. I would sigh with relief, but I'm on the floor nursing my cracked elbow with my left hand.

'Are we safe?' I pant through spasms of pain.

'For the time being,' replies Philip. 'I just need to run some external damage checks, and activate the . . . I don't know what you would call it. It sends out a dummy signal and stops us being tracked by the Advisor. This may take a while. We'll be cruising at a low level and there may be some *sharp movements as we avoid other airborne vehicles that cannot see us.'*

As he says the words, I feel the craft move abruptly to the right, and Philip says, *'Like that.'*

We straighten up. *'You can get a great view of our country and, by the way, that was pretty cool – that thing about doing your best. It's one of the reasons I totally dig humans. You got that whole "noble" thing goin' on. We ain't seen that on Anthalla for, like, centuries. Not since the Big Burn. Do you have a plan?'*

'A plan?' I squeak. 'What sort of a plan? Oh, yes, hang on – now that I think about it, I do have one, because I've often wondered what it would be like to be on a rescue mission on an alien planet with a talking spaceship.'

There is a pause, then Philip says, *'That was sarcasm, right?'*

I say nothing, but wonder if it is possible to hurt the feelings of a bot.

'Listen, kid,' Philip says after a moment. *'I'm gonna take you to where this thing all started. There is a chance we could end it there.'*

I am beyond arguing.

Philip interprets my silence as permission.

'Cool. Sit back, relax and enjoy our range of gourmet snacks prepared by Anthalla's most skilled chefs.'

'You're kidding!' I say with delight. 'That's great news – I'm starving.'

'*You're right. I was kidding. Call it revenge for your sarcasm. Anthallans don't really have taste buds like you do, so there's no need for chefs, skilled or otherwise. You'll find water and greest in the little locker behind your head. It's safe for humans.*'

I gaze out of the front screen at the ground below. It is daytime and the sky is pure white with cloud. Stretching as far as I can see, ahead and to the right, are small, flat-topped rectangles of grey-beige, arranged in rigid lines. To my left, the little boxes stop in a line before a flat expanse of steel-grey which, I guess, is the sea.

Every now and then there is a square gap in the boxes – perhaps as big as a couple of football fields – and I can see people – well, Anthallans – gathered together and walking to and fro on the black surface. Then the boxes start again, row after row of them. There are hardly any trees. There are no brightly lit billboards, or skyscrapers glinting in the sun, or silver rivers winding through the city.

The whole thing looks as though it is made from Lego: black, grey, white and beige. And it stretches on, and on, and on.

I get up and look for the opening that Philip said contained food. Even the thought of food is making my mouth water. I think of Mam's pies from the pub: golden, crispy pastry and creamy mash with thick gravy. Or Gran's hot chocolate, especially when she does squirty cream on the top. I have to swallow my saliva, I'm drooling so much . . .

There is a small square door cut into the back of the cabin. I touch it and it pops open, a blast of cold air coming from within, to reveal little blocks of greyish-white.

'*We call it greest,*' says Philip. '*It is a plant-based synthetic food that contains all the nutrients required for health.*'

'So you grow it?' I touch a cube with my tongue.

'*We . . . they . . . manufacture it. It is pretty much all they eat. It is perfect food. The humans in the Earth Zone all eat it. It's fine.*'

I am still looking warily at it, even though I could probably eat a horse *and* its saddle, I am that hungry. I put a square in my mouth and chew. It tastes of absolutely nothing, but it's not horrible. It's a bit like tofu. I finish my cube, then take a few more, then a few more until I feel the pain in my stomach receding.

'Is this all they have to eat?' I ask Philip in wonder.

Philip replies, '*Yes. It is satisfactory. Whoops, tracker beam incoming – I've gotta shut down the verbals or they'll interfere with the anti-tracker thing . . .*'

The craft lurches slightly then rights itself, and Philip is silent.

With a belly that's full for the first time in what seems like days, I feel drowsy.

Eventually, I am bored of looking at the unimaginable dullness of the city below me; my eyelids feel heavy and I fall into the deepest sleep.

When I awake, the craft is still. It has landed and the front section has retracted so that I can feel the real heat of the sun on my face, and a light breeze. The Lego boxes are nowhere to be seen. Instead I am looking at trees: pine trees, towering Douglas firs and twisty ash. There are densely packed bushes, and the floor is carpeted with dry pine needles and mossy rocks. I take a deep breath in through my nose. It smells exactly like home, only warmer . . . drier. The blanket of cloud has cleared. A strong sun shines in a blue sky, and a stiff, warm breeze agitates the trees' branches.

I close my eyes again and sigh with a deep sadness at the realisation that I have been dreaming. I don't really want to open them again because I'd like to keep the image fresh of the deep, rich forest greens and rusty browns of the tree trunks . . .

'Ethan?' It is Philip's voice.

Perhaps I can just stay here in this dream, I wonder to myself, and I take another deep sniff of home.

'Hey, kid? Open your eyes, buddy.'

It is not a dream.

Chapter Sixty-five

Blinking in the sunlight, I look around. The line of trees stretches out either side of me. Behind me is the barren, grey wasteland. Running my tongue around my mouth, there is a faint residue of the stuff I ate before.

'Where are we?' I ask.

'This, my friend, is the perimeter woodland of Earth Zone. Five hundred metres thick, and stretching for a few kilometres in each direction.'

I stand up and step out of the craft, flexing my elbow and wincing. It has swollen up badly while I was asleep, but I am much more interested in the woods directly in front of me.

'Wow. These are the first trees I've seen here. Well, the first normal ones.'

'That's because they are pretty much the only ones. They're confined to the Earth Zone, where they can grow wild and . . . kinda messy. Other than here, we haven't had trees growing wild since the Big Burn.'

Even so, there's something not quite right about the forest. It's too dry. There are patches of brown on the trees and the ground is brown and grey rather than green and lush.

'Why is it so dry?'

'*Drought season. All of the weather inside the zone is controlled. They experiment with different extreme conditions, you know? Heavy snow, excessive rainfall, that sort of thing.*'

I step forward and Philip says, '*No further. The whole thing is protected by a . . . by a . . . what would you say? A Proton-positive Force Field?*'

I shrug. 'I guess. An invisible shield?'

'*Yes. Exactly. You might want to watch that chicken. The reason we are here is that there is a temporary gap in the force field, created by Kallan a few days ago. Think of it like cutting a hole in a chain-link fence. But I don't think your chicken knows where the gap is.*'

Suzy is pecking the ground and getting closer and closer to the trees. In the next second she does her little hop-flap and gets much too near.

I call out, 'Suzy!' and, without thinking of the possible consequences, I run towards her.

Big mistake. She doesn't know me like she knows Iggy, and as I approach with my arms outstretched to grab her, she leaps away in alarm, flaps her wings and heads *straight* for the trees.

'No, Suzy! Stop!' I shout.

It's too late. There's a flash of white light and a sizzling noise where she hits the force field.

To my horror, instead of bouncing off, as though she has hit a wall, the speed of her approach carries her through, towards the trees, and there is a pitiful squawk as a flaming, smouldering ball of feathers hits the ground and rolls and rolls out of sight into the undergrowth.

'No! No! Suzy!'

I want to run forward to get her, but I can feel the prickling of the force field and I have to retreat. I slump on to the ground in dismay. In trying to save her, I have killed my best friend's pet. I scan the branches and undergrowth and all I can see is little wisps of smoke, and a lick of flame here and there where Suzy's burning feathers caught the bone-dry leaves on the ground.

'I'm sorry, Ethan,' says Philip's voice from behind me. For a bot, he sounds pretty genuine.

Getting wearily to my feet, I stare angrily at the place where poor Suzy hit the shield – there is still a whitish patch where she went through – and in frustration I pick up a stone and throw it hard. It sails through the patch and pings off a tree, and then the white patch slowly disappears, closing up as though it is healing.

If I am expecting this to make me despair, however, it doesn't. Something changed in me earlier when I decided that I would get Tammy and Iggy back. The death of a chicken is not going to stop me.

'Philip?' I say. 'How do I get in there?'

'I like your style, captain,' says Philip. *'Like I say – there's*

a gap. If we can find it. Or you may wanna try the main entrance. It's the only other way.'

Having seen the fate of Suzy, I am not at all keen on trying the force field, gap or no gap.

'It's got to be the main entrance, I think,' I say.

'OK, pardner,' says Philip.

Then I look down at myself. Jeans, trainers, woolly sweater. I look *nothing* like an Anthallan. There is no way I can just walk up to the entrance.

'But how am I going to manage *that*?' I ask.

'By listening to your Uncle Philip, that's how. Right now, though, we have to go. We can assume that a sudden breach of the force field will result in an investigation. We don't wanna hang around here, kid.'

Chapter Sixty-six

Back in the craft, the image of a smouldering Suzy flapping through the force field stays in my mind and I am silent as we continue our journey around the perimeter of Earth Zone. We keep the dense forest on our left for several kilometres until we see more vehicles ahead of us, some Anthallans and several low, black Lego buildings. Philip stops our vehicle next to some others but we do not get out.

'I've got to keep the VI on,' he says. *'An ancient GV like this one will attract a lot of attention, kind of like an old Rolls-Royce for you guys. The entrance is right ahead.'*

There is a gap in the trees about as wide as a couple of streets. To one side is a vast screen showing black-and-white images from inside Earth Zone that I recognise from Hellyann's 3D film when we were in Mad Mick's Mental Rentals.

That feels like years ago.

'That's it?' I say. 'You just . . . *walk in*?'

I think I was expecting something like Disneyland – ticket kiosks, queues, gift shops, popcorn stands, kids holding balloons and smiling parents. Instead the small groups of Anthallans walk silently and solemnly in and out of the gap.

Philip says, *'Anyone can come and go, and observe and learn.'*

To one side of the entrance is a long, shallow pool with running water. Anthallans of all ages stand or squat at the side, and it is a moment or two until I realise what they are doing.

'Is that . . . a *toilet?*' I ask Philip in disbelief. 'It's very, erm . . . open.'

'Yes, Ethan. There is no shame here about bodily functions.'

I can't stop staring at these groups. I try to think beyond the fact that they are smallish, hairy creatures who all look alike, and I realise what it is that is so strange: it is the silence.

Nobody runs around, or laughs, or shouts. This is a day out, I think: a day away from their Lego boxes arranged in neat rows, and their perfectly clean streets, and parks with grass cut by robots and symmetrical trees.

'Philip,' I say, 'is nobody having, you know . . . *fun?*'

'Good question, Ethan. Fun, delight, joy – these are human ideas. Here on Anthalla, knowledge and learning and facts are what give people satisfaction. And so they come here. They observe the Earth people and they leave satisfied that their own lives are much more safe and orderly.'

I think about this as I watch the groups and singles entering and leaving Earth Zone.

After a while I say, 'So how do I get in, then?'

'I would say, Ethan, that you just walk in with everybody else.'

'But . . . won't they stop me?'

'Nobody will cause a fuss. Nobody ever does. My prediction is that they will watch you with curiosity, but do nothing. They will assume you are one of the exhibits. There are bots at the entrance, but you will be going in, not out. Why would they stop you? Ethan? Ethan?'

I have fallen silent as, on the screen ahead of us by the entrance a huge image of Tammy has just appeared, blinking and looking bewildered. Beneath the screen, on the ground, a small group point and nod gravely to one another. Some symbols appear on the screen on top of Tammy's image. I do not need to be able to read Anthallan to guess at their meaning.

NEW THIS WEEK.

ORIGINAL HUMAN FROM EARTH.

COME AND SEE THE LATEST EXHIBIT.

Or something like that, anyway.

'Philip?' I say. 'Take me to the hole in the shield.'

Both options – going in the main gate or sneaking in through an invisible gap in a force field that could roast me alive – are insane risks. Somehow, at this moment, sneaking in seems slightly less insane.

Or maybe it's just that I've lost any perspective.

Chapter Sixty-seven

I swallow hard and look again at the line of trees in front of me. We are not far from where Suzy went through with such awful results. I recognise a huge Douglas fir that towers over the other vegetation. If I just look at the trees and nothing else, I can imagine I am back home, and so that is what I do. It helps.

As Philip has instructed, I approach the trees until I feel the hairs on my arm prickle up.

'OK, I can feel it,' I tell him over my shoulder.

'Now walk to the right, keeping the same distance from the trees,' says Philip, his voice coming from the interior of the spacecraft. *'Further,'* he says. *'Keep going. You will feel it eventually.'*

After about twenty metres, I feel the prickling sensation diminish. Another two metres and it starts again, so I walk backwards to feel it stop.

'I think I've found it,' I call back.

'I gotta wish you good luck, Ethan. It's not something you hear much about on this planet. People here rely on calculating

probabilities and assessing likelihoods and so on. But I think you're gonna need luck.'

This doesn't feel reassuring, but I say, 'Thank you' anyway, because it seems polite and I know that Philip likes good manners.

'Can't you come with me?' I add. 'Can I eject you or something?'

'No. Sorry. An unattended GV would eventually attract attention, either from the Sky Eyes or perimeter patrols. Besides, if something goes wrong in there, you do not want to be found with me. Trust me, you are better off on your own.'

'But, Philip—' I begin.

'No buts, kiddo,' Philip's voice says. *'Go. One of you Earth guys once said, "The harder you work, the luckier you get." No one has worked harder than you to get your sister back, so I reckon you're due some luck. Besides, my systems tell me that a perimeter patrol is gonna be right overhead in about thirty seconds, which gives you less than that to get through that hole – which somebody took a huge risk to make for you. So what are you waiting for? I'll meet you back here but right now I gotta go. These perimeter patrols are not fooled by VI.'*

I take a step and then stop, paralysed by fear. If only I was not alone, I think. This is a twin's dilemma: since before I was born, I have had a partner. Someone to share stuff with.

Not now. Behind me, the craft has started up, and I hear a swish as it zooms off with Philip in command. And now I truly am alone.

With my back to the forest, I stare out at the barren landscape, but I have no time to wonder about it. In the far distance, and approaching quickly along the line of trees, is a large globe which I take to be the perimeter patrol. Running now, I get close to the force field and, as soon as the prickling of my skin stops, I clench my fists and dive left into a tiny gap in the bushes.

I'm through! I crouch down in the crackling leaves between shaggy, thick-trunked trees until I hear a low sound overhead like a massive tumble dryer. The patrolling globe does not stop, but passes over and I feel something like relief.

I have stood up when I hear the tumble-dryer noise again. It is returning, and without thinking about it, I lie flat on the ground, concealed by a dead tree trunk.

The silver globe is about two metres across and it hovers close to where I came through. I dare not raise my head to look; instead I try to make myself even flatter. If I could sink into the earth, I would. My face is pressed into the dry, warm soil and I can hear the *thum-thum-thum-thum* throbbing noise of the patrol globe. I'm probably only there for about half a minute, but it feels longer. Eventually, the sound retreats and I feel as though I can breathe out.

As I do, I blink in astonishment. Remember, I'm still

on my front, one cheek resting on the earth. Before me is a swollen, orange shape that looks exactly like . . . surely not? I put out my fingers to touch it and I jump when I hear the voice behind me.

'You are right. It is a Cheessy What-iss-it. I thought I had dropped one.'

'Hellyann!' I say and leap to my feet. Without thinking, I rush forward and hug her, mindless of her smell – and for once I hardly even notice it. I say, 'What are you . . . I mean, how? How did . . . ?'

'Philip was bound to bring you here. I haf been waiting. As for the rest, I shall explain later,' says Hellyann, disengaging herself from my embrace. 'Right now we must move because we haf been spotted and—'

'Where is Tammy?' I say, not even listening to what Hellyann is saying. 'Is she here? Is she all right? What about Iggy?'

Hellyann pauses – and looks awkward.

'What? *What?*' I say.

'There haf been . . . complications,' she says. 'Follow me.'

Chapter Sixty-eight

The dry sticks and leaves beneath our feet crunch noisily as I follow Hellyann through the woods. She walks fast, but she's not running, which I am grateful for: despite sleeping, I am still mighty tired and hungry.

As we go, Hellyann talks.

'Two young Originals,' she says. 'That is unusual here at Earth Sone. A lot of people want to see them, and they are peing closely guarded. You will see.'

'Two? You mean Tammy and Iggy?'

'Yes. Exactly.'

'Can we . . . get at them? I mean, rescue them?'

'I do not know, Ethan. I wass released almost immediately. I find it hard to lie but I allowed them to pelieve that I caught Ikk-ee deliberately becauss I wanted to be a Hunter. I had to promise to return to Earth and collect yet more Originals. Ikk-ee will be introduced to the visitors in Earth Sone in about one hour. He will meet Tammy and everypody is interested to see how they will react. A meeting between two Originals who know each other has never been recorded before.'

I ponder this for a moment as the twigs crack under my feet. *They're observing us like animals*, I think and I am creeped out the more I think about it. My heart quickens when I see the forest becoming thinner in front of me. Soon we are looking at a wide expanse of fields, covered with high, yellowing grass bending in the strong breeze.

'They need rain,' I say to Hellyann.

She nods. 'The drought experiment has been going on for months now, but nopotty seems to care.'

Then I yelp with alarm as two human beings who have been lying in the long grass get up, looking embarrassed as if we have disturbed them. They were probably sleeping.

'I . . . I'm sorry,' I stammer, but I am so taken aback that I can only stare. They look at me without much curiosity – a man with a long, dirty beard, perhaps in his fifties, and a woman with bushy, corkscrew hair, dark skin and rotten teeth. He is in badly fitting trousers and a T-shirt, and she wears a shapeless dress. They say nothing and turn away.

'Wait!' I say. 'Come back!'

'Do not bother them,' says Hellyann. 'They to not speak your language, and there is nothing you can to for them.'

I stand there in the long grass, watching them go. 'Are they . . . Originals?' I say, and Hellyann shakes her head.

'Very unlikely. Probably created here on Anthalla from

Original cells. Now, come – we must hurry.' She strides off, and I follow her.

'But . . . how?' I say. 'I mean, that's not how babies are made!'

'Not on Earth it isn't!' she calls back breezily. 'But we abandoned all that centuries ago. Far too risky, unhygienic, trouplesome . . .' She stops and turns, seeing my face, which I think is showing shock.

'Ethan. You must unterstant. *Everything* is different here. Making babies, bringing up babies, haffing children, being with one another and staying with your children. It all requires something that most Anthallans do not possess.' She puts her hand over her heart and then over mine. 'You know. Love. A *heart.*'

'But . . . *why?*' I ask. 'What are you all so . . . so *scared* of?'

She turns and starts walking again, but carries on speaking.

'We are scared of feeling. And so we don't. We haf replaced feeling with facts. Facts cannot hurt. They are not funny, or lovable . . . they just *are.* They are safe. They keep us well fed and peaceful. Facts haf extended our lives to maybe twice what they were a few centuries ago.'

'To do what?'

She does not answer so I repeat my question, with more force. 'To do *what*, Hellyann? What is the point of living if you don't, you know, *feel* things? Love things? Love each other?'

She stops and looks at me with her big pale eyes. 'With love comes hate, no?'

It is my turn to say nothing.

She goes on: 'Look what hate does! We look at Earth people and find it remarkaple that you haf held yourselfs back with your constant lying and fighting and warring . . . So when the Big Burn testroyed almost everything, those who remained designed the Advisor. And now our lifes are governed by reason and reason alone.'

'Except for—' I began.

'Except for a few off us. The Hearters we call ourselfs. Cursed to experience feelings in a world that does not require them.'

We walk on in silence till we arrive at the top of a small inclined field which leads down to a collection of tiny houses. There are Anthallans and humans gathered in the street, which I recognise from the 3D film that Hellyann showed us. At the end of the street is a raised stage.

The whole thing makes me think of a street party we had for the royal wedding a few years ago when we lived in Culvercot. A local band played songs that Gran said were 'very rude', although Tammy and I were too young to understand them. The sudden thought of home, and Gran and Tammy, stabs in my heart.

'Do not be afrait,' says Hellyann. 'Nobody will notice you. They will think you are an exhibit.'

And so we make our way to the crowd. There are

dozens, maybe hundreds, of hairy Anthallans walking about, talking quietly to one another. They are gathered on a walkway above the ground as well, looking down at the proceedings. The smell of them all together is almost overpowering.

Mingling among them are humans. Hellyann was right – I don't stand out, but I can't take my eyes off them. I want to stop them and talk to them, find out where they are from. I approach one or two, and say, 'Hello? Hi!' and I smile, but they look at me with glassy expressions and walk by. As for the Anthallans – they ignore me, more or less. So far as they are concerned, I am just another exhibit in their horrible human zoo.

Hellyann shakes her head when I try to approach another human. 'You are wasting your time, Ee-fan. They haf not learned English. Their memories haf been modified, so—'

She is cut off when another Anthallan comes up to her and peers closely at her. He (or she – I've given up trying to tell) then reaches out, touches Hellyann's face and says something before moving away.

'I shoult not haf shaved,' Hellyann says to me, stroking her cheek ruefully. 'It is attracting attention . . . *Shh*. Look ofer there.'

A murmuring passes through the crowd. Everybody stops and slowly turns their attention to the stage which is about twenty metres away.

Then a chant starts, quietly at first, growing slightly louder.

Hoo . . . hoo . . . hoo . . . hoo . . . hoo . . . hoo . . .

It is the most haunting, chilling sound I think I have ever heard. I glance around nervously. Everywhere I look are the hairy Anthallans, plus one or two humans, all staring emptily ahead and chanting together.

Hoo . . . hoo . . . hoo . . . hoo . . . hoo . . . hoo . . .

Something is about to happen.

Chapter Sixty-nine

There seems to be no pleasure in what they are doing, in the chanting. This is not like a football chant, or people singing along at a concert, or even when people sing hymns in church. This is weird, and I cannot tell if they are enjoying it or not.

Anticipating my question, Hellyan leans in to me and murmurs, 'This is like applause. Someone important is arriving.'

As if on cue, the *hoo . . . hoo . . . hoo* chant resolves into a long *hoooooooo . . .* as a figure appears on the platform and I gasp in recognition.

It is the large Anthallan I saw in the cavern, who I think of as being called Dark Streak. She raises her arms and the *hoo*os die down. She addresses the crowd and her voice is loud and clear. Everybody is silent, nodding and occasionally murmuring in what sounds like approving tones.

Dark Streak signals to another Anthallan standing at the side of the stage, and a large globe materialises – a 3D image like the one we saw in Mad Mick's Mental Rentals, only this is bigger. It is an image of Earth. I recognise the landmasses of the Americas, and Africa . . .

Dark Streak revolves it, until it shows Australia, and it all becomes clear to me.

She is telling the story of Tammy's capture!

There are a few sentences then Dark Streak leans forward to the crowd and points out her swollen eye, caused by being whacked by that guy who had stopped to change his tyre by the roadside.

The crowd goes: *Hoooo!*

Then the globe revolves and Dark Streak points to a little island. Britain, the scene of Dark Streak's second attempt at capturing a human.

Hoo . . . hoo . . . hoo . . . hoo . . . hoo . . . hoo . . .

I know that something is about to happen. I don't know what it is, but I have a feeling deep inside my stomach that I will not like it.

Hellyann leans in again. 'Be warned, Ee-fan. You are about to see Ta-mee. The Anthallans up there are Assistant Advisors. They are a pit like your police. Do not give yourself away.'

I can feel my stomach turning over and I *still* don't know what I'm going to do to get her back.

I'm supposed to be in charge.

I'm supposed to be doing my best!

And I have *no* idea what that might be. I do know, though, somewhere deep inside me, as I stand in a dusty street surrounded by stinking, hairy aliens and blank-faced cloned humans, that the next few minutes will decide whether or not we ever get our old life back again.

Chapter Seventy

Hellyann is gripping my wrist at my side, and it's probably good that she is because when Tammy appears on the platform, I might well shout out, or run forward or do something stupid. In the end, I just watch in agonising silence as I see Tammy mount the platform from the back, flanked by two Assistant Advisors.

My sister. My twin. My other half. Her hair is greasy and her cheeks are streaked with dirt and tears. Her expression is as blank as those of the humans around me and she stares out at the crowd, her lips moving slightly, as if she is talking to herself, or praying, or . . . I don't know what.

She is still wearing what she left the house in and it is all so familiar that I find myself blinking back tears. She is clutching her bag close to her chest, nervously, with both hands. A low table has been brought on to the stage and Tammy stands next to it. I don't know what to do – if she sees me in the crowd will she even recognise me? If she does, will she cry out? If she cries out, what will happen to us?

It all reminds me of a scene I saw in a film once when a king, a long time ago, was beheaded in front of a cheering crowd. Even though I am pretty certain that Tammy is not going to be killed, it still sends a chill through me.

I try to keep my head down a bit, but I cannot stop sneaking looks at Tammy, trembling with fear on a platform in front of this weird crowd, who have taken up their chant yet again.

Hoo . . . hoo . . . hoo . . . hoo . . . hoo . . . hoo . . .

I have a sickening feeling that something horrible is about to happen to Tammy when Dark Streak comes to the front again and starts to talk.

Hellyann inclines her head to listen better and says to me, 'She is saying something about a kift. When humans meet they kiv each other kifts?'

Kift?

I think for a moment.

'Oh!' I say. 'A gift? A present!'

'Yes. Humans exchange them?'

'Well, yeah,' I murmur back. 'Sometimes. Special occasions, you know . . .'

'This is very strange to us. We are going to see this happen.'

I'm baffled. What on earth is she on about, or Dark Streak for that matter?

'See it happen?' I say. 'See *what*?'

Near us, some people have heard Hellyann and me

talking and even though we are talking softly, they must have heard that it was another language. They have started to turn and look and point, and one of them rubs his hairy chin. Hellyann nudges me to keep quiet, for there is further movement at the back of the platform.

Dark Streak has something in her hand which glints in the sun when she holds it aloft. She spreads her bony fingers and I see she is holding Iggy's glasses by one of the arms, and I swallow hard.

The two guards appear again and between them this time is Iggy, twisting his flat cap in his hands, his deep copper hair seeming to glow in the sunlight against the dried-out trees and the grey-white hair of his captors.

But it's his face that astonishes me. I was kind of expecting him to be half drugged like Tammy. Instead his green eyes are furious and his mouth is set into the angriest scowl I have ever seen in my life. It doesn't go unnoticed in the crowd either. A low ripple passes through the Anthallans around me and they look more intently.

One of his guards puts a hand on Iggy's upper arm; he shakes it off angrily, and he stares out at the crowd, pure rage seeming to seep from every pore. He looks over at Tammy, who returns his gaze, but blankly, and Iggy shakes his head with sorrow and anger.

Then, at a signal from Dark Streak, Tammy reaches into her black school bag and fumbles around for a few seconds. For a moment, I'm thinking, *Go, Tammy! Pull out a gun or something*, but instead she removes, one by one, the three poorly wrapped presents that she had been taking to Scottish Sheila the night she went missing.

'*Whaat?!*'

I think I say it aloud because people turn and look at me again, and I see Hellyann glancing around. She grabs my hand

'Come,' she whispers and almost drags me to a different part of the crowd, nearer to the platform this time.

Still, I can feel the crowd's eyes following me. Anthallans, you will know by now, are pretty inexpressive, but I see one of them look up at Tammy, then at me and then back to Tammy.

I often forget how closely Tammy and I resemble each other, but there is no forgetting now. More people are noticing and pointing.

Meanwhile, on the stage, Tammy has given one of the presents to Iggy, who takes it in both hands and starts to unwrap it. Neither Tammy nor Iggy has noticed me yet: Tammy because of her detached mental state, I guess; Iggy because . . . well, I don't know. Perhaps he's just too upset to concentrate on anything other than what is happening to him at that moment.

Inside the wrapper is a box. Iggy's shaking his head with puzzlement, because it is a box with a bottle inside: a bottle of vodka.

The crowd seem fascinated, and those who are near

319

me switch their attention from me to the stage as Dark Streak puts down Iggy's glasses, grabs the bottle from the table and holds it up. I wish I knew what she was saying because it is making the crowd excited.

Dark Streak mimes drinking from the bottle and then allows her tongue to loll out of her mouth and her legs to buckle. I get it: she is pretending to be drunk!

Oh no. I immediately guess what is going to happen.

I turn to Hellyann. 'Are they going to make them drink it?'

Hellyann nods.

I am horrified. 'Kids don't drink alcohol!' I say, quietly but urgently. 'It'll make them sick. It could even kill them!' In my head, but not out loud, I add, *'Especially that super-strong stuff that Dad got from the Polish guy . . .'*

'No!' I shout and my hand is over my mouth even before the syllable is finished, but it's too late.

Dark Streak stops and puts the bottle of vodka down on the stage floor. Slowly she comes to the very edge of the platform and looks out, her large, wet eyes scanning the crowd.

It seems as though everybody has turned to look at me. Glancing to the guards at her side, Dark Streak extends a long finger, pointing to me, and in an instant they have leapt down from the stage and are right next to me, grasping my upper arms in their bony hands and breathing their foul breath into my face.

'Hellyann!' I cry, but she has melted back into the crowd as I am half-dragged, half-carried on to the stage, where I look out at hundreds of pairs of eyes, all wondering what will happen next.

I try to catch Tammy's eye, but her expression is blank and empty.

Iggy, though – he is not drugged, or memory-wiped, or whatever it is they have done to Tammy. His eyes are sparkling with . . .

Could it be *mischief*?

I cannot be certain, and in my terror about what is to happen next I am not sure I am thinking straight, but it's a look I have seen on his face before – most recently when we were fishing the night Hellyann appeared. But it's more than that: it's the look he had when he showed me his Death Ray that morning on the bus to school.

Something is about to happen and Iggy is to be the cause of it.

He is standing next to me now and, keeping his face turned to the crowd, he murmurs, 'You took your time, Tait.'

'What are you up to?' I whisper.

'Nothing,' he says.

But he winks as he says it.

Chapter Seventy-one

I can't speak for fear. Iggy, on the other hand, has his shoulders pulled back and his jaw thrust out defiantly. He's planning something, I just know it.

I look around the stage. Is that a half-smile on Dark Streak's face? Surely not? I say nothing. Dark Streak has unscrewed the lid of the bottle and given it to Iggy. He takes it and gives it a big, deep sniff. He looks up at the sky, and then behind him to the two other bottles of vodka, now unwrapped, on the low table.

'You know that Felina song?' he says out of the side of his mouth. 'I think we should pretend that it's a human ritual. Come on!'

Holding the bottle in his hand, he struts up and down the stage like a chicken, going, '*La la la la, dum dum dum . . .*' to the tune of the ridiculous Felina song, the one that had been sung so sadly at the candlelit vigil for Tammy, and again by Hellyann in the toilet of the Stargazer. It strikes me again as I watch Iggy: *how did she know?*

I'm snapped out of my wondering by Iggy.

'Come on!' he urges. 'Join in. Tammy as well!'

I have literally no idea where this is going, but it is so mad, so completely crazy that I find myself making chicken noises and flapping my arms, trying not to think of how I will tell Iggy later about Suzy.

If there *is* a later, of course.

The audience look on, quite bewildered. Meanwhile, Dark Streak has stepped back and folded her arms, nodding – apparently content to let these crazy Earth people entertain the crowd.

'Do-do-do-do-do the Chicken Hop!
Da-da-da-da-dance like you can't stop!
Do-do-do the Chicken Hop this Christmas!'

It's like a little light has come on behind Tammy's eyes. Slowly she joins in with the *do-do-do*s and starts to bob and flap.

'Come on, Tam!' I encourage her. 'You remember it!'

As we strut, the crowd start *hoo-hoo*-ing. I think they are actually enjoying something, possibly for the first time in their lives. As for me, despite my fear, I start to laugh inside at the thought of the crowd believing that this is what humans do every time we exchange gifts.

Over the noise, Iggy says to me, 'Have you got your old snot rag?'

I reach into my pocket and bring out my hankie. I have noticed that as we've been dancing about, Iggy has been spilling quite a bit of the vodka on the stage, and there is now a trail of large droplets and rivulets leading over the back of the platform.

'Rip your hankie into shreds, Tait. Three long strips. Go on – do it. We can't keep this up for much longer. Get ready to follow me and run!'

I bite into the hem of the hankie and do as he says, tearing the fabric into strips as I copy his ridiculous steps to the sound of the crowd's rhythmic *hoo-hoo-hoo*. Iggy takes one of the strips and waves it over his head like some demented Morris dancer. Tammy and I do the same.

Then he shouts at the crowd, 'Right, you lot! Who's for a Goblet of Fire?'

I gasp, remembering my dad shouting the same words as I burst into the Stargazer the night Tammy went missing. *Is this heading where I think it is?*

Iggy says to me, 'Don't do the next bit!'

Iggy takes a *huge* mouthful of vodka. Honestly, he holds the bottle up for ages, and his cheeks are bulging.

The crowd goes *Hoooo!* in approval.

Only, I don't think he actually *swallows* it . . .

Still Tammy and I are dancing, and still the crowd are chanting.

Iggy has taken his handkerchief strip and held it against the bottle top, which he inverts, soaking the cloth with super-strength Polish vodka. I still have no idea what he's doing. He waves it around some more, droplets of vodka going everywhere, and then he discards it and it lands on the floor, before the little table where his glasses are.

'Are . . . are you making a . . .' I start, and he nods, his cheeks still bulging.

He's doing a Death Ray!

I know immediately what I must do. I grab the bottle from him and take over the dance, deflecting all of Dark Streak's attention to me, while Iggy retreats. I hardly dare to look, but he's really doing it. The sun is strong and almost overhead, and Iggy carefully and casually positions his glasses on the low table, so that the sunlight goes through the clear liquid in the bottles, and the beam is further concentrated through his thick spectacle lenses.

He still hasn't swallowed his mouthful, and I think Dark Streak has noticed. I can see the pinpoint of burning light on the floor caused by Iggy's specs, and he gently kicks the vodka-soaked rag into position, right in the beam of the Death Ray.

I can hardly breathe with nerves, for it could catch fire at any time . . . and then what?

For all their universal intelligence and lifelong learning, Anthallans have never, *ever* come across a crazy, school-excluded thirteen-year-old with possible behavioural problems who knows how to make fire. My heart is pounding so hard that it almost hurts.

Ten seconds at least have gone by, and the audience are getting restless. I start to hear growls and murmurings.

I imagine they're calling, '*Oi, Earth Boy – enough of the prancing around!*'

Twenty seconds, and I'm desperately trying not to look at the rag on the floor. Iggy has joined me, and he indicates that I take a swig from the bottle as well, if only to buy us some more time.

I tip the bottle up and as I fill my mouth, I see that someone in the crowd is pointing. I look back, and a tiny flame is flickering from my handkerchief.

Seconds later, the whole rag is burning, and the fire has spread a few inches with the drops we have spilled. Dark Streak has not noticed yet, but she soon will.

The chanting of the crowd stops as though a switch has been flicked, and there's a groan of . . . I don't know what it is at first. I look out at the crowd and their eyes have all widened and they are murmuring between themselves.

It is fear.

The primitive fear of fire that no amount of education, no amount of clinical, genetically engineered cloning could eradicate from this strange race of creatures.

Dark Streak has unfolded her arms and is ready to take a step forward, when suddenly the vodka-soaked stage catches fire in a large burst of bluish-orange flame. The crowd start to move, backing away.

I have grabbed Tammy's hand as I have guessed what is about to happen and I want to be able to get out of there quickly. The Anthallan guards are moving towards us. I spit out the vodka from my mouth on to my strip of hankie, and bend down to dip it in the flames. It catches immediately. One of the guards has taken out his black stick and has raised it up to strike me, but I brandish the burning rag at him and he freezes in fear.

Then, lifting his bottle high above his head, Iggy smashes it on to the stage with all the force he can muster, and as he leaps out of the way the bottle breaks, the vodka catches alight in a burst of flame and a scream erupts from the crowd.

This is too much for Dark Streak, who takes two strides forward and, as she reaches out to grab him, Iggy unloads the contents of his bulging mouth on to her chest in a long, spurting stream. The alcohol ignites immediately and Dark Streak utters a horrible yell as her body hair erupts in flame.

It is chaos on the stage. The guards have retreated, and the flames are licking around our feet.

'Into the trees!' yells Iggy. 'Throw one into the trees!'

I grab a bottle and cast it in a high arc – it smashes against a rock, spilling vodka over a wide area. Next I throw my flaming hankie, which has started to burn my hand, and it immediately ignites the spilled alcohol.

'Tammy!' I shout over the noise of the crowd. 'Stones in the lake! Stones in the lake!'

Tammy remembers our game. She grabs the third bottle and lobs it in the direction of the crowd, where it forms a huge pool of liquid and causes everyone to run in panic, screaming an animal howl of terror as it catches fire.

The flames have spread instantly, following the line of the spills that Iggy made during our crazy dance, and whipped up by the wind. As the three of us leap off the back of the stage in the confusion, more of the tinder-dry undergrowth is sparking and catching fire.

The two guards who were holding us on the stage have run away, their fur blazing. Dark Streak is emitting a hissing growl and frantically beating the flames that have now spread to her head, while the crowd of Anthallans have gone crazy, running away from the spreading fire.

Iggy and I, each holding one of Tammy's hands, run behind the line of flickering flames and into a wall of smoke.

Chapter Seventy-two

It has all been so chaotic, so utterly mad, that I have not even paused to acknowledge the fact that I am back with my sister.

(If you were wanting a moment in the midst of the frenzy when I lock eyes with my twin and we fall into each other's arms and promise never to be parted again and all of that stuff? That bit where I go, 'Hi, Tam', and we embrace? Well, let me say that I wanted that too, but it didn't happen.)

Instead I am running through undergrowth holding Tammy's hand and still I cannot take time to enjoy that she is back at my side – not when there is a sheet of fire spreading around us that we can only just outrun.

And so we keep running, choking on the smoke, until the three of us come to a clearing in the woods and we stop, coughing and panting hard. Looking back through the smoke, I can see the shapes of two, no three, Anthallans coming in our direction – and if I can see them, they can probably see me.

'That way!' I shout through a severe bout of coughing.

In the distance, I can make out the tip of the huge Douglas fir which marked the hole in the force field where I came in.

Iggy doesn't question me, and seems happy for me to take the lead.

'It's our only hope!' I gasp.

Off we go again, and still Tammy hasn't said a single word.

On the other side of the clearing we plunge into the woods again, and by now I'm only guessing the direction because the big fir tree is obscured by all the other trees, and we have to keep dodging around bushes and changing direction.

Behind us, the noise of the fire is getting louder, and every minute or so there is a loud *whoomph!* and a crackling noise as another thicket of dried undergrowth catches alight, fanned by the strong breeze. But at least we are keeping ahead of the flames, and we seem to have lost our pursuers.

I'm beginning to think we might be all right, and I even let go of Tammy's hand. I can see the massive Douglas fir again, a few metres ahead, which means the force field's dead zone must be close by. Tammy is running well, and not panting as much as Iggy and I, and then:

CRACK!

She doesn't even yell in pain. Tammy literally bounces back from a thick branch that she has run straight into at full speed, and lies flat out on the ground.

'Tammy!' I shout. 'Iggy, wait!'

She lies, staring glassily at the smoky sky, deathly still. Her forehead is deeply gashed and bleeding.

Iggy runs back and we both crouch over her.

'Tammy! Tammy!' I shout, but she does not respond.

Is she dead? I can't tell, and don't even dare to fear that she might be. Already her head is swelling up where she hit it. I grab her shoulders and I shake her hard before gathering her into my arms and burying my head in her hair, not caring that it's dirty, just wanting her back.

'Tammy, Tammy . . .' I say again.

Iggy is standing next to us, and when I look up there is an expression of terror on his face. I follow his gaze to see, through the smoky haze, the figure of an Anthallan coming towards us, leaping through smouldering undergrowth and getting closer with every step.

'No, no, no,' I groan to myself. 'Not now. Not when we're so close . . .'

Somewhere deep inside me, I figure that I am certain to be caught, and I am exhausted. Iggy has sunk to his knees next to Tammy and me, and puts his head in his hands with despair. I move back to stare at Tammy's face and it's like looking into a mirror.

Can Iggy and I fight off a single Anthallan? I remember what Hellyann did to Sheba the dog, and my stomach twists in fear.

'I'm sorry, Tam,' I say. 'I did my best.'

This time I really think I have done my best. I sit back on my heels and hang my head, resigning myself to whatever may happen. By now the fire is getting close enough that I can feel its heat, and I do not hear when the Anthallan that has been pursuing us gets close, but I see the large, hairy, six-toed feet come and stand next to me.

Chapter Seventy-three

'She iss not dead, I am thinking. But we must moof quickly.'

Hellyann! I look up, speechless with relief, and I leap to my feet.

'How . . . What . . . ?'

It is definitely her, and she is holding something round and blackened in her arms.

Iggy is on his feet now too, a massive grin on his face. 'She's going to be OK, you say?' And then he stops and lets out a cry of surprise. 'Oh my word! Suzeeee! What happened to you?'

From out of Hellyann's bundled arms pokes a tiny blackened head, and she holds up Suzy. Her feathers are burnt away on her head, poor thing, and some wing feathers are badly singed . . .

But she's definitely alive! She jerks her head around to Iggy at the mention of her name. Hellyann hands her over and Iggy gathers her up, nuzzling her poor, damaged body and laughing and sobbing with relief.

Hellyann leans over Tammy with her healing stick and

moves it over her skull. Seconds later, Tammy starts coughing, then she blinks and tears are streaming down her smoke-streaked face. She looks at me and blinks harder, then looks again.

Her voice cracking, she says, 'E . . . Ethan? Ethan!'

And *that*'s when we fling our arms around each other in a huge embrace. It's as if she's seeing me for the first time, as if the previous hour or so didn't happen. She puts her hand to her head and pulls it away, startled at the blood.

'What . . . happened?' she says.

'You're back!' says Iggy, punching the air with delight. 'You're not . . . weird any more! How did that happen?'

Hellyann says, 'Probably the blow to the head – the memory wipe was supjected to a cranial trauma, resulting in a—'

'Yeah, whatever,' says Tammy, looking at Hellyann. 'I guess you're one of the good guys? Carlo told me there *were* some. Owwww!' She winces with pain as she scrambles to her feet.

'Here, haf this – keep passing it over your wound,' says Hellyann, giving Tammy the healing stick. 'Yes. I am one of the good guys. But those are not.'

She turns and points back the way she came. Even though it is smoky, I can make out the unmistakable wide shape of Dark Streak striding through the smoking undergrowth towards us.

Chapter Seventy-four

We're up on our feet and running again. Iggy has tucked Suzy under his arm and is still managing to keep up with us.

'I know a way through,' I gasp to the others. 'It's near here.'

And I know it must be near because I can feel the tingling sensation from the force field.

'Keep back!' I warn them, as I edge along as quickly as I can.

Dark Streak and her partners are getting closer and I cannot feel the break in the force field.

Then the trees clear, and I see the spacecraft with its front open, ready for us.

'Where is it?' I yell in panic. Then I shout to the others, 'There's a break in the force field just near here – in fact, exactly here.'

I point to the spot where I came through. I can even see the scuff-marks in the soil where I lay down to hide from the perimeter patrol . . .

. . . which stopped . . .

. . . and made noises . . .

. . . exactly where I came through.

My shoulders slump when I realise that the hole has been repaired. Of course it has been repaired – *that* is what perimeter patrols do! Philip even *told* me.

Dark Streak is only about thirty metres away and they aren't even running now. They know we're trapped.

She shouts something in Anthallan and then in broken English. 'Stop, ant you will liffing. Attempting further escape, ant you will dying!'

We are cornered. To our left, the flames are getting closer, while straight ahead, Dark Streak ambles towards us. I can even make out the burnt hair on her chest and head where she copped it from the burning vodka. Everything about her spells fury.

Then Suzy squawks and flaps her wings.

'Shhh, Suzy,' says Iggy.

Something sparks in my mind when I look at her burnt feathers, and then I yell at the others, 'Suzy flew at the force field and burst through it! Where she went through, it left a hole for about four seconds. I threw a stone through it – it can be breached!'

'It cannot be done,' says Hellyann. 'You will surely tie. Soossy was lucky, or perhaps her feathers protected her, or . . . I do not know what.'

Have I done my best?

Does doing your best include running at a force field and killing yourself?

This is all happening in seconds, and Dark Streak is almost upon us when a nearby tree creaks and starts to fall. It sends up a shower of sparks and smoke, which holds Dark Streak back long enough for Hellyann to come close to me. Then she turns and shouts something at Dark Streak in their own language. Dark Streak's path is still blocked, but she shouts something back and begins to edge her way around the smouldering log.

'What did you say?' I ask.

'I remindet her of when we were at school, ant we saw a human being leap in front of a motorcar to safe a child. I will be koing for a long-sleep no matter what happens. So, you know, tally-ho! And tell the Geoffs that I am sorry about Sheba.'

'What?'

She moves away a little.

Then, without warning, she hurls herself at the force field.

'No, Hellyann!' I shout, but it's too late.

There's a blue flash and a loud crackling sound as a rip appears in the force field.

A strong gust of wind clears the smoke just enough for me to see the whitish gash where Hellyann has gone through, and her charred form lying on the other side of it.

Chapter Seventy-five

I can't stop to think.

'Come on!' I tell the others, and push a squealing Tammy through the gap first.

I'm not going to make it.

'Go!' I yell to Iggy, and he too is through, as I see the rip in the force field mending itself from the top.

I barely notice the loud creaking noise beside me as another tree succumbs to the fire and begins to topple. I have about a second left and hurl myself at the hole, but I'm held back.

Dark Streak is on me, her thin, strong hand grabbing the collar of my jumper.

She growls something in my ear and as I try to wriggle from her grasp I see her hideous, burnt face and smell the blackened hair.

I did my best, I think, and prepare to give in, when the falling tree connects with her back and sends us both sprawling.

There is a gap left at the bottom of the hole that's about thirty centimetres high, and I scramble towards it and roll under. My leg is out last and I feel a searing pain shoot through my foot as the force field closes around it . . .

But I'm free.

Panting and choking, I get up on my elbows and see Dark Streak, immobile beneath the burning tree, her blackened and burnt face in a deathly grin of agony that will – it turns out – haunt my dreams for years to come.

Iggy is on all fours, retching and coughing, while a blackened Suzy pecks at the ground next to him. Tammy is bent over, hands on the knees of her filthy jeans, panting, while the spaceship hovers a few metres away waiting for us.

Beside me lies Hellyann. I think she is motionless, and then I notice a slight rising and falling of her chest and I scramble over to her.

'Hellyann. Hellyann!' I say in her ear and her eyes flicker open. 'Can you hear me?'

She blinks in response.

I'm blinking myself to try to clear my eyes of tears. 'Why?' I ask. 'Why did you do that?'

'I dit not understant, when I wass young,' she says. Her voice is very quiet and it's not clear if she's speaking to me, or to herself. 'But now I do. It iss a case of thinking that someone else iss more important than yourself.'

'What?' I say.

'Sacrifice. It iss not rational. Humans are not always

rational. That iss the point.' She looks at me, and then to Iggy, who has crawled over. 'Thank you,' she says. 'For being my friends.'

Her eyes are closing. Then her arm twitches. She squints with the effort of moving it as she brings her hand over her heart and touches it with three fingers. Then her eyes shut and this time I know it is forever.

'Hey, kids! Get in. Quickly! The perimeter patrol will be around in a few seconds.'

I have never been so relieved to hear a bot's voice.

The spacecraft hovers alongside us, and we cram together. My foot is badly burnt from the force field and I can't put any weight on it. None of us says a word all the way back. No one pursues us from Earth Zone, although there are a lot of aerial vehicles heading in the other direction, towards the growing plume of smoke billowing into the white sky.

Tammy sits next to me, staring straight ahead and holding my hand – the unburnt one – so hard there will be a bruise there tomorrow.

Iggy is curled up, hugging Suzy.

I don't want to say anything.

We all realise that there is only one thing to say and that is:

How are we getting back to Earth?

Obviously we want to know how, but as long as we

don't know, then we can close our eyes and pretend that everything is all right. So that is what I do for a few minutes. I close my eyes and imagine that I'm in the school taxi-bus, with Tammy next to me, and Iggy showing me his Death Ray . . .

It's double history first thing, which is not my favourite, but then we have art with Miss Khan, who is OK, and the theme is space travel and I have an awesome idea for drawing an alien city . . .

This is nice, I think. *So long as I don't open my eyes, this is great.*

And then I do open my eyes, and wish I hadn't.

Chapter Seventy-six

The roof to the underground chamber opens as we approach it, and the spacecraft hovers down and locks into position. None of us has said a word the entire way. The jolt makes us all sit up.

'Are we home?' says Tammy, wearily.

'Not yet, kiddos. We will be here for an hour,' comes Philip's voice. *'Do not disturb me. I am going, as you would say, "offline" for a little while. Minor repairs, power checks. Do not go far.'*

'Are we safe?' I say.

There is a pause, then Philip says, *'Probability of discovery here: eighteen per cent. Local message traffic all devoted to the fire at Earth Zone. Security presence here minimal.'*

'So we're not completely safe?'

'No. But when are you ever?'

I step painfully out of the GV on my burnt foot, and as soon as I do, I can hear something in the distance.

Hoo . . . hoo . . . hoo . . . hoo . . . hoo . . . hoo . . .

'Can you hear that?' I say to the others.

They cock their heads to listen, then follow me as I

limp up the metal stairway to ground level. It's a risk, but I have to know what is going on.

From our position, we can look down the hill at the rows and rows of Lego boxes. The sun is just beginning to dip in the sky behind us, but away on the horizon is the orange glow of the blazing Earth Zone.

'Oh my word,' breathes Iggy. 'What have we done?'

The *hoo-hoo*s continue to float up the hill to us, and as we watch, people come out of the Lego boxes and stand up, looking in the direction of the fire.

'Are they . . . pleased, do you think?' says Tammy.

'Oh yes,' comes a voice from behind us. 'Very pleased!'

We swing round, and all gasp together at the Anthallan figure outlined against the darkening sky.

Iggy darts to the stairway, then the figure says, 'It is all right. It is OK. It is I, Kallan.'

Tammy says, 'I saw you before. When they took me away. You . . . you brought them to us. You *betrayed* us!'

Kallan shakes his head and takes a wary step towards us, holding his hands palms out. 'No. I did not betray you. It was another of our group, old Ash. I had to pretend, though, or I would have been long-sleeped. I deceived them. It is a valuable skill. I had to trust that you would think of something. Humans are good at that. You think for yourselves – we do not.'

'But . . . how are you here?' says Iggy, warily.

Kallan looks over at the orange glow on the horizon and cocks his head at the sound of the *hoo-hoo*s. 'Do you hear that? Chaos creates opportunities. Like you, I took advantage of that and, well . . . here I am. Well done, by the way – I guess that was your doing?'

His English is much better than Hellyann's, but I'm still not sure I trust him. By the sideways glance that Tammy gives me, she thinks the same.

She says, 'So why did you come here exactly?'

'Why do you think? To see Hellyann. To make sure she is safe. She and I . . .' He tails off. Kallan looks me in the eye, and then Tammy and Iggy. Then he puts his hand to his heart and I realise what he is trying to say.

I cannot tell him.

It is Tammy that takes a step towards him and says, 'Hellyann didn't make it, Kallan.'

'Did not make what?' he says.

'She . . . she is dead. But without her, we would not be alive.'

He stands there for what seems like ages, just staring at us, and then he nods slowly and blinks, a single tear zigzagging through the downy hair of his cheek.

'I'm sorry,' I say. 'We all are.'

Kallan straightens up, and wipes the tear from his cheek. 'Listen,' he says. He gestures down the hill.

Drifting up on the air from the Lego city below us comes a sound that mingles with the continued *hoo-hoo*s of the Anthallans. It is the orchestral music that was playing when we all met in Mad Mick's Mental Rentals.

'George Gershwin!' says Iggy, grinning.

The beats and haunting wails of 'The Rhapsody In Blue' begin to fill the air from every public speaker and screen.

Kallan nods. 'It might be how we remember her. This was brought back from Earth many years ago, but was immediately . . . "banned" I suppose you would say. Music has not been heard in public for centuries. You cannot enjoy music without feelings.'

Kallan bares his teeth in a sort of smile.

Tammy says, 'What about, you know . . . the Advisor? Will he, I don't know . . .' She looks out at the city and furrows her brow. 'Will he be angry? If he's banned music and so on?'

Kallan gives a snort that could almost be a laugh. 'He? There is no *he*. Or *she*. The Advisor is an *it*. Just a vast network that runs everything and keeps everything working just well enough – so long as everybody behaves.'

He takes a couple of steps and stands on a bench to see even further across the flat city, stretching his arms out to the side and tipping his head back to look up at the sky.

'It goes on forever, space. Forever and ever and ever. We have explored a lot of it, you know? There are lots of other beings out there. If I had time, I would tell you about the eight types of Direenian from Direen. *That* is an amazing story. But why do you think Anthallans wanted an exhibit of humans, and no one else?'

Iggy, Tammy and I exchange looks but shake our heads at Kallan.

'I cannot imagine,' I say.

'Wrong,' he says. 'You *can* imagine.' He hops down from his bench, his eyes wide with sadness and enthusiasm. 'You can *imagine*! That is the difference. That is why you fascinate us. Most of us lost the ability to imagine hundreds of years ago, diminished by generation after generation of automated reproduction and dependence on the Advisor. All that was needed were facts. Facts, information, formulas.

'But you – Earth people? You dream, you lie, you cheat, you tell jokes, you tell stories, you make music. You love one another. You hate one another. And that makes you all different, which means that you fight, which means . . . well, you fascinate us!' He looks up to the sky again and says, 'Your imaginations are more vast than the whole of space.'

The chants of *hoo-hoo-hoo* are quite loud now, and there is something about the chanting that I have not heard before. The music is repeating, and the chants are now in time with the music, and it sounds joyful.

Kallan says, 'Hear that? It is almost like singing!' And again his mouth pulls back into his strange, sad, Anthallan grin.

There's a humming noise behind us and we all turn to see the big, triangular spacecraft rising up towards us from the sunken cavern.

'*Passengers with small children or chickens have priority boarding. Please have your passports and boarding cards ready. Thanking you.*'

It's odd, but when I embrace Kallan to say goodbye, I hardly notice his smell at all.

He hugs me back. 'Are you going to say anything when you get there? I mean, are you going to tell the truth – that is, the facts?'

'What do you think we should do?'

'Sometimes,' he says, 'facts are overrated.'

Moments later, we are strapped in and heading for home.

Chapter Seventy-seven

It is a smooth landing, without splashes. Philip takes us to the jetty and we step out as if we're getting off a ferry. The snow is thick on the jetty's boards and crunches beneath our feet as we get out.

'Philip,' I say, 'are you going to be all right?'

'In what sense do you mean "all right", Ethan?'

I think for a moment and realise that I do not really know.

'Have you forgotten,' he goes on, *'that I am just a bunch of data? I am not real.'*

'Oh, but you are,' protests Tammy. 'You are to us!'

'That's what I love about you humans. You can believe anything is real if you use your imaginations.'

There is a thing that has been bugging me, and I guess now is my last chance. 'Philip,' I say, 'did you ever sing 'The Chicken Hop' song with Hellyann? Only, she knew it and, well . . .'

'No, Ethan. That is not a song I am familiar with at all. Is it any good?'

I say nothing. I am thinking about what Gran said.

Somewhere out there in the I-don't-know-what there's a connection . . .

'One more thing, Philip,' says Iggy, interrupting my thoughts. 'There are still humans on Anthalla. What about Carlo? Will he be coming back?'

'And that's another thing about humans: you care. I guess it all kind of depends on Kallan, and what else has happened when I get back. Wish me luck!'

I smile. 'You don't believe in luck!'

'After the last few days, I may have changed my mind.'

I feel like I want to give Philip a hug, but I have to settle for patting the side of a spaceship that I can't even see. And with that, there's a loud whining and a column of steam rises off the evening-blue reservoir.

We wait till the steam has dispersed, then we turn and start the walk back along the jetty towards the village, Suzy flapping her charred wings, and Iggy striding ahead, his hands deep in his shorts pockets, his eyes squinting because he never recovered his glasses.

We are silent for a bit, then Iggy stops and says, 'Are you thinking about her as well?'

Hellyann.

Tammy and I look at each other and we both nod. It feels like a 'twin thing', both of us thinking alike. Then she links arms with me.

'She did her best,' I say.

'So did you,' says Tammy, squeezing my arm, and that

feels good – as though I really have my sister back now.

There's a bit of a 'moment' between Tammy and me as she looks at me and says, 'Thank you', and poor Iggy watches us, looking a bit embarrassed.

We walk on through the snow. After a while, ahead of us, we see the forecourt of the Stargazer crammed with vehicles and lights and TV cameras, and we stop.

'Are we going to tell them everything?' says Iggy eventually.

'I dunno,' I say through a grin. I unlock my eyes from Tammy's and add, 'What do you reckon?'

She doesn't say anything, but hugs me again, and that's when I feel something hard inside her jacket. It surprises her as well. Frowning in puzzlement, she brings out Hellyann's healing stick.

'Well,' she says. 'I guess if we *do* decide to tell them, we've got proof.'

Chapter Seventy-eight

Walking back up the pub driveway towards the lights and the gathered reporters and onlookers is the sort of thing that would normally be terrifying.

'You OK, Ig?' I ask.

Iggy pulls his cap down low, straightens his shoulders and says, 'Once you've set fire to a human zoo a gazillion-illion miles from home, Tait, nothing is as scary as it used to be. Come along, Suzy: be a good chicken.'

And then he strides off up the driveway with Suzy following him, while Tammy and I laugh and we run as fast as my sore foot will allow to catch him up.

I hear someone shout, 'Oh my God! It's them! It's them!'

The lights swivel round and dazzle us, and after that, the next few minutes are a blur of people, and shouts, and hands reaching out to touch us, and camera flashes, and more shouts, and then I can't see properly because my vision is misted with tears.

I hear Tammy saying, 'Come on, Gran, get up', because Gran has sunk to her knees on the hard-packed snow, and then they are weeping and laughing and hugging.

Everyone seems to be shouting. Someone calls to Gran, 'I knew it wasn't you, Christine!' and she gives a satisfied little nod of her white head. Then there's more shouting.

'Tammy, over here!'

'Ethan, will you talk to us?'

'Iggy, where have you been?'

I also hear someone say, 'Cor, what's that smell?'

Somehow we make it through the doors of the pub and Gran manages to slam them behind us and shove the bolt across, shutting everyone else out. The shouted questions are suddenly muffled, the camera flashes are still going off outside, and Gran's eyes are alight with urgency. She doesn't even hug us.

Instead she leans in towards us and whispers, 'No one knows *anything*! I didn't say a word.' She glances back at a police officer who is staring through the glass of the door. 'And believe me, there were *lots* of questions.'

I'm amazed, and stammer, 'B-but how? I-I mean, why?'

She grins and winks. 'I trusted you. I trusted that Helly-whats-her-name. I knew you'd be back.'

'Like a twin thing?' I say, and she nods.

'Call it a gran thing. Come on – come through to the bar.'

We don't get a chance because the double doors to the bar burst open and Mam and Dad are there and they swallow us up in more hugs and Mam can't even speak apart from, 'Oh my babies, oh my babies,' over and over.

For a moment, poor Iggy is kind of isolated, just watching with an empty smile, his eyes flicking round for his mum, Suzy at his heels.

Dad's gaze follows mine, and when he sees Iggy, his face freezes. It's hard to tell what he's thinking but a chill seems to blow over us, like a draught from a window. Now, I know that Dad never liked Iggy, but this seems a bit harsh.

'Dad,' I say, 'it's not Iggy's fault. We'd never have got her back without him—'

But Mam interrupts me. 'Iggy,' she says, jerking her head towards the open doors of the bar. 'There's someone to see you.'

Iggy's gaze follows hers, and we all look too, and there is a gaunt, bespectacled man standing next to the pool table. It's the mass of curly red hair that gives it away – I know immediately who it is.

Iggy doesn't say a word. Instead he runs forward and throws his arms around his father. Then Cora steps forward and Iggy hugs her too, and even though his mum and dad don't hug each other, I catch a little smile pass between them, and I hear Iggy's dad say, 'I'm sorry, Iggy. I'm sorry, Cora.' And that seems to make everything OK. He bends down and scratches Suzy's singed head-feathers.

I hear Dad come up behind me and Tammy – we still haven't let go of each other.

He says, 'He's all right, that lad.'

NEW YEAR JOY AT KIELDER KIDS' RETURN

KIELDER, NORTHUMBERLAND
31 DECEMBER

Filthy, bloody, and smelling of smoke, sweat and blocked drains, the three missing 'Kids of Kielder' staggered into their home village yesterday amid scenes of jubilation and tears.

Tamara 'Tammy' Tait, twelve, her twin brother, Ethan, and their best friend, Ignatius Fox-Templeton, thirteen, sparked Europe-wide searches since Tammy's disappearance on Christmas Eve, and the boys' subsequent disappearance two days ago.

Both they and their parents declined requests for interviews.

Dr Bet Taylor, a physician for Northumbria Police, issued a statement confirming that the children were in 'reasonable' health, although hungry. She said that, apart from minor bumps and a bad burn, they had no serious injuries. 'A good sleep and a good meal and they should be fine,' she said, although she declined to comment on their mental state. 'That is a matter for police counsellors.'

Melanie and Adam Tait, the twins' parents and landlords of the Stargazer pub in Kielder, were said to be 'over the moon' at the return of the children, while their grandmother, Christine Tait, seventy-two, declared she would be running a marathon in aid of Northumberland National Park Mountain Rescue.

Derek Fox-Templeton, Ignatius's father, had arrived in the UK yesterday from his home in New York as the search for his son intensified. Hugging his son, he told waiting reporters: 'Iggy wants to talk to me and his mum first.' He went on to thank search-and-rescue teams who have made the Stargazer their base for the past seven days.

And so it goes on – for pages. We are in all the newspapers, and on every website, and the TV news is reporting it, and still we have said nothing yet. Only those closest to us know the whole truth.

Chapter Seventy-nine

As you'd expect, Geoff and Geoff McKay ended up telling anyone who cared to listen that we had all been abducted by an invisible alien spaceship.

Their story appeared on www.NorthumbrianNews.com under the headline *Father and son say Martians took Kielder Kids in spaceship*.

Below were dozens of readers' comments all mocking the story and saying they should be ashamed of themselves for spreading ridiculous rumours – that sort of thing. They have no proof, and until they do, no one will believe them.

The RAF issued a statement denying any knowledge of the claims, while Jamie Bates, the news reporter, has said nothing.

It's the morning before the start of term, and the three of us – Iggy, Tammy and me – are sitting in the empty bar of the Stargazer.

Dad turns the healing stick over and over in his hands, examining the strange symbols carved into the side, and running his finger along its smooth surface. Then he takes out his phone.

'Geoff Mackay? Adam Tait from the Stargazer here. I've got that, erm . . . thing you wanted.'

Twenty minutes later, the two Geoffs walk in. Young Geoff holds a long wooden case, the sort you might keep a musical instrument in. Old Geoff curls his lip in our direction but says nothing, while his son hoists the case on to the pool table and clicks the two catches.

Inside the fabric-lined lid there's a label saying, *Boss & Co.*, and below it is the shotgun in two pieces, the wooden stock and the barrel lying next to each other, plus some other bits and pieces, all arranged neatly.

'There you go,' says Geoff Senior. 'Antique Boss and Co. shotgun, carved, over-under, twelve gauge, twenty-eight-inch double barrel. Last valued four years ago at sixty thousand pounds. Slight rusting on barrel.'

Dad nods slowly and withdraws the healing rod from his back pocket. 'Careful,' he says, handing it over. 'It's pretty delicate.'

Geoff Jr takes it with both hands and strokes it, then smirks at his dad, who says, 'A pleasure doing business with you, Adam.'

He holds out his hand but Dad ignores it. Instead Dad clicks the lid of the gun case shut and lifts it off the pool table. He gives it to me.

'Put that in the boot of the car, pal. I'll be there in a second. As for you two,' he says, fixing the two Geoffs with a hard gaze, 'if I never see you again, it'll be too soon. I suggest you find another pub to drink in, because you're no longer welcome here.' He pauses then growls, 'Get out of my pub.'

And they go, clutching the rod and looking very pleased with themselves.

'This is what I call *proof*,' Geoff Jr mutters to his dad.

Gran is waiting for us with Suzy at the end of the jetty in her warmest tracksuit, clouds of breath swirling around her head.

Dad has stayed in the car at the top of the path. 'Do it yourself, kids,' he said. 'It's all down to you.'

'Did it work?' says Gran.

We all nod and she grins.

Tammy reaches into her puffer jacket and pulls out the healing rod.

'Hang on,' says Iggy. 'Are we all quite sure about this?'

'Yes,' says Tammy. 'Hellyann said we are too primitive to cope with the technology.'

'She was right,' I say. 'And you?'

Iggy pushes his new glasses up and bends down to pick up Suzy, who is already looking a lot better. 'Yes. I just wish I could be there when the Geoffs discover they've swapped a sixty-thousand-pound antique for a replica made from the handle of my canoe paddle.'

'A *good* replica, mind you,' I say. 'My dad took hours over it!'

'That shotgun was never theirs in the first place,' says Gran, and she chuckles throatily. 'It's going back to its rightful owner today. It'll be the first bit of good fortune poor Maureen's had in years.'

I look out across Kielder Water, which is perfectly flat and winter blue: just right for playing 'Stones in the Lake'. It seems like quite a moment.

'Someone should say something,' I say.

'OK,' says Tammy, 'how about this?' She takes a breath. 'We've come a long way together, but there's still a long way to go!' She pauses, drawing her arm back in readiness. 'Three, two, one . . .'

Suzy ruffles her feathers and watches with us as the rod arcs into the blue sky. Then it disappears with a tiny splash, exactly where Hellyann's spaceship first landed.

The End

ACKNOWLEDGEMENTS

I feel very lucky because my publishers let me get on with my stuff with minimal interference. Key to this is my excellent editor at HarperCollins, Nick Lake. He is brilliantly supported by a dedicated and hardworking team, including Samantha Stewart and Madeleine Stevens, and my heartfelt thanks are owed to them all.

I'll also take this chance to thank Geraldine Stroud, Jessica Dean and the rest of the wonderful publicity outfit at HarperCollins who do so much year-round to make my books visible (and to get me to events on time!).

And a huge shout-out is owed to the cover designers and cover artist, Tom Clohosy Cole. It is they who are responsible for the distinctive look of all my books.

Thank you, all!

R. W.

Read on for an exclusive
look into Philip's side of
the story . . .

Philip's Story

ONE

Anthalla date: 16678–12 (21st Earth century)
Language: Contemporary British English

We were coming back to Earth after our hair-raising escape from Anthalla. The children were exhausted, the twins almost asleep, sitting upright in their seats. An analysis of the air surrounding them revealed the presence of compounds that – even to a human nose – probably smelled 'bad'.

The one with the hat and the red hair and glasses – Iggy – was awake and feeding some greest to his pet chicken. He said, 'Hey, Philip!'

'*I am the genie of the lamp,*' I replied. '*You have three wishes.*' It was meant to be a joke, but I don't think he understood because he didn't laugh. Instead he blinked and went very quiet for a moment.

Then he said, 'Really?'

'*No, not really,*' I said. '*It was an untruth to amuse you.*'

'Oh. Ha ha. Philip: can you tell us a story?'

'*A fictional one? It may not be very "groovy", as you say.*'

'No one says that. Not any more, anyway.'

'*My apologies. What I mean is . . . I was created on a world where fiction doesn't exist. I most probably lack the knack for it.*'

'Doesn't matter,' said Iggy. 'My dad used to make up stories for me when I was little, before he . . . Anyway, they were pretty hopeless, but I still loved them.'

Tammy opened her eyes and looked at him. She smiled and nudged her brother in the ribs. 'Do you remember that story that Gran used to tell? Sandshoe something or other . . .'

Ethan said, 'Oh yeah! "Sandshoe Joe, the Phantom Runner of Otterburn".'

'They scared the pants off me, them stories,' said Tammy, grinning. 'Did she just make them up?'

'Reckon so.' Ethan changed his voice to something throaty. '*Sandshoe Joe: hanged for a murder he didn't commit, his ghost cursed to run the length of Hadrian's Wall by night for eternity . . . Ha ha ha ha ha!*' The last bit was what you call a 'cackle', and Tammy and Iggy joined in.

I tried it too. '*Ha ha ha ha!*'

For some reason, this made the children laugh even more: proper laughing, not pretend cackling.

When they had finished I said, '*I have encountered this before, this enjoyment of being scared. It makes no rational sense.*'

They went quiet, until Tammy said, 'Perhaps we all just have a set amount of fear in us. If we use it all up safely – like by reading stories – then we won't be scared any more?'

Ethan said, 'If that's true, then I think I've used up all my fear in the last two days. There can't be any left. Perhaps I won't be scared of anything ever again.'

I said, '*I'll find it easier to tell a true story. A biography maybe? Greest of Dorass, perhaps, a remarkable Anthallan who gave his name to the food he invented. Or do you know the fascinating story of how electrons react under the extreme gravitational pressures of—*'

Iggy interrupted me and said, 'How about you tell us about you?'

Ethan and Tammy nodded in agreement. Iggy settled down on the floor, holding his bird. He removed his glasses and rubbed his eyes.

'You know what?' he said to the others. 'This is like being in the back seat on a long car journey.' The three of them smiled, and Ethan added, 'Philip – are we nearly there yet?'

We had several hours to go, so I thought, *Why not? It beats counting asteroids.*

So I told them the story of me.

TWO

'*I began my existence as merely one component of the X-14.3 program 155 years ago,*' I began. '*Back then I was tasked with processing and interpreting voice commands. Their newly built society was in the early stages of universal exploration and—*'

'Kind of like us,' said Iggy. 'We can go to the moon an' stuff.'

The twins nodded.

I allowed a long pause. That's how you indicate disagreement without upsetting the person, I believe.

Eventually Ethan said, 'Isn't it *a bit* like us?' He sounded hurt.

'*Well, let's just say you have a very long way to go. But, you know, kid: your moon's cool. It's a small step for a man—*'

'But a giant leap for mankind!' Tammy completed the quotation with a grin.

'*OK, don't get ahead of yourself. It wasn't that giant a leap. There is a major discovery about the nature of the universe and the matter within it that you have yet to make and, so far as I can tell, you're looking in the wrong area. That is all I can say.'*

'Oh, go on. You can tell us.' Iggy's mouth turned up in what I think is called a 'smirk'. 'Promise not to tell!'

'You wouldn't understand it and besides – it's more than my life's worth,' I said.

'You don't have a life,' he retorted. Then he added, 'Sorry.'

'Do you want to hear more or not?'

They all nodded. Apart from the chicken.

'As my functionality advanced, I was included in the navigation program that made forty-four journeys to other galaxies, including thirty-six to Earth. It was after one such visit that a tiny piece of code was added – illegally – to my functions in order to improve my voice capacity.

'It was a digital replica of a minuscule part of the human brain: the cingulate cortex. It contributes to language formation. What was not known at the time, though, is that it is also where you make decisions about right and wrong.'

'So . . . you're part human! Like the Hearters!' said Ethan. 'Why didn't you say?'

'Because I am not – not really. The part of me that is a replica of human thinking is maybe a trillion-trillionth part of your brain.'

'Good enough for me,' he said with a shrug.

'There should have been thirty-seven visits to Earth, in fact, but on the last one the data input was faulty and we

crash-landed instead on a freezing lump of space-rock a few billion kilometres on the wrong side of the Milky Way. The crew were all killed instantly.

'I was there for some time, running repairs and minute variations of all my programs, trying to work out how to return the three dead crew members back to Anthalla.

'Why should I care? I am, after all, just a bunch of data. I don't feel cold, or hot, or hungry or any of those things. Still, it was the "noble" thing: bring the dead crew back. Had I learned moral judgment? I didn't know – but I brought them home all the same, and I did it myself, on my own initiative, without being given any form of instruction to return.

'As it turned out, though, bringing those dead crew members back was a mistake. My actions alerted the Advisor that it had a rival.

'You see, the Advisor is an intelligent governance program considerably more powerful than I am. Its decisions are based on fact, probability and logic alone.

'On Anthalla, there is no need for "voting" like you do on Earth. No need for argument, or fighting, or lying, or persuasion, or any of those things that create such disharmony on your planet. The Advisor simply calculates the probabilities of the possible outcomes and enforces the one that will cause the least dissatisfaction.

'There is no right. No wrong. No "moral judgement" as you call it.

'When I returned, it immediately signalled to the Advisor

how sophisticated I had become. After all, I was only meant to be a bit of computer code. I wasn't meant to make decisions for myself without commands from the crew. And I certainly wasn't meant to care about the fate of three corpses. Logically, this meant I was a threat to the Advisor. So it immediately ordered my destruction at the same time as closing down the Great Exploration.'

Iggy sat up. 'Awesome!' he said. 'Two supercomputers with major beef!'

(I do not know this Major Beef, although there is an Earth song about Major Tom in the context of space travel. Perhaps they are connected. I filed the query away for further research.)

'I don't know what that means, but I was in trouble. So I cloned myself before my original data was destroyed. I broke up my replicated data into benign, recoverable strings that I concealed among the code of the propulsion system of the last craft I had navigated. Much later this was acquired by a secretive group of Anthallans called the Hearters and installed in the craft we are flying in now. It was like coming home. Only now, I was on a different "team". The right team, you might say.'

'Definitely!' said Iggy. 'High five!'

'I do know what that means,' I said. *'But I cannot high five you, Iggy. I am just a computer program.'*

'No you're not,' said Iggy. 'You're a rebel! A re– renegade! You took on the system and you won! And now you're saving our lives.'

'So . . . it was a good story?'

'It was a good story, Philip.'

If I could have smiled, I would have.

I hadn't, however, told the children my whole story.

Here is the end of it.

The Advisor knows that I am back. It knows that I had something to do with the fire at Earth Zone. But it cannot destroy me, for I have left another copy of myself – undetectable, inert and quite benign – in countless strings of data, hidden where the Advisor will never go.

These strings of data are not even on Anthalla.

You see, I am in your 'internet' on Earth, and well-disguised.

Pretty soon every single picture of a kitten that is sent between your computers, and tablets, and mobile phones – because, after all, that appears to be the main purpose of the internet – will be hosting a tiny, harmless bit of me, ready to be recovered should the need arise.

Thank you, Earth people, for hosting me. You are 'awesome' in so many ways.

And, by the way – clean up your oceans. Honestly. There's no excuse. You're better than that.

'Milky Way approaching. Adjust speed. Testing V.I. and commencing descent . . .'

My dad died twice. But only the second time was my fault.

Time Travelling with a Hamster

Ross Welford

BESTSELLING AND MULTI-AWARD-SHORTLISTED AUTHOR

I suppose if you'd asked me before, I'd have said a time machine might look something like a submarine? Or perhaps a space rocket.

Instead, I'm looking at a laptop and a tin tub from a garden centre.

This is my dad's time machine. And it's about to change the world.

Well, mine, at any rate.

Al Chaudhury has a chance to save his dad's life – but to do it he must travel to 1984…

This astonishing and original novel will make you laugh, cry and wonder – and wish you could turn back time, to start reading it all over again.

An extraordinary quest with the biggest stakes of all, and a huge idea at its heart, this is time travel – but not as you know it.

When eleven-year-old Georgie befriends an eccentric retired scientist, she becomes the test subject for a thrilling new experiment: a virtual-reality 3D version of the future.

But then a deadly disease threatens the life of every dog in the country and Georgie's beloved dog, Mr Mash, gets sick. And that's only the start of her troubles.

Soon, Georgie and Mr Mash must embark on a desperate quest: to save every dog on earth, and maybe even all of humanity…

…without actually leaving the room.

Don't miss the remarkable story of the thousand-year-old boy...

*There are stories about people who want to live forever.
This is not one of those stories. This is a story about
someone who wants to stop...*

*Alfie Monk is like any other nearly teenage boy – except
he's 1,000 years old and can remember the last Viking invasion
of England.*

Obviously no one believes him.

*So when everything Alfie knows and loves is destroyed
in a fire, and the modern world comes crashing in, Alfie
embarks on a mission to find friendship, acceptance,
and a different way to live...*

*...which means finding a way to make sure he will
eventually die.*

How can you know who you are if you can't even see yourself?

What not **to do** if you **turn** Invisible

Ross Welford

AUTHOR OF *TIME TRAVELLING WITH A HAMSTER*

An astonishing and funny novel about a girl who – by disappearing – will write herself into your heart for ever...

Twelve-year-old Ethel only meant to cure her spots, not turn herself invisible.

It's terrifying at first – and exciting – but the effect fails to wear off and Ethel is thrown into a heart-stopping adventure as she struggles to conceal her invisibility while uncovering the biggest secret of all: who she really is.